ANGEL CRUSH

By
Violette L. Meier

VIORI PUBLISHING

VIORI PUBLISHING
P.O. Box 5283
Atlanta, GA 31107

This book is a work of fiction. The characters and events
portrayed in this book are products of the author's imagination.
Any similarity to real persons, living or dead, business
establishments, events or locals is coincidental and not intended
by the author.

ISBN: 978-0-9887805-0-7

Printed in the United States of America

Cover and Interior Designed by Viori Publishing

DEDICATED

...to God. Thank you for blessing me.

...to the loves of my life: Ari, Xoe, Ruah, & Zahyir.
You are why God blessed me to do what I do.

...to my mother, family, friends, and supporters.
Thank you for everything. I am humbled by your
perpetual faith in me. I truly adore you.

ANGEL CRUSH

1

Sadie Covington was a naturally beautiful woman. Her paper-sack brown skin was smooth and even toned with nary a freckle, stretch mark or mole. Thick black curls crowned her head like an ebony halo. Milk chocolate eyes stared out from a kind and cherubic face. She was short in stature with a perfect hourglass figure, ample breasts, tiny waist, and round hips.

A stunning beauty she was, but very approachable. She had the type of personality that made everyone around her feel comfortable. Intimidating, she was not. Pretty, but a bit clumsy; sexy, but a bit silly; the type that looked stunning in a one-dollar thrift store dress and four hundred dollar shoes. She ate Froot Loops from a crystal bowl and wore evening gowns with Minnie Mouse thongs. Her toes spread when she laughed; open mouthed, teary eyed, loud, and full of sincerity. Nothing was too fine or too common. She knew when to be a lady and when to raise sand. She was honest, but not hurtful, funny, but not vulgar, sweet, but not stupid. Sadie was the kind of woman that was easy to talk to, easy to please, and easier to fall in love with.

Every Sunday morning she sat on a small iron stool, leaning on her kitchen counter, eating fruit salad, and doing a new crossword puzzle. And, this Sunday morning she was doing the same. The sound of lead touching paper filled the room. The smell of Fragrant lilacs and vanilla rose from burning candles as she scribbled odd vocabulary words on the wrinkled newspaper. The phone rang. She dropped her pencil on the floor, grabbed it with her toes, passed it to her hand, and placed it upon the counter.

"Hello," Sadie spoke into the mouthpiece, as she rolled her eyes upward. She hated her Sunday morning peace to be disturbed, but she was glad to have to get up from the stool. Her legs were asleep. She tried shaking off the pins and needles feeling and massaged her calves with her free hand.

"Hello," she said again, this time with an obvious level of annoyance in her voice.

"Hey, baby. What're you up to?" a man's voice echoed through the receiver. His voice was baritone and penetrating with a slight southern drawl, the kind of voice that echoed with strength and sent your soul back to times of muscled farmhands, aching Hebrew backs breaking under Egyptian whips, Nubian princes wearing crowns of gold, clay inhaling and becoming a living soul. It was raspy, ancient and immortal, reeking with virility.

"Relaxing," she answered. She sat back on the stool and picked up her pencil once more. She held the phone with her shoulder and took a sip of white grape peach juice. "Mr. Tucker, is there anything in particular that you need?"

A new word was scribbled onto the puzzle.

"I need to hear your voice," he replied in a tone that indicated that he was smiling.

She smiled and put down the pencil.

"You have my attention," she cooed. "Now that you hear my voice, is there anything else you need from me?"

Sadie took a bite of fruit and attempted to chew it as quietly as possible. She plunged her fork into her bowl for the last chunk, but the fruit missed her mouth, leaving a sticky juice trail down her chin. Abandoning the fork, Sadie picked the fruit up off the counter with her teeth and savored its tangy sweet taste.

"No, your voice is sufficient. To hear it makes me realize how lucky I am to have you as a fiancé. Relax yourself. I'll call you back after you finish your puzzle. I know how important your quiet time is to you," said James.

"Aren't you the sweetest thing in the great state of Georgia?" she asked rhetorically in her best southern belle accent, grinning as she wiped her chin with her forearm.

"Baby, I'm the sweetest thing in the world," James laughed. "You know how this chocolate tastes; the cream too."

"Oh shut up! You're so nasty! I was wondering when the modesty would fade." Sadie joined in with the laughter. "I'll have to talk to you later. I do want to finish my puzzle and then run some errands. Maybe you can come over for dinner if you're not busy. My parents are coming in from their retirement home in Florida and I would like you to finally meet them. They're very curious about the man who has asked their daughter to marry."

"Around what time?" There was a bit of nervousness in his voice. The thought of meeting her parents made him uncomfortable. He was not the kind of guy who cared about others approval, but Sadie's parents were important to her. James prayed that they would like him. After all, he felt he was a pretty cool guy.

His parents loved her. His mother talked about Sadie nonstop. She was the daughter his mother never had. James' parents thought Sadie was perfect for him and liked her more than any other woman he had dated. James hoped that Sadie's parents would feel the same way about him.

"Maybe seven," Sadie answered, twirling her short hair with her fingers. The tiny curls hugged her fingers like onyx rings. "They can't wait to meet you. I've told them so much about you. I'll have all the ones I love together. Dinner will be perfect."

"I don't know about that. Are you cooking or are we going out?"

"Boy, you need to stop. You know I can cook," Sadie giggled.

"You do a'ight, I guess," James joked. "I haven't had to go to the emergency room yet."

"Whatever! I'll cook. I really don't feel like dressing up," she said, dismissing his remark. Sadie knew James loved her food. He ate at her table like a runaway slave finally getting a meal after running barefoot through six states. A matter of fact, sometimes she felt he loved her food more than he loved her.

"So, I can just throw on some jeans and a T?"

"Sure, why not. You look amazing in simple jeans and a T." A naughty grin curled her lips. An image of James in a fitted white T-shirt filled her thoughts. She could see his ripped arms, his broad shoulders, and reminisced on the way his abdominal muscles formed a perfect eight pack and how his legs were so large and well made. His skin was so black that it looked purple and it was so smooth that it felt unnatural. The room seemed to get a bit hotter. She took a sip of juice and tightly crossed her legs to curb the tickling pang in her loins.

"Thank you, baby. I'll be there. Is there anything that you want me to bring?"

"Dessert. Anything, but cake. I went to two weddings and three baby showers last month and I ate so much cake that I'm surprised I'm not sweating icing," Sadie complained. I think I still have a couple of slices in my refrigerator."

James laughed. "I'll see what I can do."

"I appreciate that, baby. I really can't wait to see you tonight. You're going to really love my dad. He's ultra charming and loves to talk. He'll trip you out with his stories. And, you will absolutely fall in love with my mom after she gets to know you. She can seem a little distant at first, but she comes around fairly quickly. They are truly great people. But I'm a bit biased." She laughed.

"I'm sure," James' voice cracked. He was a ball of nerves.

"You don't sound sure. Everything will be great. You'll see," Sadie assured him. "Well, my love, let me get back to me-time."

"Okay, sweet stuff. I'll talk to you later."

"I love you," cooed Sadie.

"I love you more."

"Goodbye."

"Bye," James responded and hung up the phone.

Sadie placed the receiver back on the hook and sat back down. The back of her thighs stuck to the soft leather of the stool. Every move sounded like flatulence. Her tiny shorts provided no buffer. She adjusted her legs and picked up her pencil once more.

After fifteen minutes, she finished the puzzle and folded the paper. She yawed loud and stretched her entire body until she formed a gigantic "X." With a lazy push, she slid from the stool, making her shorts ride above her cheeks. She pulled them down and inserted her index finger in her ear and wiggled it as fast as she could, secretly loving the ear orgasm. The silence of her condominium seemed to squeal in her ears. She walked into the kitchen. The cold floor was like ice to her bare feet so she rose upon her toes. Sadie hit the power button on the radio that sat on the counter. Nothing. She checked the plug. It was plugged in.

"I just bought this radio. I can't believe it's not working," she mumbled. Sadie unplugged it and the music came on. She flipped the unit upside down. There were no batteries. Instantly the volume blared. Sadie dropped the radio to the floor, barely missing her foot. She bent down to pick it up. The entire room dropped at least twenty degrees in temperature. She could feel her skin like it was a foreign object. Her heart thumped. She bolted up. Her feet were glued to the floor as her eyes searched every corner of the room. A flapping-fluttering sound filled the room. Sadie pressed her palms tight against her ears. A single tear ran down her face. Chill bumps cascaded down every inch of her body. A strong breeze wrapped around her like a blanket of ice. Her T-shirt waved like a hand with no bones. The gust of wind became so strong that she could hardly keep her footing. She turned her eyes to the window. It was closed. Everything outside seemed undisturbed. Even the leaves on the trees stood suspended in motionlessness.

"What's happening? Who's here?" she screamed. "I'll call the police!" She opened a drawer and pulled out an electric mixer, looked at it helplessly, then dropped it back into the drawer. "I have a gun!" she lied. "Show yourself!" Sadie screamed; the wind seemed to blow her words back into her mouth.

The kitchen light flickered. The sound grew louder. She wrapped her arms around her head. A gust of wind blew her to the floor. Sadie fell hard on her behind.

"Oh God! What's going on?" she cried, looking around the room, her hands vigorously massaging her tailbone. She saw movement. Sweat formed on her brow. Sadie reverberated off the floor and pulled a butcher knife out of the knife rack. She held the knife above her head ready to strike anyone or anything that came near her.

A dark shadow fell upon her face. Her skin turned as pale as the moon. The knife hit the floor, its wooden handle making an echoing thud. Sadie's eyes stretched in horror and disbelief. Her mouth opened and her lips tore back, exposing all teeth and gums. A scream fell silent upon her lips as two large hands grabbed hold of her shoulders and lifted her unconscious body into the air.

2

The sunlight peaked through the kitchen blinds and made horizontal lines across Sadie's face creating glinting pinstripes. She opened her eyes and sat up. Darting to and fro, her eyes searched the room frantically. Looking down at her completely nude body, fear conquered her, wreaking havoc in her heart causing irreversible demolition and marching to her brain raging psychological warfare. Sweat covered her from head to toe. Her skin tingled with heat and uncomfortable redness. She could smell her feminine scent in the air. Her shorts and T-shirt laid balled up next to the refrigerator. The kitchen floor was cold against her back and her apartment was unearthly quiet. She screamed. Her fingers dug into the sides of her face. She screamed. Her fists pounded against the floor. She screamed.

Her howling rang through her home and fell into silence. Sadie was spent. Her lungs could push out no more screams. Sanity came back to her. She decided that what she was experiencing was not real. She had imagined it all. She must have fallen asleep while doing her crossword puzzle.

"This has to be a dream." Sadie pinched herself. It hurt. She was awake. "I cannot understand."

Tears flowed down her cheeks, piquant tasting like salt water taffy into her gaping mouth. She placed her hands on the counter and pulled herself up.

"I'm losing my mind." Her voice trembled as she wept. Uneven breaths rushed from her mouth. "This cannot be real."

A warm liquid with a strange tingling sensation ran down her inner thigh. Sadie reached down and touched the tepid goo. She rubbed the creamy matter between her fingertips. It was as slick as lotion. She smelled it. It smelled faintly vanilla, but bittersweet, like resin. No, like spice, like myrrh. She tasted it. It tasted like almonds and honey.

"What is this?" she howled as she spat the sweet substance on the floor. "What is this?" she cried as the horrific realization of its origin invaded her near slipping mind. Sadie smeared the thick liquid with her hands, trying hard to wipe the creamy matter off. The more she wiped, the more irate she became. Her eyes swelled with fresh tears. Thick mucus ran from her nose and glazed her top lip. Myrrh odor covered her hands. To no avail, she flung her hands insanely trying to rid herself of the infuriating scent.

She stumbled out of the kitchen and went into the bathroom. With quaking hands, she turned the sink faucet on and rinsed her hands, scrubbing franticly almost on the brink of madness. She rubbed her skin so hard that her natural melanin threatened to rinse down the drain. Sadie ripped open the linen closet, pulled out a fresh towel and washcloth and threw them on the powder blue toilet lid. She turned on the shower and crawled underneath the warm water. Vigorously, Sadie scrubbed her flesh until it was sensitive to the touch. She turned off the water, dried her body, and walked slowly to her bedroom.

"No one will ever believe me," she wept aloud. "I've been assaulted and I can't call the police. They would throw me in the crazy house!"

Sadie dropped the towel to the bedroom floor, gathered some jogging clothes and dressed quickly.

"No one will have to know as long as it doesn't happen again!" she exclaimed. "I'll take it to the grave."

Sadie let her body fall into a seated position. She pulled a pair of tennis shoes on her bare feet. She felt sick to her stomach. Dragging and slowly pressing her knees into the floor, she crawled back into the bathroom. Gripping the toilet, she emptied her stomach, stood up and confronted her reflection in the mirror.

"Girl, you have to get yourself together. You are stronger than this. Mom and Dad will be here soon and I can't afford for them to get suspicious," she scolded herself. Her eyes welled up again. "Stop it!" Sadie yelled at her reflection as she drove her fist into the counter. Her pinky finger popped out of place, but she refused to wince. With a quick jerk, she popped the finger back in place. "Strong!" She wiped her face clean and flicked off the light, involuntarily pausing to internalize the pain in her throbbing finger and maimed spirit. She jogged through her apartment to the living room (tripping and falling at least twice), grabbed her purse, exited with cheetah speed, and drove herself to the grocery store.

3

Tall pine trees and hardy oaks lined both sides of the street. Perfectly preened grass and exotically designed bushes decorated the lawns. Expensive cars sat in each driveway complimenting lavish homes. At the very end of the cul-de-sac loomed a three-story Georgian mini-mansion with four ivory pillars gracing its facade. Inside of the house, James Tucker and his two roommates — Forrest Cohen and Luis Rivera — sat before a gigantic flat screen television.

"Jay, you gonna go wit' us tonight? We're gonna hit the new club that opened up on Peachtree Street," Luis asked while palming a basketball. He bounced the ball twice then rolled it over to a corner.

A handsome man he was, darn near pretty. Luis was well built, medium height with a Caesar haircut, and a deep New York Puerto Rican accent. His skin was golden like sunsets born and his eyes were dark, deep set, and hidden beneath brows so tamed that they looked professionally arched. Full lips and perfect teeth made him supreme eye candy.

"Naw, man. I have to go and meet Sadie's parents," James answered. "They're coming in tonight." He placed his feet upon the coffee table and picked up the TV remote. He flipped the channels slowly, absorbing just enough content to see if his interest was elicited.

"Are you nervous?" asked Forrest, his honey brown eyes twinkled. Forrest had a smile that lit up the room and an innocence that was rare. His face was dark olive, narrow with high cheekbones, a dimpled chin, a large but complimentary nose, bright eyes, and full lips. A small yarmulke sat in the middle of thick silky curls. Forrest was very tall and slim, but muscular. His arms were the sexiest part of his body. He was quite attractive to most women, but his ignorance of his attractiveness was one of his best qualities.

James looked into Forrest's energized eyes and laughed. "You seem more excited than me."

Forrest smiled and said, "I am. I can't believe that you're getting married. You're breaking up the three musketeers. This house gonna seem empty without you."

"I'm getting married not dying," James laughed. "I'll come by to visit."

"Marriage. Death. Same thing," Luis said. "I can't believe you're goin' out like that. You gonna let that broad tie you down. Won't be me."

"You stupid," James laughed. "First of all, I love her. And second of all, she ain't no broad! She's a good woman and we all know that is rare these days."

"I don't trust no woman. They're worse than men these days," Luis retorted. "Chicks are ruthless. They all just sniffin' after a brotha's doe."

"It's scary that you're a mentor and social worker, Lu," James said, muffling his laughter. "I hope you don't be teaching those kids all your ignant-ass ideas."

"Whateva!" Luis raised his hand. "I speak the truth."

"That's not true," Forrest said. "There are plenty of good women."

"I don't know one! Oh, I'm sorry. A good woman like old girl." Luis looked up at the ceiling like he was trying hard to remember. Luis snapped his fingers thrice. "Oh yeah." He smirked. "What's her name? Sarah, who cheated on you with her quote unquote best friend," Luis spat blithely.

James held his side. The laughter would not stop coming.

"That's not funny," Forrest grumbled. "She broke my heart. I let her bring that trifling dude with us everywhere." His eyes frowned. "And my mother told me she was a sweet traditional Jewish girl. That was the last time I allowed my mom to set me up with anyone. I think I'm going to marry a gentile just for revenge. Mom is already pissed that I joined Jews for Jesus. If I marry a gentile, she will really have a heart attack."

James and Luis laughed so hard; their voices combined into one great roar.

Forrest's countenance fell. He was not amused. Thinking of his overbearing mother was anything, but amusing. She was sweet and meant well, but Forrest was tired of the endless blind dates with her friends' daughters. He felt like she was his pimp.

"But seriously," Luis began after he contained his laughter, "all broads are the same. They all have a price and will do anything or anyone for money."

"Not my girl," James said. He put the remote down and dropped his feet to the floor. "My girl is a quality woman. She's smart, sexy, and makes good money. Sadie don't need mine. She has morals and respects the body, mind, and spirit. Sadie isn't materialistic and best of all she can cook and wear a brother out in the bedroom."

"Blah, blah, blah, blah, blah," Luis mocked. "I'm sure she had lots of practice."

"Don't make me smack you!" James playfully grabbed the neck of Luis' T-shirt. Luis squirmed out of James' grasp and fell down on the ottoman across from Forrest's chair.

"Don't hate because you've been played," Forrest said while spinning a towel into a twist then popping Luis with it.

"Ouch!" Luis jumped. "Stop playin'!" He yanked the towel out of Forrest's hand and tossed it across the room. "I don't get played. I play."

"Whatever," Forrest said. "You weren't playing last year when that tall blonde Asian chick got two thousand dollars from you and disappeared."

Luis extended his middle finger.

Forrest smirked and continued, "Jay, don't listen to Luis. He only dates hood rats and gold diggers. Sadie is a great girl and she loves you."

Luis nonchalantly mouthed a stream of obscenities and gave Forrest the middle finger again. Forrest waved him off. James laughed.

"You know I'm not paying attention to that fool," said James.

"Can I ask you a personal question?" Luis asked James.

"Sure."

"You sure you ready to sleep wit' one woman for the rest of yo life?" Luis' face was suddenly serious. "Marriage is supposed to be forever and forever is a mighty long time to be wit' one woman."

Forrest leaned in closer. His eyes peaked with curiosity.

"Yeah, man. I love her and just want to be with her," James answered. He threaded his fingers. "She's the one. She never gives me drama and she makes me happy. I've never met a woman like her in my life."

"How can you be sure?" asked Forrest. "Even the thought of marriage scares me and I'm a hopeless romantic."

"I don't know, but I know she's the one and I'm ready. She's the only woman I have ever been faithful to. I mean I don't even look at other women," answered James.

"Negro, please!" Luis laughed.

James paused and leaned in. "Look, I haven't had sex in five months and you know how I used to get down. I never thought I would survive a week, but she is worth the wait. That's love."

"Get outta here!" Luis shouted. "Why not? She cut you off?"

"Naw, man. After we got engaged, we decided to not sleep together again until we are married," answered James.

"You mean she decided," Luis shot. "Ain't no way you came up wit' that idea."

"That's beautiful," Forrest said, smiling.

"That's stupid!" Luis snapped.

"No it's not. They're saving themselves. The anticipation will make the wedding night ultra intense," Forrest retorted.

"You always talkin' that crazy stuff. Open your shirt. Let me make sure that you ain't growin' titties." Luis waved Forrest off. "James, you stupid, man. While you sitting around with blue balls, I bet she givin' it to some thug dude," Luis laughed. "You know you a career brotha so she gotta get it on wit' a rough neck before she gets tied down her whole life to Mr. Straight-laced." Luis laughed hysterically. "You see, she lookin' for the thug she thought you were when she met you. You ain't rough enough no more. When she first met you, she saw you all dirty and workin' wit' yo hands. You had dirt under your fingernails and sweat all over your face. Now you all clean cut carrying a briefcase. You used to sound gutta now you sound all proper like you been studyin' the dictionary 'cause we know you are allergic to school." Luis laughed.

Forrest joined in with the laughter and soon so did James.

"Lu, you know Sadie is better than that. She's the faithful type," Forrest said.

"Everyone is capable of everything and that includes Sadie. Believe that!" Luis shouted.

"Man, I hear what you're saying and I understand where you're coming from, but Sadie is a winner and she will be my wife. I trust her. I love her. She makes me happy," James said, looking Luis directly in the eye.

"As long as you happy, man." Luis walked up to James, grabbed his hand and pulled him close into a brotherly hug. "As long as you happy. All I ask is for you to keep your eyes open."

4

The smell of sun-dried tomatoes, garlic, and bread permeated Sadie's home. Sadie stood in the kitchen stirring homemade tomato sauce and sipping red wine from the bottle. Memories of the strange creature that visited her earlier dominated her thoughts. It filled her head so much that she felt as if her brain was being forced out of her facial orifices. A chill crawled down the back of her neck like a millipede. Sadie dropped the spoon and leaned against the counter in quiet reflection. She could faintly picture his face, large wings, and then blackness. Recollection of what occurred after the creature took her was nonexistent, but she knew in her heart that it had violated her. Her body ached intimately. The myrrh smell lingered on her. It aroused her and fueled her anger simultaneously. She hugged herself tight and let the tears come. Her intercom buzzed.

"Yes," Sadie said quickly, leaning close to the intercom and holding down a pink button not wanting to portray the pain in her voice.

"It's us," a husky voice answered.

"Dad? Mom? I'll buzz you in." Sadie pushed a red button to unlock the door downstairs. She wiped her face with an unused dishrag and checked her reflection in the toaster. Quickly she picked up the olive oil and rubbed the tip of her finger over the opening then rubbed the oil on her lips. She combed her hair with her fingers and took a deep breath. Two knocks on the front door. She shuffled over to it and opened it wearing a grin so wide that it seemed to stretch across her whole face.

"Hello sweetheart," her father warmly greeted.

Mr. Covington was a very tall and extremely handsome man. He was the male replica of Sadie with honey brown skin and thick curls. A full beard edged his face. One of his large hands grabbed the back of Sadie's neck and pulled her face to his. He planted a hard wet kiss on her cheek. His other hand rested within the tiny hand of his ebony skinned wife.

"Daddy!" Sadie squealed. The wet kiss began to cool on her cheek. "I'm so happy that you're here." She looked at her mother's high cheekbones and huge slanted eyes and smiled. "Mom, it seems as if you've gotten even younger than me! My, you look radiant."

Mrs. Covington smirked dryly. She was never able to take compliments well. Fawning always seemed insincere to her. She lovingly touched Sadie's cheek and frowned.

"Why are your eyes puffy?" Mrs. Covington inquired. "Have you been crying?"

"I haven't been sleeping well," Sadie sputtered.

"Why is that?" Mrs. Covington questioned. "Is something wrong?"

"Are we going to stay out here all day?" Mr. Covington interjected.

"Well come on in." Sadie stepped aside to allow them to walk past her. She exhaled a sigh of alleviation. Lying to her mother was not what she wanted to do and telling her the truth was not what she was going to do.

"It smells good in here, ladybug," Mrs. Covington said. She tossed her coat on the sofa and marched straight into the kitchen. She pulled a big wooden spoon out of the dish rack and stirred the sauce. Blowing the sauce ever so gently, she tasted it and frowned. "Way too much garlic, honey."

"That's the way I like it. Daddy likes it that way, too." Sadie plopped down on her father's lap and tousled his hair. "Don'tcha?"

"That's right, sugar." He playfully slapped her hand away and tickled her until she hit the floor.

"I wasn't aware that you and your father were the only ones eating," Mrs. Covington grumbled.

"Maaaa!" Sadie whined.

"Maaaa!" Mr. Covington joined in.

"You two cut it out," Mrs. Covington laughed. "Sadie, my love, would you mind if I finished the dinner?"

"Mom, I'm supposed to be cooking for you." Sadie got up and placed her hands on her hips. "Go and sit down next to Daddy and relax yourself." She walked into the kitchen and took the spoon, bent down and gave her mother a quick peck on the lips.

Mrs. Covington smiled a great smile and grabbed her daughter and squeezed her tight.

"It's good to see you, baby," she said and pulled back. "Let me look at you." Her eyes examined Sadie from head to toe. "You look good but your hair is cut way too short, and what is that smell?"

"What smell?" Sadie's smile disappeared and her eyes shifted from her mother's face to the wall.

"You smell like incense or sharp spices or something. Is that some new lotion you bought from Lotions and Bath Potions?" Mrs. Covington asked while shaking her head.

"Yeah, exactly," Sadie lied. Her hands began to shake. It was an unnerving thing to lie to her mother. Sadie always felt that she could tell her mother anything, but she knew her mother would never believe what she had experienced. Her mother did not believe in anything that science or simple logic could not explain. So, the supernatural was definitely out of the question. Sadie could imagine her mother dismissing it as a foolish dream induced by cold feet and stress. Mrs. Covington would give the number to a reputable shrink and tell Sadie to lay her burdens on them.

Mr. Covington was different though. He believed in everything supernatural from ghosts to demons to aliens to fairies. Sadie's father had a spooky tale for every night of the week. The spiritual plane was a personal fascination to him. Ever since he was a boy, he believed that life had to be more than what his eyes could see. Mr. Covington naturally migrated to religion, spirituality, mythology, and the imagination.

He was not religious, but deeply spiritual. In his early twenties he believed that he received a call from God. He served as a Baptist minister for a few years before stress, induced by the church, inflicted pain on his spirit. The back biting and church politics made him disfavor religion in general. He quit and never looked back, but he kept his mind open to God and the spiritual realm. Maybe Sadie could tell him. Mr. Covington would surely understand.

Sadie's parents were an enigma to her. It was amazing to her how two people with such different outlooks on the realm of reality could coexist. But they did and they did in perfect harmony. They proved that opposites really did attract.

"What happened to classic fragrances like rose or musk? Now you young people walk around smelling like ancient Roman funerals or Ethiopian Magi thinking you will seem more refined knowing good and darn well you ain't fooling no one but yourselves," Mrs. Covington chastised. "You young folk try to make everything more complicated than it is. Just use some nice soap and you will be fine."

Mr. Covington laughed hysterically.

Sadie smiled a fake smile. All of a sudden she felt ill. A bubbling sensation filled her belly. She held her breath to fight the vomit that was climbing up her pharynx. The face of the creature was fresh in her mind again. She could see his flaming eyes, his countenance aglow with a strange light, his strong cheek bones and angular features, his inhuman complexion. Her eyes began to water.

"Baby, what's wrong? I didn't mean to hurt your feelings. I'm sorry," Mrs. Covington apologized. She patted Sadie's shoulder and kissed her lightly on the cheek. "If you like that perfume I'll learn to also. I didn't mean..."

"You did nothing wrong, Momma. I just have a bad case of indigestion. I'll be alright soon. Don't worry about me."

"Would you like a glass of milk? That could sooth you," Mrs. Covington asked.

"No," Sadie answered.

"Well, you just sit down and I'll finish the cooking." Mrs. Covington went back into the kitchen and started rambling.

"Ma, you don't have to do that," said Sadie.

"Let her go ahead and cook," Mr. Covington said, grabbing Sadie's hand. "She won't feel comfortable unless she's doing something. You know that's what she wanted to do since she stepped foot in here anyway."

Sadie decided not to protest. She knew what her father was saying was true. Her mother could never just sit down. She always had to have something to do. Sitting still was a punishment that Mrs. Covington could not endure. Sadie was convinced that her mother had ADHD (Attention Deficit Hyperactivity Disorder).

"Okay." Sadie sat down on the sofa next to her father. It took every bit of will power to not weep in front of her parents. They were so close and she felt that she could pour out her soul but Sadie knew in her heart that her mother would never believe her and her father would turn it into some sort of *Twilight Zone* or *Tales from the Crypt* episode. She laid her head on her father's shoulder and closed her eyes. She allowed a few tears to creep out of the corners of her eyes but refused to sniff. Discovery was not an option. This was her cross to bear.

5

James stood in front of Sadie's apartment building looking up towards her fourteenth floor window. The sun was setting behind him casting his shadow upon the ground before him like an animated ink blot. Rubbing his hands together and smoothing his eye brows, he took a deep breath and walked to the glass doors slowly. He could not bring himself to push the intercom button yet. The idea of meeting Sadie's parents made his stomach flip. He had heard so much about them. Sadie said that they were wonderful people but he wondered if he would be fully accepted into her family. After all, he was just an average street guy with good business sense.

Sadie's father was a college professor of Paranormal Studies at a prestigious university in Miami. He held a PhD but he became very annoyed when anyone outside of academia referred to him as Dr. Covington. Mister suited him just fine. He felt that his educational accomplishments only needed to be acknowledged in an academic setting. Any other time, being called doctor was just for vanity reasons and a vain man he was not. From what James heard, humility was one of Mr. Covington's greatest attributes. James felt reassured by that. A humble man was usually a kind one.

Sadie's mother was a housewife, a successful furniture upholsterer, an English tutor, and a piano instructor. She was a master of all of her trades and a very meticulous woman.

Sadie was a Creative Arts Therapist for a retired nun community where she made an obscene amount of money. Sadie had a Bachelors Degree in Art and Philosophy, a Masters Degree in Recreational Management, and a PhD in Psychology.

James was very successful but not in the same way as Sadie and her parents. He was intelligent but not extensively educated. After he graduated from high school, he wanted nothing more to do with academia and took a job at a car detailing shop. Having business savvy, a great work ethic, and extraordinary people skills, he built a small auto empire. Now he owned seven auto detailing shops, four of which catered to luxury vehicles and exotic automobiles. James had done pretty well for himself. He was not ashamed of his accomplishments but felt a bit intimidated by the potential smugness of her parents. Maybe he was prejudging them and thinking way too much. He pushed the buzzer.

"Yes," Sadie said, her voice sounding fuzzy through the small speaker.

"It's..." He cleared his throat. "It's James."

"Baby!" Sadie squealed. "I'm glad you made it."

"You know I wouldn't miss coming for the world," he said.

A buzz sounded in James' ear and he opened the glass double doors. With swift feet, he walked into the elevator and pushed button "14." *It's silly how in this day in time buildings still called the thirteenth floor the fourteenth floor because of superstition.* James thought. He leaned against the elevator wall and breathed deeply and slowly. Letting his eyes close for a moment, he let his head fall back against the gold mirrored wall. The doors opened and he stepped out of the elevator and turned the corner. He walked slowly, letting his feet drag across the Asian inspired carpet while allowing his eyes to linger upon the cream painted walls and gold trimmed ceiling with mini gold and crystal chandeliers hanging a few feet apart from one another. Within seconds, he was standing in front of Sadie's door. Before he could knock, the door swung open and Sadie had her arms wrapped tightly around his neck slowly pulling him inside.

"Mom, Dad, this is James," Sadie introduced him grinning from ear to ear.

Mr. Covington stood up and extended his hand. James accepted it and Mr. Covington pulled him into a full embrace, hugging him so tight that James could hardly breathe. With his face pressed hard against Mr. Covington's bear-like shoulders, he felt like his back would break within the trap of the big man's arms. Mr. Covington had to be at least six feet and six inches tall because James was over six feet himself and the older man made him feel like a dwarf.

"Nice to meet you son," Mr. Covington laughed as he let go. "We've heard so many great things about you."

Letting out a massive exhale, James stepped back, pleasantly surprised and taken aback by the man's genuineness and affection. Immediately James felt at ease.

"Nice to meet you too sir." James smiled. "Sadie never stops talking about how wonderful y'all are."

Mrs. Covington stood next to her husband, a small smirk on her face. James bent down and kissed her hand. She blushed.

"Nice to meet you Mrs. Covington," James said and then looked at Mr. Covington. "If you don't mind me saying sir, your wife is an extraordinary looking woman. Now I understand where Sadie gets her beauty from."

Mrs. Covington buried her cheek into her husband's forearm and smiled.

James grabbed Sadie's hand and they all made their way to the dinner table. He leaned close to Sadie and whispered, "I forgot the dessert."

"That's okay. We ladies have to watch our hips," Sadie responded.

"That's my job," he whispered in her ear and took an inconspicuous nibble causing Sadie to giggle quietly.

The dining room was brightly lit by a modest but eloquent chandelier and the room was almost filled from corner to corner by a huge mahogany table with matching china cabinet and ruby cushioned chairs. Dark red carpet complimented the chairs and the ruby dinner napkins folded neatly upon the table. Expensive silverware adorned the napkins as tropical imprinted china, shining with warm reds and crisp greens, waited to hold delectable food. A plastic vase decorated with various African American cartoon characters filled with wild plastic flowers made the centerpiece uniquely Sadie.

"You smell good sweetie," James whispered into Sadie's ear. "What is that?"

She immediately let his hand fall. Sadie pulled her chair away from the table so clumsily that it almost fell to the floor.

"Are you okay, baby?" James asked.

"I'm cool," Sadie unintentionally snapped.

All eyes rested upon Sadie. Her father's brow furrowed and her mother's face revealed a tinge of worry. Sadie refused to look at any of them and sat down. They all followed her example.

In silence the food was passed from hand to hand and each plate was filled with delicious Italian dishes. Minutes passed as the clinging sound of silverware and china filled the air.

Sadie decided to break the ice. A forced smile bent her lips. She laid her fork upon her plate and placed her hand upon James' hand.

"James, did I tell you that my dad is a spirit-monger?" she laughed.

Everyone laughed in unison.

"Not exactly," James laughed. "But you did tell me that he dealt with weird happenings." James smiled, looked at Mr. Covington, and took another bite of pasta.

Mr. Covington's eyes lit up. He placed his fork down and folded his hands on the table and said, "I teach and do research regarding supernatural occurrences. You would be surprised how many people experience things not of this world."

Mrs. Covington rolled her eyes.

"You don't believe in those things ma'am?" James asked, as he hungrily refilled his mouth with food between words. Sauce covered his lips. Sadie motioned with her napkin for James to wipe his mouth. Embarrassed, he quickly wiped his mouth and slowed down.

"I think it's all foolishness," Mrs. Covington replied. "I don't believe in any of that stuff. I would protest against all supernatural craziness but it has been so lucrative for our family." She grinned. "I think it's all products of over active imaginations. Isn't that right Sadie?"

Sadie placed her fork down slowly and wiped her mouth with her napkin. Her forlorn eyes looked deep into her mother's with a thoughtful pause.

"I'm not sure if I agree with you anymore Momma," Sadie replied.

"Since when?" One of Mrs. Covington's eyebrows rose.

Sadie's eyes fell to her plate. She whispered, "I just think that there is more to life than what we know. Strange things happen. Unbelievable things," she let her words linger with quiet apprehension.

Mrs. Covington folded her arms. "James," she called. "Have you been filling my daughter's head with spiritual mumbo jumbo?" A crooked smiled slanted her lips.

"No ma'am but I do believe that there is something greater than us. I believe in God and Jesus but I don't know about religion too much and I'm not really into the ghost thing. But once I thought I saw something," James said with a silly smile on his face.

"And what was that?" Mr. Covington asked, intrigued.

"Well, when I was a kid, I lived with my great grandma and she had furnace vents in the floors and I used to stand over them to let the heat blow up my pajama pants," James laughed. The others smirked a little. He continued, "One morning I was standing over the heater when I leaned forward and looked into the living room. Standing right before me was this little boy. I could still see him as clear as water. He was smiling at me and he had golden skin and a yarmulke on his head. I blinked my eyes and he was still there. I leaned back into the hall and then looked back in the living room and the boy was gone. I figured I was still half sleep but it seemed so real."

"I think you were whole sleep," Mrs. Covington teased.

"My wife doesn't believe in anything that she can't see. She is a natural heathen," Mr. Covington joked.

Mrs. Covington punched him softly on the arm.

"I am no heathen. I am a realist," she retorted. "Some omniscient creature that runs the earth from space and a bunch of dead folks aggravating others is just ludicrous to me. I believe in evolution, the Big Bang Theory, and that the dead go the way of the dodo and turn into dust like all things do."

"Well, I believe that God caused the big bang and I don't believe that men came from monkeys although all things evolve in the natural cycle of life. But I do agree with you about the death thing. I think that once something is dead. It's dead," James paused. "But science says that energy never dies but transforms so maybe it's possible for us to come back as a spirit or ball of light or something. I don't know," James said with his mouth full. He turned to Mr. Covington. "What do you think sir? Sadie told me that you used to be a preacher man."

Mr. Covington smiled and signaled for James to wipe his mouth. James dabbed his lips with his napkin and nodded his head with thanks.

Mr. Covington took a sip of wine then leaned back in his chair. He said, "That was many moons ago. Another lifetime it seems." He paused in quiet reflection, a hint of sadness filled his eyes. A smile slowly curled his lips. "Well, I agree with you about creation. I believe that the heavens and the earth is the product of a grand design. Only a supreme intelligence could have set such things in motion. As a researcher of phenomenon, I have seen and encountered some of the strangest things and those experiences have led me to believe that there is more to this world that we live in."

James put down his fork, intrigued. "What have you seen?" he asked.

Mrs. Covington rolled her eyes, shook her head, and mumbled under her breath, "Here we go again."

"For example," Mr. Covington said, ignoring his wife. "I went to Brazil a few years ago and this old chiromancer died and I saw her spirit leave her body. It was like a pale smoke that swirled into the air and lingered over her body for a fraction of a second. When it vanished, a cold chill passed through me like ice passing through my body. Even frosty breath left my mouth. It was at least ninety degrees in her little cottage." Mr. Covington shivered just thinking about it. "Another example is when I went to Israel and my colleagues and I were dining in a small café. A terrorist set off a bomb outside of the window where I sat. All I remember is that a shining being grabbed me up and I was transported across the street. Many people died that day including two of my colleagues. The other three were severely injured. There was no way I could have made it out of that place on my own. It had to be an angel that grabbed me."

Sadie glowered. A small bit of vomit reached the back of her mouth. She swallowed it down quickly.

"Carlos Covington, stop beguiling the boy with your fanciful tales. All of those lunatics you investigate got your imagination soaring like theirs," Mrs. Covington jeered. "I'm blessed that you were spared in that bombing but I feel that you just moved out of the way at the right time and the shining being was the glare from the explosive."

"One day you will believe," Mr. Covington retorted. "And when you do, your little world will be turned upside down."

"There is nothing to believe," Mrs. Covington snapped and began eating again.

"Well, I know that there is something else out there," Sadie mumbled under her breath.

"What did you say, baby?" James asked.

"I'm going to get more wine. Anyone want some?" Sadie asked.

"Sure," Mr. Covington said, raising his glass.

Sadie pushed her chair back with the back of her thighs and walked down the hall to her wine closet. She opened the door and entered the dark room. While she stooped down to pick up a bottle of wine, thick myrrh odor thurified the air. The strong smell filled her nose, making her cough uncontrollably. Sadie dropped the bottle, breaking the glass on the floor. She spun around with her mouth agape.

Before her, a beautiful being stood. His face was as bright as the sun and his skin an unearthly gold. His eyes looked into hers and paralyzed her where she stood. A pair of gray wings protruded from his back, spreading from wall to wall casting the room in shadow.

"Wh...wh...what do you want? Who are you?" Sadie fell to her knees. Vomit poured from her mouth, splashing all over her clothes and the floor. The myrrh scent camouflaged its sour odor.

"I am Turiel, one of the Grigori, a Watcher. My soul has burned for you since your conception. Your beauty is like a bane to me. My heart you control with every breath you take. I love you," the angel confessed, its countenance shining brighter burning Sadie's eyes. She pressed her face into her thighs with her arms wrapped tightly around her shins.

"Leave me be!" Sadie sobbed. "I want no part of you!"

"Do not fear me, mighty vessel. My longing for you has a purpose greater than you and I. Soon we will behold the fruit of our union," the angel whispered. His voice was like the sound of many waters.

"Leave me alone," Sadie mewled, her head now between her legs. His countenance was too bright to behold. "Leave me alone!"

"For now my love," his voice echoed faintly. His nude body rose into the air and floated above her head. He opened his arms and she was taken up into them. With burning lips he kissed her. Sadie's spirit was stirred in rapture and pain. She drifted to the floor like a leaf in the wind. He was gone.

"Sadie?" James turned on the light. "Sadie!" he yelled as he ran to her unconscious body spread eagle on the floor covered in vomit and smelling of pungent myrrh. It felt like spiders were crawling all over him. His instincts told him to run and to never look back but he could not. Love held his fear at bay. He kneeled down and lifted her head. Her breath was coming slowly. Ashen and glowing with a strange luminance, her face was changed. Strands of silver hair curled from her temples. Sadie's lips were raw and pulsating scarlet. James shook her shoulders. Her body flopped as if dead. She was so hot to the touch that he let go quickly. After a moment, Sadie cooled down and James pulled her torso into his arms.

"Sadie!" he yelled. "Wake up!" Sweat ran down the side of his face. His eyes bucked. His heart was beating so hard that his shirt seemed to visibly move with the rhythm. James picked her up like a baby and carried her into the living room.

"My goodness!" Mrs. Covington leapt from her seat. Mr. Covington was behind her. "What happened?" she screamed.

"I don't know. She was lying on the floor!" James exclaimed. He placed Sadie upon the sofa, propping her head up on a pillow.

"I'm going to call..." Mr. Covington was cut short.

Sadie sat up. She opened her eyes, blocked the light with her hand, and looked around her. "Water," she whispered, her voice raspy and cracking.

Mrs. Covington ran into the kitchen to get a glass of water.

"Are you okay?" James asked.

"What happened?" Mr. Covington questioned.

"Here." Mrs. Covington handed Sadie the water.

"I fainted," Sadie replied after taking a sip.

"Your hair, your lips...," James said as he touched the platinum strands. The invisible spiders came back crawling down his back and arms. He shook the feeling off and swallowed hard. "That fragrance you're wearing is stronger. What is it? Something more than a faint happened. Tell me!"

"I'm okay. Don't worry about me. I just need to rest," she breathlessly mouthed.

"Do you want me to stay?" James asked angrily, livid with himself because of his inner cowardice. Truly he prayed for her to say no although he would faithfully stay if her answer was yes. Every inch of him was filled with fear.

"Go on home son," Mr. Covington answered. "We'll clean her up and take care of her."

James' eyes flared. "Do you want me to stay?" he asked Sadie again. James needed her permission to leave. Only then would he feel like a decent human being for leaving her in her time of need.

"No sweetheart. I'll be okay. Call you tomorrow, okay," Sadie murmured. She winced. Her lips hurt. She raised her fingers to the tender skin and she saw a smear of blood on her fingertips. A fire stirred within her loins. Her eyes closed. "I'm so tired. I must sleep."

James kissed Sadie's cheek and Mrs. Covington walked him to the door.

"It was nice to meet you," she said.

"You too," James responded, looking over his shoulder at his resting fiancé. "Take good care of her for me. I know she's in good hands but this whole situation doesn't feel right. Something is in that room. I think Mr. Covington and I should check it out before I leave."

Mrs. Covington turned to her husband. Mr. Covington stood up and said, "You're right James. Let's go check things out."

The two men cautiously approached the door to the wine closet. The wood seemed to be moving in and out like a maple bosom drawing breath.

James looked into the eyes of his future father-in-law then back at the door looming before them.

"Ain't no time like the present," James whispered under his breath and grabbed the brass knob. He pushed open the door, forcing it to hit the wall on the other side.

Mr. Covington walked into the dark room, his eyes darting through the darkness. Nothing dwelled inside but the thick pungent smell of myrrh. James followed behind him quietly searching each corner of the room. Upon finding nothing suspicious, the two men exited the room and went back into the living room.

"What did you see?" Mrs. Covington asked.

"There was nothing there," James answered.

Mr. Covington's eyes darkened. Although he had seen nothing, he could feel in his bones that something had been there. He knew the feeling all too well. A chill shot down his back. He shook off the frightening sensation and said, "James, we can take care of Sadie. Go home and relax. Everything will be fine."

James walked to the door. He didn't feel comfortable leaving just yet although he knew Sadie's parents were perfectly capable of taking good care of her. Soon she would be his responsibility. Maybe he should just go and let them have her one last time. James hoped it would be under different circumstances. He placed his hands in his pockets and bit his bottom lip. The thought of Sadie being hurt molested his heart.

James said, "Call me if you need me."

"We will," Mrs. Covington agreed, slowly closing the door, hoping that he would leave without taking offense.

She gave a quick nod. James turned and walked away. She locked the door and rejoined her husband and daughter.

6

"Why are you home so early?" Forrest asked as James walked in the front door. The clock read *8:29* p.m. "Didn't the dinner start at seven? Y'all must've been eating pretty fast."

"Sadie's sick," James mumbled as he dropped his jacket on the couch and plopped down next to it, his face wrinkled with concern. He held his head in his hands and exhaled loudly.

"What's wrong man?" Forrest dropped his feet from the table and leaned forward with his elbows on his knees. He turned off the news and placed the remote on the arm of the chair.

"Something strange happened," James whispered, his eyes glazed and staring into a far off place.

"What do you mean?" Forrest asked, his thick eyebrows furrowed.

"I don't know man. Something happened to Sadie tonight and I feel crazy inside. An eerie feeling was all over me when I left her place," James answered.

"You still aren't telling me what happened," Forrest pestered.

"I'm not sure." James paused. He leaned forward and looked Forrest in the eye. Worry and a bit of tautness traced the rim of his eyes. "Is Lu here?"

"Naw," Forrest answered, deeply concerned about his friend. It was not like James to be stressed out. He was always cool and calm and whatever he felt like he could not handle, he just let it go. Now James sat before him on the brink of fearful frustration and Forrest felt as if he had to help him in any way he could.

"Good. I don't feel like hearing his mouth. I'll tell him about it later when I process it a little more," said James.

"Are you gonna talk to me or not?" Forrest asked, drumming his fingers together. Curiosity was killing him.

He was always impatient when waiting for potentially ground breaking news.

"Just give me a minute to gather my thoughts," James snapped. "Can you just calm down?"

"Sorry dude. I'm just trying to help. You walked in here like someone slapped your mom and beat you up in front of her," Forrest solemnly joked.

James cracked a smile. "You crazy man." He smirked. "But on the real, I met the parents. They're cool people. Nothing like I thought they would be. All was going well until I asked Sadie what kinda perfume she was wearing and she started acting funny. It was just a question. She smelled like an incense shop."

Forrest laughed. "Like an incense shop?"

"Yeah, like some kind of tart, bitter, vanilla scent. It wasn't bad, just strong and making a brother lightheaded," James laughed uncomfortably. "Anyway, we were all eating dinner, right, and talking about ghosts and the supernatural."

"Sounds like this is going to be an ironic incident," Forrest commented. He leaned back into a more relaxed position.

"Ya know! Anyway, Sadie got up to get some wine. Next thing you know, I heard a crash like a breaking bottle so I went to check on her. When I got to the wine closet, she was lying on the floor covered in vomit. The room was so thick with that incense odor that it made my stomach turn. I rushed over to her and she was limp like she was dead. Her lips were a little bloody, her body feverishly hot, and some of the hairs in the front of her head had turned gray. I mean sparkling silver like it was glowing or something!" James exclaimed. "I was spooked," he paused. "What kinda craziness is that?"

"Man that is some wildness!" Forrest exclaimed. "I don't know about that bro. I see a lot of wild things at the hospital but I can't tell you what would have caused that within the span of a few minutes. Maybe something frightened her. There are some rare cases where people are frightened so badly that the stress of the horror changes the color of their hair. Did you check out the room to see what could have caused it?"

"Yeah. It was nothing there, but that smell. Her dad and I checked it out together. I could tell by the way Mr. Covington looked that he was just as creeped out as I was," answered James.

"Maybe you need to leave her alone. Sounds like something sinister is at work. What happened next?" Forrest's heart was beating so fast that he thought that it would burst with anticipation. He leaned forward and started to drum his fingers again.

James chuckled at Forrest's dramatic choice of words.

"I carried her into the living room and her parents tended to her. Sadie said she would be fine and asked me to leave." James leaned back and closed his eyes. "Something ain't right man. I've never felt such a feeling of horror in all my life. I wanted to get out of her place so fast but I felt too ashamed to run for the door."

Forrest shook his head. "I don't know what to say man."

"Me either," James sighed. "Me either. But, I love her and I'm gonna make sure that she's okay."

"You be careful dude. That story crept me out. I got chill bumps all over me. You were right when you said something ain't right. I would've run out of there so fast," said Forrest. "It all seems so hard to believe."

"I know," James said as he stood up and picked up his jacket. "I'm gonna go to bed. Talk to you tomorrow."

"All right. You have a good night sleep. I'll pray for y'all. Everything will work out fine," Forrest said as he picked up the remote and turned the TV back on.

"Thanks man. We both need it. A matter of fact, I'll be praying too. Only God knows what's going on," said

James as he made his way up the stairs and disappeared from Forrest's sight.

7

Chirping, chirping, chirping was all Sadie heard when she opened her eyes. Her window was open and the loud sound of birds chirping outside really irked her. Usually she would welcome the peaceful sound but she was tired, physically drained, and the thought of wings made her skin crawl.

The sun had not poked its head above the horizon yet. The moon was still the ruler of the heavens with its bright beams lacing her window pane with silver ribbons. Oblivious to the lunar beauty, all she wanted to do was sleep but it seemed that every bird in the world was perched on the tree outside her window like they were holding a rally protesting her sleep. It was extremely odd to hear birds that time of morning. Maybe they were bewitched birds holding a secret meeting, connecting their wings and fluttering around the tree in a spell casting circle. Sadie laughed at the thought as she sluggishly crawled out of bed, closed the window and drew the curtains. With weary steps, she made her way back to her bed when the hall light flicked on.

"Dang!" she barked under her breath. She was not in the mood to talk and she knew it would be no one else but her dad. Her father was a perpetual night owl. She would believe that he was a vampire if he didn't have a day job.

A second later Mr. Covington was standing in her doorway in pinstriped pajamas. Despite his nocturnal nature he never stayed up past three a.m. He made himself get in the bed at that time whether his eyes closed or not. But her dad could never sleep when he felt that his little girl was in distress. He tapped the open door with his knuckle.

"You awake, baby?" Mr. Covington asked, staring at her as she sat down on the edge of the bed.

In the dim light he looked older. The shadows rested upon the lines of his face strangely highlighting his mortality almost rendering him mildly frail and ancient of

days although his days were not yet three score and ten. It unnerved Sadie to know that time would one day suck her father up into its black hole of nothingness and he would be gone from this world without the slightest shift of reality. The world would go on as if he had never been and only a select few would know that they were once in the presence of greatness. Nevertheless, she was too tired to revel in his grandiloquence.

"Yeah Daddy," Sadie slurred.

"Can I come in?" he asked.

"Of course Daddy," Sadie whined. "I'm soooo sleepy."

"I know. I just want to talk to you," he said as he stepped inside the room. "I'm sleepy too but thinking about you won't allow me to rest."

"Daddy! It is so early in the morning. Can't this wait?" Sadie begged.

"No. I'm worried about you. I want you to tell me what's going on," Mr. Covington demanded. "And you better not say nothing!" he scolded.

Sadie rolled her eyes and said, "Keep your voice down. You're gonna wake mom."

"Well, you better start talking," he demanded with his arms crossed across his chest like a correctional officer.

"Come sit down," she invited as she tapped the bed next to her.

Mr. Covington sat down and faced her. He reached out and twirled one of her silver curls around his finger. The color looked strange yet beautiful.

"What happened to you, baby?" Mr. Covington asked with a shaking voice. "You look like you saw a ghost. Whatever it was, it scared you so badly that your hair turned gray. That is a momentous matter in itself. Moses' hair turned gray when he descended from the mountain after his encounter with the burning bush. Supposing that no bush was burning in your wine closet, you must have seen something else. Now, I have seen many things in my lifetime and studied many peculiar phenomena and I know that whatever you experienced was awe inspiring. You have to tell me what transpired in that closet."

"You wouldn't believe me if I told you." Sadie laid her head on his shoulder and he wrapped his arms around her as she began to sob heavily. Her tears fell upon his shoulder in warm heavy puddles. Aching bellows climbed up her throat and leapt from her mouth, ricocheting from wall to wall then recoiling back down the sorrowful tunnel it emerged from in one trembling swallow.

"Please don't cry," he begged as a rebel tear forced its way out of his eye duct. "Who do you think you are talking to? I'll believe almost anything," he laughed. "Tell me, baby."

Sadie looked up into his eyes and laughed through tears.

"Daddy," she whined. "Please don't tell Momma."

"Okay, baby, but you have to tell me something that I can't tell." He rubbed her arm as he rocked her.

"An angel came to me," she whispered.

"What?" Mr. Covington pushed her shoulders back and looked into her eyes. "What did he say?"

"An angel came to me," she repeated. "He said that he was watching me or a watcher or something." Sadie paused to think. "He spoke as if he loved me. It was the first time he spoke to me but the second time he had come. The first time he took me." Sadie swallowed hard and buried her face into her father's chest.

"I don't understand," Mr. Covington's voice trembled. He held Sadie so tight that she could hardly breathe. She forced her head to the side so that she could catch her breath. Mucus ran from her nose and mingled with her tears, both soiling his pajama shirt terribly.

"Daddy, he did things to me!" she wailed, gripping his shirt with angry fingers.

"What on earth are you talking about?" he asked through clinched teeth. His trembling chin rested upon the top of her head. Tears escaped the corner of his eyes. They were coming so fast that he did not know that they were there until he tasted their salty warmth upon his tongue. Mr. Covington's breathing escalated.

"I think he raped me," Sadie cried.

"You don't know?" he snapped. "Rape?" he roared. "How can you not know for sure?"

"I don't remember the act but I remember waking up naked and this pungent smell all over me," she wept.

"This is impossible!" her father proclaimed. "Are you telling me that a son of God mated with you?"

"I think so." Sadie looked at him with pitiful eyes. She trembled as her father withdrew his arms and placed them upon his lap.

"This is insanity!" Mr. Covington stood up. Anger filled his voice as his nostrils flared and he gnashed his teeth.

"You believe me don't you Daddy?" Sadie fell onto her side and balled up into fetal position. Her body shook uncontrollably. She never imagined that her father would doubt her. She felt like a fool. He thought that she was insane. Who could she turn to? She damned herself for telling him.

"I believe you. It's obvious that something happened. You wouldn't lie about such a thing." He paused. "I'm not sure about the angel," her father whispered. "If this is true, I'm afraid for you. Not since ancient times have such preternatural perversity occurred." Mr. Covington leaned over and kissed Sadie's forehead. "Tell no one. Let me do some research."

"You've heard of this happening before?" Sadie asked.

"Sweetheart, it's Biblical. Genesis 6:1-4 says:
'Now it came to pass, when men began to multiply on the face of the earth, and daughters were born to them, that the sons of God saw the daughters of men, that they were beautiful; and they took wives for themselves of all whom they chose. And the Lord said, "My spirit shall not strive

with man forever, for he is indeed flesh; yet his days shall be one hundred and twenty years." There were giants (nephilim, fallen mighty ones) *on the earth in those days and also afterward, when the sons of God came in to the daughters*
of men and they bore children to them. Those were the mighty men who were of old, men of renown'.

Such an experience is of legend my love. Hopefully what you say isn't what you really experienced."

Fear embraced her. It dug its fingers deep into her flesh and squeezed out every bit of courage with its serpentine arms. She did not like what she saw in her father's eyes. They betrayed his calming voice and any ounce of hope she may have had of being alright.

"Daddy, will I be okay?"

Mr. Covington reluctantly nodded his head and answered, "Of course, baby. Of course. Get some rest. I'll see you at breakfast in a couple of hours."

Mr. Covington walked out of the room, refusing to look back, and clicked the hall light off.

Sadie tucked herself under the covers and said a prayer for the first time in her life.

"God, I know that I have ignored you my whole life. Please don't be angry with me. Now I realize that you are real. Forgive me for my doubt and my ignorance. I'm not sure if ignorance is the correct word because I knew about you but I didn't believe. I went to work every day among your humble servants and thought them foolish for worshiping a silent and inactive deity. You were just too abstract to me. Now that I have seen an angel, I know that there is a God that it serves. Lord, forgive me! I'm sorry. Please, help me. I don't know what's happening. Protect me from this thing that boldly defiles me at its will," she wept silently. "I don't know what to do but I do know if you refuse to help me..." Sadie closed her eyes and allowed sleep to come.

8

The aroma of sweet blueberry muffins floated through Sadie's apartment on a cloud of fragrant wholesomeness. Mrs. Covington stood in front of the oven wearing one of the fancy aprons that Sadie collected.

Sadie had a fetish for the cooking garments and she went to flea markets from coast to coast to find the prettiest of them. They reminded her of an era of feminine strength when women were proud of being mothers and wives and felt just as empowered as modern women in their man suits and short hair cuts. Make no mistake, Sadie had no quarrel with the working woman, she was one herself, but she equally respected the sacrificial importance of the homemaker.

Mrs. Covington opened the oven to see if the muffins had browned and closed it once again after seeing their yellow heads. She pulled a pan from the cabinet and filled it with turkey bacon. After grabbing a few dishes and juice glasses to set the table, she went into the guest room where her husband was still sleeping and kissed his inanimate cheek.

"Wake up Carlos," she whispered.

"Ebbie, give me a few more minutes," he pleaded through unmoving lips.

"I will not," she hissed playfully. "It is after eleven and you and that daughter of yours are still hibernating like bears. Were you two up last night?"

"Yes, baby," Mr. Covington said as he rolled over onto his back and opened his eyes. "We were up pretty late talking."

"Did she tell you what happened to her?" Mrs. Covington questioned. She placed her hands on her hips.

Mr. Covington closed his eyes and lied, "No. She couldn't remember."

"Are you being frank with me?" Mrs. Covington questioned.

"Yes Ebbie," he mumbled.

Her eyes morphed into slits. She could feel it in her bones when her husband was lying and her bones were twitching like a bad nerve.

"Keep your secrets," she pouted. "But come to breakfast now!" She grabbed the pillow from under his head and hit him in the face with it. Mrs. Covington stormed from the room and banged on Sadie's door.

"Get up girl!" Mrs. Covington yelled. "It's time to eat."

"Okay, Mom. I'll be out in a minute," Sadie responded.

"You better be!" Mrs. Covington threatened as she made her way back to the dining room to set the table.

After a few minutes, all three sat at the table with faces aching with worry and fear, each of their fears different.

Sadie had a fear of the angel seeking her out again, of her father revealing her secret to her mother, and of the news her father may bring back after his research.

Mr. Covington feared for his daughter in the worst way that a father could. He felt that he could not protect his little girl and that she may be violated again by some lust drunk phantom. The images that ran through his head were maddening. If he could crack his head open like an egg and stick his hands in to grab the slimy images and cast them away from him he would. With all his experience and training, there was nothing he could do to help her and he felt like fecal matter.

Mrs. Covington feared that she would be left out of the most exciting news that has ever entered her tiny family. Subconsciously she felt that something was very wrong and that maybe her time of naturalism may be suddenly coming to a frightening end. There was something eerie going on in this place and for the first time in her life she felt a deep boding.

In fear and silence the Covington family ate until the awkwardness of the meal was interrupted by the buzz of the doorbell.

"Who could that be?" Sadie asked as she hopped up from the table and made her way to the door. She pushed the button and asked, "Who is it?"

"It's me."

"Come on up." Sadie pushed the button again and unlocked the door. She went back to the breakfast table and sat down. Both of her parents stared at her in silence waiting on her to tell them who rang. She ignored them completely. Sadie picked up a slice of bacon, sucked it, took a sip of juice, a bite of toast then ate the bacon in calculated nibbles. Her lips were still very tender so she tried to eat with a skinned back grin and tried to move her mouth as little as possible.

Irrespective of her feelings, Mrs. Covington laughed and said, "You have been eating bacon like that since you were two years old. I cannot believe that you are still doing it. Remind me not to serve bacon at your wedding breakfast."

Everyone laughed quietly.

The door opened slowly and James walked into the apartment.

"I hope that I'm not interrupting. I was in the neighborhood and decided to swing by and check on Sadie," James said. James was never in the neighborhood unless he intended to be. Sadie lived in the opposite direction of his home, office, and his most frequented places.

"Baby you are welcome here anytime," Sadie responded. "Would you like something to eat?"

"Sure," James answered as he walked into the kitchen and fixed himself a plate. He sat down next to Sadie and poured himself a glass of juice. "How are you feeling babe?" he asked. He kissed her cheek softly and gave her hand a little squeeze before he took a sip of juice.

"I'm okay."

"What happened to you last night?" James asked.

Sadie and her father's eyes locked.

Mrs. Covington placed her fork on the table and waited for Sadie to answer. It was obvious that Sadie and her father were harboring a horrible secret. The look in both of their eyes made the hairs on the back of Mrs. Covington's neck become erect.

Sadie began to eat slowly. She sat quietly for a few minutes hoping that everyone would forget the question asked.

"Did you hear me, baby?" James asked, his brow furrowing, as he turned his eyes to her.

"I heard you," Sadie whispered. She kept eating.

"Why are you behaving so rudely?" Mrs. Covington scolded. "Answer the young man's question. I'm curious about what happened too." She wore a crooked frown.

Sadie dropped her fork and shot her mother a wicked glare.

"I can-not re-mem-ber. I faint-ed," Sadie said pronouncing ever syllable of every word.

"You have never been a good liar," Mrs. Covington snapped. "It's unfair to hide things from me and your fiancé. Your father isn't the only one who loves you!"

Sadie grabbed her mother's trembling hand.

"I know Momma. I know that you are concerned about me. I really don't know," Sadie lied. "I was trying to piece things together with Daddy last night but I can't remember anything."

Mrs. Covington twisted her lips in disbelief. She couldn't believe that Sadie sat before her spewing a bold faced lie.

Mr. Covington put his arm around his wife and kissed her forehead.

"Sadie will be just fine," he said. "Don't worry your pretty little head off."

Mrs. Covington knocked his arm away.

"Don't patronize me! A fool can understand that something is wrong here and both of you know exactly what it is!" Mrs. Covington howled. "Why would you want to keep me in the dark? Don't I deserve to know what is going on with my child?"

Mr. Covington smiled sadly.

"First of all, Sadie is our child. You didn't make her by yourself; so, stop it. Secondly, no one is going to keep you in the dark." He turned to Sadie. "Baby, we're going to have to cut this trip short. I have research to do at the university and I have to get back to work. I'm sure you understand."

Sadie nodded her head. Fear was ever present in her father's eyes. His fear seemed as if it had grown tenfold since last night. She had a feeling that her situation was more precarious than she imagined. An aching chill zigzagged down her back and arms. It took every bit of courage she could muster not to fall to the floor and wail.

"When are you leaving?" James asked.

"We're leaving after breakfast," Mr. Covington responded.

"Why so soon Carlos?" Mrs. Covington asked. Anger echoed through her voice. Now her suspicions were hyperbolized.

"I received a bit of troubling information last night and I may be embarking on the most preternatural event of my life and career," Mr. Covington answered truthfully.

"You're cutting our vacation short because of more eerie foolishness?" Mrs. Covington barked, still hurt by her daughter and husband's secrecy.

Mr. Covington smiled a weary smile and kissed his wife hard on the lips. She smiled through her sulking face.

"Are you going to be okay?" he asked Sadie.

"Yes Daddy."

"I'll take good care of her Mr. Covington," James interjected.

"I'm counting on that son," said Mr. Covington leaning across the table holding James in an iron eye lock. "Keep an eye on her and if she allows you to, stay over a few nights and keep a close watch over her."

"Yes sir." James nodded.

"Well, baby, we better be going," said Mr. Covington as he stood up and went straight into the guest room to pack. In minutes, he was carrying their suitcases to the door. "Come on Ebbie. It is time for us to go."

Mrs. Covington took off the apron and laid it across the back of her chair.

"Goodbye Sadie. Take good care of yourself," Mrs. Covington uttered. She suspiciously kissed her daughter. Sadie nodded her head in agreement.

"It was nice to meet you," Mrs. Covington said as she turned to James and gave him a big hug.

"It was a pleasure meeting you both. Hopefully when we meet again things will be under better circumstance," said James.

Mr. Covington came over to the table and kissed his daughter and hugged his future son-in-law. He grabbed his wife's hand and they both sped from the room in supreme urgency.

9

It was noon when the Covington's arrived at Miami International Airport. The hot sun burned in the sky like an unquenchable flame beating upon their skin with unmerciful fists. Sweat began to pour from their pores as soon as they stepped outside into the humidity. The air was thick and palpable. It felt as if a heavy coat was draping their shoulders. Their clothes stuck to their bodies like bandages as they drug their bags to the pick-up curb. Each second took an eon in the sweltering heat. Mr. Covington wiped his brow impatiently. Mrs. Covington fanned herself with her hat. They grabbed the first taxi they saw and arrived home within half an hour.

The taxi pulled up to their three story beach home. The salmon colored structure was topped with a sienna tile roof and the yard was adorned with citrus fruit trees and tall waving palms. Bushes of wild flowers bordered the lawn as plastic pink flamingos hid their beaks within their petals. From the sidewalk, a perfectly leveled flagstone path led to a large porch with a wooden emerald green bench swing and what seemed like an endless assortment of flowerpots. Lots of windows decorated with warm colored fabric covered the home's façade. Vivid life pulsated from every inch of the Covington's home.

The cab driver took their bags to the door where he dropped them heavily on the "Home Sweet Home" doormat and stuck his hand out in Mr. Covington's direction. Mr. Covington gave the driver a very generous tip and the Covingtons entered their home.

"Why did we leave Atlanta so early? What was the rush?" Mrs. Covington questioned. "Are you going to tell me what's going on?" she dropped her bag and sat on the couch. She took off her wide brimmed purple straw hat and sat it next to her. The bright floral dress she wore looked heavenly against her skin. "I'm worried about Sadie and I want to know what's going on."

"Honey, you wouldn't believe me if I told you," Mr. Covington answered, taking off his straw fedora and fanning his face with it. "Besides, I'm not in the mood to convince you. I'm worried about our girl too and I have a lot of work to do." He unzipped his bag and pulled out a white T-shirt. He slipped out of his tropical print button down and put on the T-shirt, tucking it into his khaki shorts. "I'm going to the university to do some research. Call me only if it's an emergency." Mr. Covington bent down and kissed his wife's cheek. He grabbed his keys and headed for the door.

"Carlos, I demand that you tell me what's going on!" she yelped.

"Not right now. I really have to go. I love you Ebbie. Talk to you later," said Mr. Covington as he walked out of the door.

Outside Carlos Covington could hear his wife slamming doors. He knew her anger would subside soon. It always did. Her anger was like fire on an inch of paper. It flared high but died quickly. She was a reasonable woman and he would make it up to her by plucking her some lemons from the tree in their front yard and making her a pitcher of sweet lemonade. Ebbie loved his lemonade. He would throw a few strawberries and orange slices in it also. She would be just fine. Besides, she knew that he loved their daughter as much as she did and he would always do everything in his power to protect their family.

Mr. Covington jogged down the driveway, jumped in his silver Jaguar and sped down Bird Road, arriving at the university within minutes.

Thoughts of Sadie would not leave him. Mr. Covington knew exactly what she described. It was impossible for him to conceive of it being true. But he knew Sadie was not a liar and she would never make up such a thing. Sadie was a skeptic like her mother. To make such a claim was downright alien to her personality. Sadie was a proud and optimistic atheist. A staunch believer in human divinity and that nature was the creator and humans were the sustainer of all things. She believed that everything was created and destroyed in its own time and that there was no need for God when humanity was the captain of its own fate. Sadie would never ever lie about a supernatural experience unless it really happened. Like when Saul in the Bible became Paul, something mind boggling occurred to change his entire perspective on life. A person usually does not change their core beliefs unless something mind boggling occurs.

Mr. Covington was credulous when it came to the spiritual world. He believed a lot of things, but he never believed in the legends concerning angels falling in love with humans. Those stories were nothing more than silly myths, tales spun from the fabric of an ignorant and paranoid society to explain why some women gave birth to strangely tall children. Today giants are called basketball stars.

The hairs on the back of his neck rose. *What does this mean for Sadie?* He thought. The thought of a creature mounting his little girl like an incubus nearly made him homicidal. Quickly he jumped from his car and ran full speed across campus to his office. Random students stood in amazement of the old man's swiftness.

Mr. Covington's office was huge and very well lit. Books lined every wall. A small refrigerator sat in the corner and a small sofa was up against a far wall. A crescent shaped desk sat in the middle of the room stacked with papers and a high tech computer.

Mr. Covington logged onto his computer and cross referenced the words "sons of God" and "nephilim." He went to the religion section of his personal library and pulled out a Holy Bible, a copy of the Ethiopian Bible, a copy of the Dead Sea Scrolls, the book of Enoch, the book of Jubilees, and a few books on Jewish and Christian mythology. He sat the books on his desk, picked up his pen and notepad, put on his glasses, and began to read.

10

Sadie rested silently within James' sleeping arms. It was nice to have him in her bed again. Under different circumstances the temptation would have been far too much for her to bear, but now sex was the furthest thing from her mind. Her body ached. Her womb tingled nonstop as if she was suffering from a strange infection. Sadie was too ashamed to tell James about it. Not only would he not believe her, he probably would not want to marry her either. The scent that constantly enveloped her made her head swoon. No matter what she did, it would not wash off. When she looked in the mirror, she did not recognize the stranger in front of her. She felt like she had lived twenty years within the last few days. The gray hairs on her head didn't help. But she did notice a youthful glow that radiated from her skin. It was as if she wore an ultra glittering bronzer that twinkled like pixie dust every time the light hit her.

Hearing from her father was her main objective besides ridding her life of the unearthly intruder. Her dad would find out what was going on. He would tell her what to do. He would make things right.

Sadie snuggled closer to James. His chest smelled of soap. His heartbeat was strong and steady, his breath deep and nearly silent. She kissed his chin lightly and traced his cheek with her fingers.

"What would I do without you?" she whispered and kissed him again.

"What would I do without you?" a ghastly voice whispered in her ear. The bitter smell wrapped around her. Tears poured from Sadie's eyes as her body was torn out of James' sleeping embrace. He did not stir. He lay as if dead, but she could tell by the rise and fall of his chest that life was still in him.

The angel held Sadie close to him, his nude body filling her with ungodly heat. His wings lifted them to the ceiling. He pressed her back against the ceiling and folded his wings around them forming a feathery shield, a plumy dome hanging from the ceiling. He showered her neck with fiery kisses leaving red marks on her flesh. She flinched at the heat and moaned with unwarranted pleasure.

"I will not share you," his voice echoed in Sadie's ear. "Make him go away. You are mine now. Do not make me destroy him."

"Who are you?" Sadie groaned as the fiend became one with her. Light flashed around her. Fire shot through her body. Hot pain racked her flesh then cooled with orgasmic delectation. Blistering liquid filled her from within. Her heart stopped for a moment and rebooted quickly to keep her among the land of the living.

"I am Turiel, your lover. Your only lover," he crooned in her ear. "You will honor me in a way that a wife is required to honor a husband."

"No..." she whimpered. "Demon, be gone from me..."

"Soon, my love, you will have no choice." The angel pulled away from her limp body and let her fall upon the bed with a heavy thud which rocked the bed with great force.

The angel vanished leaving the room in the suffocating scent.

"What the hell!" James popped up. He looked down at his wife-to-be in utter horror. James slowly slid off the side of the bed and stood up. His pilomotor reflex activated. James blinked his eyes and took a deep breath thrice to ensure that he was not hallucinating.

Sadie's naked body lay unconscious, her face and neck covered in smoking purplish red marks. Her hair was so bright silver that the shine hurt his eyes. The myrrh fragrance covered her so thickly that he almost gagged on the taste of it. Her eyes looked as if they were covered in golden cataracts. James reached out his trembling hand and touched them. The scale-like lenses fell onto the bed turning into gold dust. Her eyes closed.

James let his eyes search the rest of her body. Her gown was nothing more, but tiny pieces of scorched cloth. The insides of her thighs were singed and smoking, but her flesh was smooth and unscarred. Her genitals were misshapen, grossly swollen to the point that it looked like bubbling flesh and most of her pubic hairs were burned off. The ones that were left were bright silver. Sadie's legs jerked uncontrollably as fulgid ooze dripped slowly from her womb.

"Sadie," James called. Tears rolled down his face. He knelt down and rubbed her head. "Sadie, wake up, baby," he cried. "Please wake up." James sobbed. "I need you to wake up."

Sadie lay still.

James bolted to her nightstand and picked up the telephone. He dialed 9-1 then hung up and dialed his home number instead. The phone rang twice.

"Yo," Luis answered.

"Is F…F…Forrest there?" James stammered.

"Yeah, dude. Calm down. I'll get him on the phone. Is everything a'ight?" Luis asked.

"No, everything is not alright! Please put Forrest on the phone," James yelled.

Luis yelled up the stairs telling Forrest to pick up the phone.

"James, is there anything I can do?" Luis asked, bothered by the fact that James asked for Forrest instead of him in time of trouble.

"I'll let you know," James snapped.

Forrest picked up the phone. "I got it," he said through the receiver. "Lu, you can hang up now."

"A'ight." Luis reluctantly put the down phone.

"What's going on, man?" Forrest asked.

"I need you over Sadie's house immediately. Something has happened and I don't know what to do," James forced out on the brink of tears. "Come now."

"You want me to bring Lu?"

"I don't care. Just get here!" James yelled and slammed the phone down.

About half an hour later, Luis and Forrest rang Sadie's doorbell. James buzzed them up quickly and let them into the apartment.

"What's goin' on, man?" Luis asked. He walked into the living room and looked around. "This is a nice place," he said as he picked up a small piece of African art and sat it back down. "But I'm sure you didn't have us rush up here to see the décor."

"Shut up, Lu. I should have left you at home," Forrest snapped.

"You couldn't have left me nowhere," Luis spat as he got up in Forrest's face.

Fire was in James' eyes. He rushed over to Luis and pushed him so hard that he fell flat on the floor. James pointed his finger in Luis' face and said, "Now you listen to me. Shut the hell up and chill out! I need help here and I ain't got time for your crap. Do we understand one another?" James roared.

"Yeah, dude," Luis responded as he got up from the floor. Shock and embarrassment was painted across his face. "Sorry, man."

"Sadie is in here," James said as he instructed them to follow him.

The three entered Sadie's bed chamber. James lagged behind his two friends. Forrest's eyes bulged like a fish and Luis belched out a loud curse word.

"Bro, you into some freaky stuff," Luis exclaimed. "What in the world did you do to her?" He gasped when he saw all the little marks on her neck. "Are those hickies or bruises?" He leaned in closer to her. "What's that smell?"

James' eyes narrowed as he looked at Luis. "I didn't do this. When I woke up, she was lying next to me this way." He turned to Forrest. "Help her. You are the only doctor I trust right now."

"Is this the smell you were talking about the other day?" Forrest asked as he bent over to examine Sadie's neck and shoulders. They were terribly bruised. "It smells like myrrh." He brushed his hand across her sterling silver hair. It looked metallic and not humanly gray at all. Her forehead was hot to his touch. "She's feverish." Forrest took her pulse and found it normal.

"Yeah. The odor is stronger than ever now." James began to pace. "I don't know what happened. I was asleep and the bed rocked real hard like she was dropped from the sky and I popped up. She has been sleeping and unresponsive for about a half hour now and I...I don't....don't know what to do," James choked on his words. "What you see isn't the worst of it. I had to cover her up so you couldn't see her naked, but her thighs are all charred looking and her private parts are all swollen and wet."

"Did you two have sex?" Forrest inquired, his arms folded and his eyes full of skepticism. "Do I need to examine her?"

"No. We were fully clothed and cuddling when I fell asleep," James answered spitefully. He did not appreciate Forrest's judgmental attitude. James felt that Forrest had already mentally tried and convicted him for assault and battery.

"Well someone did somethin'," Luis said as he lifted the sheet covering Sadie. "There's a huge wet spot under her," he squealed as his eyes rested upon her blistered private parts. "What the hell happened to her down there and what's wit' the smoke? Her stuff is smoldering!" He covered his mouth to stop from vomiting. He dropped the covers and turned away.

"You stupid jackass!" James shouted before he landed a firm punch across Luis' temple. "Why would you do that?" he screamed, standing over his fallen friend. "Why would you look at her?" he seethed, his hands balled into pulsating fists.

"Sorry man," Luis apologized dizzily. "I was just curious about the rest of her. She's messed up real bad." Luis held his swirling head. "Real bad." Luis sat up and looked at James with a look that would make a serial killer blush. "I know things are messed up, but that's your last time putting your hands on me. We boys, but if you touch me again all bets are off."

Forrest pushed James to the side and helped Luis to his feet.

"There was enough violence in this house already tonight. Need there be more?" Forrest asked looking straight into James' eyes.

"You think I did this?" James asked through his teeth. He was hurt by the sharp accusation in Forrest's eyes. James stepped close to Forrest with balled fists, but Forrest did not back up an inch. Both men exchanged dangerous glares.

"I don't know. You were the only one here. You were in bed with her," Forrest answered. "I'm calling the police." Forrest picked up the phone.

"Don't do that man," Luis said as he took the receiver out of Forrest's hand. "Even I know that James couldn't have done what was done to this girl…"

"James," Sadie whispered. Her eyes were still closed as she tried with great difficulty to lift her head. "James."

"I'm here, baby." James rushed to her side.

"Call Daddy," she uttered. "Daddy will know what to do." Her eyes flickered then opened completely. Quickly they filled with fresh tears. "I hurt all over," she moaned.

"What happened sweetie?" James rubbed her head and kissed her face. Her body quaked violently then calmed. He propped her head up with his cradling palm. "Who did this to you?" he questioned angrily.

His friends gathered around the bed and waited with great anticipation; Luis getting back to his senses and Forrest with his arms crossed and eyes resting on James.

"Turiel, tell my father his name is Turiel," Sadie slurred as she fainted once more.

James laid her head down.

"Get her phonebook off of the night stand," he told Luis, "so I can call her dad."

"Look," Forrest yelled, pointing at Sadie. He gripped James shoulder so hard that the bones could have snapped under the strength of his fingers

Right before their eyes Sadie's body began to heal. The dark marks on her skin became lighter and lighter until they faded from sight. Her smoking flesh ceased to make vapors. Charred skin regained their natural color. The odor surrounding her diminished into a faint pleasing aroma. Sadie's eyes popped open and she sat up.

"James, what are they doing here?" she questioned, pulling the sheets around her.

James' mouth hung open. Words were so far from his mouth it was as if he had been mute all of his life. His friends were dumbstruck also. They had witnessed the supernatural and each man wanted to run from the room screaming with their arms flinging madly, ripping their shirts from their torsos, and casting the rags to the wind.

"James?" Sadie called again.

"You...you ... you were b...b...badly bruised," James stammered. He flopped down in a chair near the bed. "J...j...just moments ago you looked like...like death had you." James dropped his head into his hands. "N...n...now you are like you...you...you have never been t...t...touched." Full of helplessness and confusion, he looked into Sadie's eyes. James could not stop shaking his head. "W...w...what's going on here?"

"I don't know," Sadie wept. "I really don't know." She buried her face in the pillow.

Luis came over and placed his hand on James' shoulder. Forrest went to his other side and did the same.

"I think we should take him home," Luis said. "He's had enough craziness for one night."

"Okay," cried Sadie through the pillow. "Take good care of him for me." She lifted her head slightly. "I love you James."

"We'll take good care of him," Forrest said, helping James to his feet and pulling James' arm around his shoulder. Luis took James' other arm.

"Make sure you take care of yourself. When I examined you, you were in pretty bad shape. It's simply impossible how you just..." Forrest stopped mid sentence. There was no way he could describe what he had just witnessed. It was scientifically impossible. As a doctor he had seen many medical miracles, but this was beyond his scope of reasoning. "Are you going to be okay here alone?" Forrest asked.

"What does it matter? She ain't comin' wit' us!" Luis spat.

"Be quiet Lu," James mumbled as he hung his exasperated head. "Baby..."

"I'll be okay," Sadie whimpered.

"Are you sure?" James lifted his head and looked at her.

"Yes, I'm sure."

James let his head drop once again. Every bit of life was sucked out of him. He did not know how to feel or what to think. He let his weight fall upon his friends and whispered, "Please let's leave this place."

"I love you James," she repeated, this time reaching out. Her hand touched the side of Luis' leg and he slapped it away vehemently.

"Girl, I don't know what's happenin' in this damn house, but stay the hell away from me," Luis growled.

James looked at Sadie with confused and horrified eyes. He turned his head away from her. The men carried him out of the apartment and they disappeared into the night.

11

Mr. Covington poured over his studies. With every word he read, his fear escalated. Every story brought new horrors to the surface of his mind. Every myth in every book he read reconfirmed his worst fear that the angel was trying to create a mutant breed with his daughter.

The office phone rang, startling him so badly that he almost fell out of his chair.

"Hello," Mr. Covington answered. "This better be an emergency because I asked not to be disturbed."

"It's your daughter sir," the receptionist said. "She said that it's urgent that she speaks with you."

"I'm sorry for being rude Mandy. I haven't slept in two days. I thought it was my wife raising sand again about me not being home for the past two nights," he said guiltily. Never had he spent a night outside of his home in nearly forty years of marriage. His wife was absolutely frenetic. "Please put Sadie through. I don't want to accept any other calls today from anyone outside of my family unless I say otherwise. And if my wife calls again, tell her that I love her and I'll be home soon. Hopefully she won't give you too much trouble. If she continues to call, put her through."

"Yes, Dr. Covington," the receptionist said as she transferred the call.

"Daddy," Sadie called through the phone.

"Yes sweetheart."

"It came back to me. It bathed me in its fire," she sobbed while filling him in with all the details from the myrrh scent to her smoldering flesh.

"James was here. He didn't see it, but he saw the condition the angel left me in. I was bruised and violated. Then he saw my flesh mend itself as if nothing happened," Sadie paused to catch her breath. "He's horrified Daddy. James probably never wants to see me again," her words rushed out in high pitched agony. "I think the angel left me in that condition to frighten James on purpose because it told me to get rid of James," Sadie cried.

"Let James worry about James. All I care about is you!"

"But I love him so much Daddy," Sadie bawled.

"Well, if he loves you too, he'll be back. Nothing could keep me away from your mother. If James can't love you unconditionally, I hope he never comes back!" Mr. Covington barked although he could not blame James for his reaction.

"Don't say that Daddy. What James witnessed wasn't an everyday occurrence. He saw me regenerate. Any human would be freaked out. I don't know what I would do if the shoe was one the other foot."

"Are you okay? Did the demon hurt you?" Mr. Covington irritably asked, changing the subject.

"Yes, Daddy. The demon hurt me, but I'm okay now. My body healed itself. Most of the pain is gone now. Every string of hair on my body is completely silver," Sadie sobbed. "Truly chrome! I look like an alien off the Sci-Fi channel."

"Calm down, Sadie. I need for you to be at ease so we can fix this thing."

"Okay, I'll try, but it's kinda hard to be at ease when you are being attacked by a demon!"

"Calm down I said!" her father snapped. "I can't pretend to understand what you're going through, but I need you to try to focus so we can figure out how to get rid of this fiend. Understand?"

"Yes," she agreed and tried to steady her voice.

"Did he tell you anything? The angel?" her father asked.

"His name is Turiel. He said that he was my husband and something about offspring," Sadie paused to think. "I don't know Daddy. The beast said lots of things."

"Turiel?" Mr. Covington questioned. "He is one of the Watchers."

"The Watchers?" Sadie asked.

"Yes," Mr. Covington answered. "Do you have time to listen to what my research reveals?"

"Yes," Sadie replied cautiously.

Mr. Covington straightened his reading glasses and picked up his note pad.

"Before I start, I need you to be completely silent and hear me out. Ask me questions afterward. Do you understand?"

"Yes," Sadie whimpered.

"It's going to sound like a lot of fantastic information, but bear with me and just listen, okay?"

"Okay, Daddy."

"In the Bible, we assume that the *sons of God* are referring to the angels by examining the following scriptures: Job 1:6 and Job 2:1 which says, '*Now there was a day when the sons of God came to present themselves before the Lord, and Satan also came among them.*' and Job 38:7 which says, '*When the morning stars sang together, and all the sons of God shouted for joy?*' as well as Genesis 6: 1-4 which I quoted for you when I was at your home. Christian theology declares that Satan is a fallen angel and these scriptures include him as a son of God therefore we must conclude that the sons of God are angels."

"So I'm having sex with the devil?" she blubbered.

"Don't be foolish! You agreed to listen. Please do so." Mr. Covington took a deep breath and began again, "According to my research in the Book of Enoch, which is an ancient text written hundreds of years before the New Testament around 160 B.C. It was very popular and well known during the Maccabean times through the time of Christ and beyond. It was an accepted part of the Biblical canon for many years before the final revisions of the Bible we know today. The Book of Enoch was quoted by many of the Church Fathers, deeming it as an inspired work of God. However, some future Church Fathers abnegated the canonicity of the book."

"Why?" Sadie asked.

"Some did not find it to be divinely inspired. But for whatever reason, it didn't make it into our Bible. However, that doesn't make it less valuable. Lots of great books didn't make it," said Mr. Covington. "For example, the Catholic bible has more books than the Protestant bible. Canonization is all a matter of politics and opinion."

"What does the book say?" Sadie asked. Her voice revealed that she was getting weary of hearing about Enochian history and she had no interest hearing about the process of canonization. She wanted to get to the meat of the matter.

"The Book of Enoch says that there were about two hundred angels, called Watchers, who lusted after mortal females. They fell to earth to mate with them. The ring leader of this wanton troop was the angel Semyaza. Turiel was named as one of the angels leading the fall under the command of Semyaza.

1Enoch 7[i] states:

'And all the others together with them took unto themselves wives, and each chose for himself one, and they began to go in unto them and to defile themselves with them, and they taught them charms and enchantments, and the cutting of roots, and made them acquainted with plants. And they became pregnant, and they bare great giants, whose height was three thousand ells: Who consumed all the acquisitions of men. And when men could no longer sustain them, the giants turned against them and devoured mankind. And they began to sin against birds, and beasts, and reptiles, and fish, and to devour one another's flesh, and drink the blood. Then the earth laid accusation against the lawless ones.'

Not only did these demons take mortal women as wives, they taught them witchcraft, gave women cosmetics to inspire vanity, and instructed men in the art of war.

The unholy union between the sons of God and the daughters of men produced giants also called the Nephilim.

2 Enoch 18:3-4[ii] says:
'These are the Grigori, who with their prince Satanail rejected the Lord of light, and after them are those who are held in great darkness on the second heaven, and three of them went down on earth to the place Ermon, and broke through their vows on the shoulder of the hill Ermon and saw the daughters of men how good they are, and took to themselves wives, and befouled the earth with their deeds, who in all times of their age made lawlessness and mixing, and giants are born and marvelous big men and great enmity. And therefore God judged them with great judgment, and they weep for their brethren and they will be punished on the Lord's great day.'"

"Daddy, is this angel truly a demon?" Sadie asked, her voice quivering uncontrollably.

"I know this is a lot to digest, but please let me finish telling you my findings," Mr. Covington said. "Stay with me and listen, baby."

"Okay," Sadie reluctantly agreed. Her father's findings only made her anxiety worse. All she really wanted to know was how to keep the angel away from her forever. She could care less about the history of the beast. But she decided to be quiet and listen because her father always told her that the future can be predicted by studying the past.

"Also fragment seven of the Book of Jubilees (a former book of Jewish canon and still a part of the Christian Ethiopian canon) found in the Dead Sea Scrolls state:
'(5:1-3)[iii] And it came to pass when the children of men began to multiply on the face of the earth and daughters were born unto them, that the angels of God saw them on a certain year of this jubilee, that they were beautiful to look upon; and they took themselves wives of all whom they chose, and they bare unto them sons and they were giants. And lawlessness increased on the earth and all flesh corrupted its way, alike men and cattle and beasts and birds and everything that walks on the earth -all of them corrupted their ways and their orders, and they

began to devour each other, and lawlessness increased on the earth and every imagination of the thoughts of all men (was) thus evil continually...

(7: 21-25)[iv] For it was on account of these three things [fornication, uncleanness, and injustice] that the flood was on the earth, since (it was) due to fornication that the Watchers had illicit intercourse - apart from the mandate of their authority - with women. When they married of them whomever they chose they committed the first (acts) of uncleanness. They fathered (as their) sons the Nephilim and they were all unlike, and they devoured one another: and the Giants slew the Naphil (Naphelim), and the Naphil slew the Eljo (Elioud), and the Eljo mankind, and one man another. And every one sold himself to work iniquity and to shed much blood, and the earth was filled with iniquity. And after this they sinned against the beasts and birds, and all that moves and walks on the earth: and much blood was shed on the earth, and every imagination and desire of men imagined vanity and evil continually. And the Lord destroyed everything from off the face of the earth; because of the wickedness of their deeds, and because of the blood which they had shed in the midst of the earth.'

This human-angel species was so depraved and greedy and their hunger was so unquenchable, they literally ate man's food resources and ultimately began to eat man. Many myths claim that they were the reason God flooded the earth although there were surviving clans of giants reported in later books in the Bible.

Numbers 13:30-33 says:

'Then Caleb silenced the people before Moses and said, "We should go up and take possession of the land, for we can certainly do it.' But the men who had gone up with him said, "We can't attack those people; they are stronger than we are." And they spread among the Israelites a bad report about the land they had explored. They said, "The

land we explored devours those living in it. All the people we saw there are of great size. We saw giants (the Nephilim) *there* (the descendants of Anak come from giants {the Nephilim}). *We seemed like grasshoppers in our own eyes, and we looked the same to them.'*

Deuteronomy 2:10-11 also refer to the giants and uses the names Anakim and Emin. Deut. 3:11 tells about the king of Bashan who was the last of the giants and was over thirteen feet tall." Mr. Covington explained.

"What does all of this mean for me?" Sadie questioned, her voice trembling with anger and frustration. The information dump did little to quiet her pounding heart. It only escalated her fears and confirmed her feelings of hopelessness. Her father only confirmed the identity of the problem, but gave no resolution for getting rid of it. There was no way she could fight such a foe. "Am I to birth one of these fiends?"

Mr. Covington was silent. He could not pick the right words to say. It was evident what this Turiel creature was up to. It was to breed the Nephilim once again and it had chosen Sadie to be the mother to its offspring. Mr. Covington swallowed hard. What could he possibly tell her to comfort her?

"Daddy?" Sadie pleaded. "Help me!"

"I'll do all that I can," Mr. Covington paused, choking back his desire to weep and wail his daughter's eminent demise. "All we can do is to ask God to protect you. If it is all possible, try to prevent the demon from mating with you again."

"How am I supposed to do that?" Sadie wept angrily. "I have no power over him. I have begged him to leave me be, but obviously he has other plans for me!"

The sharpness in Sadie's voice surprised him. Mr. Covington sympathized with her frustration, but the anger in him begged to bubble out like a shaken soda can praying for the top to be popped. Maybe it was selfish for him to feel angry, but angry was all he could be. There was no way he could cause harm to the celestial culprit and ease all her worries. All in all he was as useless as a shoe without soles.

"I don't know, but pregnant you can't become," Mr. Covington declared. "I have to go now," his voice trembled. "I have more work to do. Be strong my love. We will find a way," he said free of confidence.

"Call me soon," she cried.

"Of course my dear, and please ask a friend or someone you trust to stay with you. I would feel a lot better if you were not alone," Mr. Covington said.

"Okay, Daddy."

"I love you, Sadie. Everything will be fine. I promise," he whispered then hung up the phone. As soon as the receiver was down, he wept, head pressing into hands, and body shaking furiously.

12

Sky Dawn moved through the farmers market with wondrous grace. Each step was like a toe pointed leap. She walked as if the world belonged to her and her feet were supported by clouds. Her fiery red hair waved from her head like kinky scarlet banners folding upon heavily freckled shoulders and tickling the middle of her bony back. She was a gypsy by nature with bracelets up to her elbows, silver rings on every finger and toe, and a green ruffled skirt hanging to her ankles lightly brushing her sandaled feet. A red half shirt stopped just above her navel exposing her golden red skin. Giant hoop earrings pressed against high freckled cheekbones that dipped into deep green eyes. A yellow ink pen with a feathery top was tucked snugly between her breasts and a brown leather journal was sticking out of the top of her purse.

One by one she sniffed fresh fruit, inhaling the savory confections by the second and filling her cloth purse with those to her liking. She relished the sweetness of their odors and delighted in the bright colored skins covering their edible flesh.

"How much for this?" Sky asked an old woman sitting behind a fruit stand.

"Kiwis are five for a dollar," the lady responded with a happy smile and a deep Cantonese accent.

"Then, I will take five," Sky said as she filled a small paper bag with the furry fruit. She paid the woman and made her way to another vendor when she heard her cell phone play Beethoven's Symphony Number 9.

"Hello," she answered with a great grin on her face when her caller ID read Sadie.

"Sky?" Sadie asked.

Sky answered, "Yes, who else would it be?"

"Hey girl, you didn't sound like yourself," Sadie said.

"Well, if you called me more often you would remember what my voice sounds like," Sky joked.

"How have you been?" Sadie asked. "I just bought your new book. It was absolutely wonderful. Your imagination is limitless. I had all my clients purchase one and you know I bought quite a few copies to hand out as gifts."

"I'm so glad that you liked it. It seems like people are becoming less interested in fantasy novels and fairytales," Sky said. "But for the moment I'm doing just fine. I'm blessed."

"That's good to hear. You're very modest about your success although you are number three on the best seller list." Sadie's voice smiled. "I wish that I could feel blessed at the moment," she whispered.

"What's wrong sweetie?" Sky asked while purchasing a Jamaican vegetable patty and cocoa bread from a street vender. She put it in her bag for later.

"Sky, I need you. I'm in trouble down here and I need my best friend near me. Can you come to Atlanta?" Sadie whined.

"Of course I can sweetie. I need a break from New York anyway. I just moved to Harlem from Long Island. Ask me why in the heck did I do that? I left quiet for constant racket. I guess I secretly love the hoopla. I'm engulfed within the city twenty four hours a day. You have to come see my brownstone. It's hot! You would love it. It's huge girl. I have three large bedrooms and three floors. Can you believe it? I finally own my own property. But the noise...," Sky intoned. "Although I'm just settling in, I could use a break. This crazy town has me buggin'. The movers broke some of my antiques and spilled coffee on one of my priceless books. I could've killed them. Then, this crazy cab driver tried to run me down the other day. He splashed mud all over my new skirt that I had this up and coming designer named Carl Carter make for me. You talkin' 'bout someone being mad! I was on fire! Girl, steam was comin' out of my nose and ears like one of those cartoon characters. I wanted to pull him out of that cab by his bushy beard and beat him senseless. Not to mention my new neighbor, Mrs. Morris, who knocks on my door every two seconds askin' me if I would like to meet one of her nine sons. All of them are ugly and broke. And girl you know I'm not materialistic or shallow so they gotta be monsters if I don't even want to have a conversation. Worst of all, I went to an art auction with a friend and scratched my head and ended up bidding seven thousand dollars on a painting which looked like some old man's butt." Sky took a quick breath. "Don't get me started on the guy on the subway playin' with his nipples and singing *Twinkle Twinkle Little Star*. And girl, this dude I went on a date with last week has been callin' my house fifty times a day. He even popped by my crib and I went ballistic. I can use some peace and quiet. Besides, I miss you so much. When do you want me to come?" Sky asked.

"As soon as you can get a flight out," answered Sadie, trying to process all the information that just flew at her. Sky talked a mile a minute, but Sadie loved to hear the joy in her voice. She knew that Sky being in her presence would alleviate some of the fear and stress she felt. Maybe the angel would not come with her there. Maybe it would feel less threatened by a female in her presence. Sadie asked, "Can you come tomorrow if I purchase your ticket?"

Sky answered, "Yes ma'am. I can and I will. Are you sure you want to buy the ticket? You know you don't have too. I make nice loot now. I just received a major three book deal and…"

"I don't mind. I have a million sky miles and I really need a friend to stay with me. I haven't been feeling well. I've taken off work because of all the stress I'm under. Things in my life are torn asunder and I just can't be alone," Sadie said.

"Well, don't fret. I'll take good care of you," Sky promised.

"I know I can always count on you," said Sadie.

"Always. Are you sick?" Sky asked. "A few weeks ago I thought I was comin' down with a..."

"My health is fine," Sadie interrupted before Sky went on another long spiel. "Being ill would be so much easier," Sadie murmured.

"What's going on?" Sky asked.

"It's a very long story and not a story I want to start telling over the phone. We will talk when you get here. Please hurry," Sadie pleaded.

"Of course. I'll go home and pack now. See you tomorrow sweetie," Sky replied, hung up the phone, and dropped it in her huge cloth purse. She ran to the nearest subway station and rushed home to pack.

13

James lay upon his bed with his eyes counting the stucco flowers on his ceiling. His head lay within the cradle of his palms as the quiet sound of his breathing echoed through the cool room, floated up into the ceiling fan, and wisped out of the open window. The moonlight lit the otherwise pitch black room in a luminescent gray. Every object blended into one another forming a bland continuum. The image of Sadie's flesh regenerating right before his eyes played over and over again in his mind. He could see the purple flesh fade into new brown skin like a drop of water on a hot pan. The bruises were there and then gone as if he and his pals imagined the whole morbid scene. The choking smell of her faded into a pleasant aroma and the strange steam that rose from her skin dissipated. He imagined her intimate parts folding back into itself and becoming recognizable again. Sadie was as right as rain as if she had been sleeping all along, sweet and serene.

James felt sick. His stomach churned with fear. Liquid bubbled to the back of his throat then fell back into his troubled organ in acidy waves. His chest felt tight. He could feel his blood moving through his veins. James' heart was troubled. Marriage was a fearful thought in itself, but now he had to consider marrying a woman who was experiencing some sort of supernormal abuse like in that old movie *The Entity* where a ghost was sexually assaulting a woman. The movie was based on a true story. James wondered if Sadie was battling a poltergeist. He shook off a hard chill.

What if Sadie was brutalized again and the police arrived before she rejuvenated? He could go to jail. What if it started happening to him? If something could attack her it could certainly put a hurting on him. The thought of his genitals being mangled made him want to smash his skull against his steel bedrail. That was reason enough to leave Sadie alone for life.

James closed his eyes and sighed. He knew in his heart that he still loved her. She was everything to him, the only woman he had ever loved and he had been with many women. Sadie was the only woman he even considered being faithful to. Most women he viewed as fun time girls with no potential for anything, but a headache. Sadie was different. She didn't tolerate his foolishness. Like when he thought he could speak to her any kind of way, she put him in his place so fast, so firmly, and so politely that he ended up an apologetic jerk and minded his manners from then on.

Sadie was independent, but she knew how to let a man be a man. There was never a struggle for power in their relationship. Money was never an issue. She was generous in every way, accepting even the tiniest of gifts with total gratefulness and giving with sincere thought and love regardless of price.

She was very strong, but not argumentative. He loved the fact that she could express her views without getting overly emotional, loud, or obnoxious; although, she could really show her tail if she needed too. Sadie was never combative. She always spoke with confidence and security. It was clear what she was and was not going to tolerate.

She understood him and supported him. Sadie was his cheerleader, the biggest fan of his life. Everything he did she celebrated it as if he had just found the cure to all the world's ills. He felt like a real man when he was with her. Sadie made him want to be a better person for her and himself. Consequently, he made it his life's mission to cater to all of her needs and desires for he knew that she would always be appreciative of his efforts to please her. James honored her in every way his heart would allow. How could he possibly spend his life without her?

He picked up the phone and dialed her number.

"Hello," Sadie answered.

At the sound of her voice an icy cold grabbed his feet and imbued up his leg, cramping his calf and locking his knee. It wrapped around his thighs, gripped his loins, and slithered up his heaving chest. The image of her steaming flesh and bruised genitalia flashed before his eyes. He saw the golden cataracts turn to dust. An eerie feeling churned within his bowels.

James hung up. He was not ready to speak to her. There was nothing he could say. James wasn't sure if there was anything he could ever say.

A light rapping on his bedroom door broke James' train of thought. His eyes shifted to the closed maple wood door and he pushed up on his elbows.

"Yeah," James yelled.

"Can I come in?" Luis asked through the door.

"Sure dude. Give me a sec," James answered as he sat up on the side of the bed and quickly pulled on a pair of basketball shorts that were lying on the floor. "Come in." He rubbed his face and watched his friend enter the room wearing sagging jeans, an extra extra large T-shirt, a baseball cap turned to the side, and a thick platinum chain with a diamond medallion of a naked lady riding an eagle hanging from it.

"How you feelin'?" Luis asked as he sat down in the black leather chair in the corner of the room.

"I'm cool. Just a little overwhelmed. You understand what I mean?" James asked.

"I know what you mean, but I can't understand it." Luis paused in speechless reverence. "Jay, what we saw the other day really scared the hell out of me. I never seen no mess like that in my life," Luis confessed. "I didn't know whether to run or to get help. I'm sorry I was ugly towards your girl, but..."

"I understand where you're coming from. You saw what I saw and I still can't digest it." James lay back on the bed and stared at the ceiling. "I don't know what to do. I love her, but I don't think that I'm strong enough to handle whatever she's going through and I feel guilty and terrible that I'm not by her side. I'm freaked out, but she must be going insane. Something is happening to her and no one can help. She's in that apartment alone and something could be attacking her as we speak. I should be there, but... but...I can't. I know I'm acting like a scared little punk."

"Man, this ain't no movie! Real people ain't gonna be sticking around after something like that happens. Don't feel bad. You bein' smart. I know Sadie is cool and all, but she obviously got problems that you can't handle," Luis spat. He removed his baseball cap and sat it upon his lap.

"I just can't abandon her. She needs me. I'm a coward. I called her and at the sound of her voice I hung up. I just don't know how to be," James whispered.

"Well, I can't tell you what to do, but I think you should come with me and Forrest and have some drinks. You've been up in this room way too long and some fresh air will do you good. Bro, you need to get yo stankin' self in the shower. You smell like forty four dead rats."

"I really don't want to deal with Forrest," James admitted, ignoring Luis' insult.

"Why not?" Luis asked.

James sat up and looked Luis in the eye and said, "He believed that I hurt Sadie. That man has known me for seven years. He has lived with me for five and he is supposed to be one of my best friends and he was going to call the cops on me."

"Sadie was pretty messed up. Forrest was scared," Luis explained.

"But the way he was looking at me, like I was some hoodlum, like he didn't know me from a cat on the street. He believed that I was capable of torturing another human being. He thought I could do that to Sadie. He knows I love that woman more that I love anyone. Forrest didn't respect me enough as a friend, as a man, as a brother to trust me. I would never have assumed the worst of him. He didn't even give me the benefit of a doubt. Damn Forrest. He can go to hell for all I care!" James shouted.

"Don't be like that Jay. You know Forrest loves you. He was just analyzin' the situation. Think about it dude. If you walked in and saw a girl in my bed all beat up and sexually molested and no one was there, but me, you might think about callin' the cops too. So don't get all huffy and full of pride. He was just as shocked as I was. The only reason I didn't call was because I got too many traffic tickets," Luis joked, but then added seriously, "Forrest may have handled it wrong, but he didn't call the cops and he didn't leave after your girl started in with the magic tricks and he did help carry yo heavy dumfounded ass out of her apartment. Not to mention the fact that he has taken off work for the last couple of days to cook and be here for you in case you wanted to talk. He's worried about you. You know how hard it is for him to get time off at the hospital. He works in the emergency room and they page him a hundred times a day. So don't be like that man. You acting like a punk right now. People can't always do like you think they should. We are who we are."

James stared at the ceiling in silence.

"Now you speechless?" Luis asked. He picked up a pillow and hit James across the face with it. "I ought to kick yo butt for punching me in the head the other night. If it wasn't an emergency I would have given you the business."

A smile curled James' lips. "You wish you could give me the business! Give me a few minutes to take a shower. I'll be dressed soon and I'll meet y'all downstairs."

"Bet. Wear something fly because when I change clothes all the ladies are gonna be attacking me. Try to look your best so that somebody might notice you're alive. I know it's hard to have a friend that looks like me," Luis said with a mischievous grin on his face. He got up and walked out of the room with a cocky swagger.

"Lu!" James yelled.

"Yeah man," Luis peeked his head in the door.

"Thanks."

"No problem. We all brothers up in this piece," said Luis and walked down the hallway.

14

The Atlanta skyline was always pretty to Sky. The circular lights of the Westin Peachtree Plaza and the gold sparkly dome of the State Capitol building brought a smile to her face. Although it was tiny compared to New York City's skyline, it was an interesting mix of modern and classical architecture that was comparable in beauty. Sky sat in the back of a yellow taxi cab and admired the twinkling streetlights and tree lined roads. It was amazing how an hour and a half flight could take a person from the concrete jungle to southern eloquence. Towering pine trees and full bosomed oaks hovered over the city like emerald guardians protecting the people from invisible foes. Friendly faces in charming chocolates and proper pinks, peppered with assorted shades defining the spectrum in between, intermingled on every corner. Cars puttered down the street nose to tail like elephants marching in the circus.

Sky marveled at the relaxed sophistication called Atlanta. She drank in deeply the quality of life swirling around her as she let the sights disappear and form something new at every turn. Soon she arrived in the heart of Buckhead and the taxi came to a halt. Reflecting in Sky's green eyes was Sadie's beautiful apartment building. The towering structure attempted to touch the sky with its arched windows decorated with kissing cherubim and gold trimmed doorways as inviting as the gates of heaven. Sky tipped the driver and grabbed her bags and headed to the door. She adjusted the many strands of multicolor beads that hung around her neck and pushed her untamable hair behind her shoulders. Sky pushed the buzzer and waited.

"Yes," Sadie answered.

"Open the door girl. My feet are tired," Sky declared.

Sadie let out a high pitched scream of excitement that made Sky place her hands over her ears, causing her bracelets to clang and fall to her elbows. Sadie buzzed her in and within minutes the two were locked in a lovesome embrace.

"How are you?" Sadie asked as she picked up one of Sky's bags and walked her to the guestroom. "You look absolutely beautiful. That dress is fantastic. The colors really compliment your complexion."

"I know," Sky jested as she tossed her hair behind her shoulders, placed her hands on her hips and gave them a roll.

"You are still the most arrogant thing in the universe," Sadie laughed. *And you have the right to be.* She thought. Sadie always admired Sky's unique beauty. Sky had the kind of look that either a person loved or hated. You either thought she was amazingly beautiful or weirdly unattractive. Not very many people had her golden red freckled skin and scarlet hair. That combination mixed with round voluptuous African lips, considerable height, and emerald eyes laced with ruby lashes, was truly a divine creation graciously brought forth by her Nigerian mother and Irish father.

"You know it girl. Look at you. You are almost as pretty as me, even when you are wearing sweat pants and a tank top," complimented Sky.

"Almost huh?" Sadie laughed.

"Almost," Sky joked. "But what's with the silver hair. Where on earth did you find that color? It looks good. Your face can pull anything off, but that silver looks like real metal." Sky gently pulled one of the silver curls and let the silky loop wrap around her finger. "Unnatural. I can make a killing in New York selling that stuff."

"Look at you," Sadie said. "You're always thinking of a hustle."

"And you know this," Sky replied as she raised her hand in a high five. Sadie slapped Sky's palm lightly.

"Believe it or not," Sadie said, running her fingers through her sterling curls and placing Sky's bag on the bed.

"My hair turned this color naturally. I don't know how, but it did. My father said that it was stress induced."

"That's a heck of a lot of stress. I wonder if Harlem will turn my hair green." Sky laughed. "What kind of perfume are you wearing? It's a bit too strong."

Sadie shamefully remained quiet, but put on a false smile.

"How are your parents doing?" asked Sky, unpacking in the meantime.

"They're just fine. They're really living it up in Florida. Ma is at the beach almost every day and shopping like a mad woman. Daddy still travels a lot looking for the next real life horror story. He just found his latest project," Sadie said sourly. "How is your father? Is he better now?"

"He's so-so. He's been mourning for mom for three years now. My brothers and I hired a good doctor and found a nice minister to visit him weekly so he can talk and really cope with her death. He loved her so much."

"We all did," Sadie interposed.

"When she died so suddenly of natural causes, he just couldn't understand. His mind couldn't wrap around the injustice. She was perfectly healthy. She exercised, ate right, went to church, helped the needy, had never had any serious illnesses, and was only fifty-five years old. She died for no apparent reason except that God wanted her back in heaven. Her death devastated us all. You know how Mom was the life of our family. But, Dad just can't seem to move on. He sits around that big house in silence, doin' nothin', and goin' nowhere. When he does speak, he is cursing God for ruining his life and taking the only truly good person he has ever known. He has turned into an angry atheist hermit. The only people he interacts with are the maid, me, and my brothers," Sky explained.

"I am sorry to hear he is still in such bad shape," Sadie sympathetically whispered.

"How much stress have you been under?" Sky changed the subject as she plopped down on the bed, her floral sundress clashing with the paisley comforter.

Sadie sat down next to her and sighed. "Girl I don't even know where to start. I don't want to talk about it tonight though. I just want to enjoy your company before reality sets back in. Is that okay with you?"

"It's okay with me," Sky said as she hugged her best friend as tight as she could. She let go and looked into Sadie's eyes. Never had she seen such sadness in Sadie. Usually Sadie was all rainbows and sunshine. There was something disturbing behind Sadie's eyes. It was as if her irises were infected with a crawling darkness that reeked with foreboding. It almost caused Sky to gasp. "Whatever you're going through, we can get through it together."

"I hope you're right," Sadie said as tears formed in the corners of her eyes. "I sincerely hope that you're right."

"I'm always right," Sky laughed softly and wiped away Sadie's tears. "Don't you know this by now?"

Sadie nodded and laid her head on Sky's shoulder.

"It's still pretty early," Sadie said as she looked at the clock sitting on the night stand. "Do you want to go out to dinner? I don't feel like cooking and I don't really want to order in. I have been confined to this apartment for days."

"Well, Miss Lady, that means we will have to go out. I wanna go somewhere hot! Somewhere all the fellas can sweat me." Sky winked and smiled. "You know. Where we can listen to a little music and dance a little and eat a lot."

"I sure do," said Sadie. "There's this new place that everyone has been talking about. It's one of those places where the bouncer has to pick the most stylish people to get in. Like the old Studio 54 in New York. It's supposed to have the red carpet and a lot of celebrities. Last week they said that it had more stars than the sky. It costs an arm and a leg to get up into the VIP. It has a huge dance floor and supposedly good food."

"Good thing we both have two arms and two legs," laughed Sky. She unzipped another suitcase and started to place her items in the drawers and her toiletries on the vanity.

"Can you be ready in about an hour?" asked Sadie.

"Of course. Just get out of my room so I can get dressed," Sky said as she gently pushed Sadie towards the door.

15

Carlos Covington sat on his living room couch, next to his wife, clicking the remote control with unblinking eyes. His hair was wiry and his eyes were terribly bagged and heavily veined. Slouched posture made him look eighty years old sitting in his wrinkled T-shirt and striped boxer shorts. He had been sitting silently on the couch for what seemed like forever eating only dry cereal, playing hooky from work, and accepting no phone calls. The rancid odor emanating from his armpits and mouth verified that he had not used a washcloth or toothbrush during his time in front of the flickering TV that was casting dim light on his downcast face.

Ebbie Covington gently tugged on the remote until her husband reluctantly loosened his grasp. She placed it down and she sat next to it on the cherry mahogany coffee table, blocking the TV screen.

"Carlos," she whispered. His eyes looked through her as if she was a hologram. "Carlos, I know that you hear me."

He looked into her eyes, his face as blank as a white wall.

"Sweetheart, are you okay?" she asked.

Mr. Covington remained silent.

"Carlos Covington, don't make me jump on you!" her voice trembled. "You answer me when I'm talking to you."

"What?" Carlos grumbled without moving his lips.

"What's going on?" she asked tenderly, folding her hands on her lap.

"Nothing," he murmured.

Ebbie stood up, her fists balled and her eyes tearing up.

"Enough of this foolishness! You will tell me everything. Everything! Do you hear me?" she huffed. "If you leave out one detail I will strangle you with my bare hands!"

"It's no use. We can do nothing to help her," he whispered and reached for the remote control.

"There is always something! Tell me what's going on!" Mrs. Covington screamed, picking up the remote and throwing it across the room. The clicker hit the hard wood floor and popped apart sending its batteries flying in all directions.

"I will tell you if you promise to just listen and not to disregard anything that I say. I will not tolerate your doubt or criticism. Do I make myself clear?" Mr. Covington said between his teeth, seething with choler.

Mrs. Covington sat down on the heavily pillowed sofa, placed her hand upon her husband's knee stroking it gently and said, "I will listen. I promise. Just tell me." She placed both of her hands on the sides of his face and pulled his lips to hers kissing them lightly. "I promise, baby."

Mr. Covington dropped his arm on the back of the sofa, around his wife's shoulder, and let his head fall back against a ruby pillow trimmed in shimmering gold. He took a deep weary breath and began, "Sadie is in trouble and I don't know what to do." Tears streamed down the side of his face and disappeared into the cushions of the luxurious sofa.

Ebbie's eyes bulged and watered at the sight of his tears. She had only seen her husband cry twice in her life, once at his father's funeral and the other when Sadie was born. Seeing tears trickling down his face sent an alarm ringing through her being. Fright chilled her chest so badly that she thought she may have been experiencing a small heart attack. "Don't cry..."

"You promised to just listen," he interjected and began again. "Our baby is in grave danger. She was...," he paused, painfully squeezing his eyes shut and gritting his teeth, "was...," he bit his bottom lip, "sexually assaulted."

Ebbie gasped in terror. She grabbed her chest and fell hard against the pillows, bumping her head against his arm. Maybe she was really having a heart attack for sure. Pain shot through her chest in uncompassionate bolts, but in moments they mercifully subsided showing Death's blasé indifference for taking her with him.

Mr. Covington continued with his eyes still locked on the ceiling oblivious to the panic on his wife's face, "She was violated by a creature not of this world. It came to her thrice and its lust seems to be affixed on her. It came to her for the second time when we were there. It didn't take her at that time, but it made its affections known." Carlos Covington thoughtfully paused. "I don't know what to do to help her. I researched this creature and Sadie and I both think that it's an angel."

"An angel!" Ebbie squealed. "You mean a messenger of God with wings, a halo, and a heavenly abode?" she questioned, utterly astounded by the preposterous news.

"Yes, an angel. It gave her its name. My research verified that it is in the ancient books. The scriptures insinuate that it may be trying to impregnate her," he stated quietly. Carlos turned to Ebbie. He could see the doubt and suspicion in her eyes, the way they narrowed into leery slants. He hesitantly continued. "Long ago, a mutant breed of man and angel walked upon the earth before the great flood. They were the giants of folklore, the great heroes of old, mighty warriors."

"I can't believe this!" Mrs. Covington declared.

"I know. I can't believe it either, but Sadie wouldn't lie about such a thing," Mr. Covington said. "She was just as cynical as you are. Sadie is afraid and suffering greatly. She said that the angel came to her again when James was there. James didn't see it because he was asleep, but he found her badly bruised and sexually violated. He called his friends over, one of them is a doctor, and Sadie said that her body regenerated right before their eyes. Scared the living soul out off all of them! Now James is afraid to be around her and she is living in perpetual fear."

"Maybe she had some sort of mental break. Maybe she imagined the creature. Maybe James violated her and she created this thing in order to vindicate her fiancé. Maybe they all misinterpreted what they saw," Ebbie whispered. To even consider the possibility of an angelic rapist was insanity. How could she honestly pretend to believe an angel had sex with her daughter? It was true that Sadie would not make up such a thing, but this story just made no sense at all. "There has to be a logical explanation for all of this," she shook her head slowly.

"Sure there is dear," he spat. "Maybe she turned her own hair as silver as the rims on my car! That is what she was doing when she went into her wine closet. She was dyeing her hair!" he ranted. "Maybe she created her own myrrh perfume that won't wash off! Maybe she burned her own flesh without fire! Maybe she is simply a sexual deviant that violated her own body until it became swollen and misshapen! Maybe she is just a lunatic liar! That sounds pretty logical to me!" Carlos roared. Venom radiated from his eyes. Acid spewed from his tongue.

Ebbie was taken aback. Carlos had never looked at or spoken to her like that before. She could feel the hate pulsating from his heart. A dark shadow settled over his eyes as his lips transformed into a horrid knot. His nose flared and his jawbone tightened. The man sitting next to her wasn't the man she married almost forty years ago. This menacing stranger chilled her to her core.

"I should've never told you. I knew you wouldn't listen or believe. You look at me daily as if I'm a fool. I have bountifully provided for this family by searching for the unknown and I have told you year after year about the miracles I've witnessed. You have dismissed me as a fragile minded buffoon who believes anything not even considering the fact that your nescient narrow mindedness makes you the fool because you believe nothing," he roared. "Now, the supernatural has imposed itself upon our girl and you dismiss her as you have me. You see dear, I don't care about you not believing the things I have seen, but I do care about you refusing to believe my child when her very life is in danger."

"I...I...I'm sorry," she uttered. "But how can you ask me to believe something so...so...crazy," she cried. "I love her as you do. I just can't..."

"From now on, ask me nothing! Sadie and I will handle this situation ourselves. You don't worry!" he yelled and bolted from the sofa, his eyes two lasers aimed to fire. "Please do me a favor." Mr. Covington glared at her angrily. "Don't discuss this with your psychiatrist buddies or anyone else. It would only make matters worse. Stay out of it all together!" Hurriedly he left the room. Moments later, the bedroom door slammed and the lock clinked.

16

Three feet in circumference, a half gold half silver disco ball hung twirling from a rhinestone cord in the middle of the high ceiling casting diamonds of light on the faces of those dancing on the gigantic oval dance floor. Hip Hop music blasted from chrome speakers, positioned on the four corners of the ceiling, pumping like metal hearts beating to its own life rhythm.

Three bars tended by absurdly attractive male and female bartenders were stocked from end to end with exotic liquors, expensive champagnes, effervescent beers, and eloquent wines. The bars were placed strategically near dozens of small marble topped tables surrounded by matching bar stools with plush leather cushions where tipsy patrons sat momentarily until revisiting the bars to expunge their pockets and their wits.

In the very back of the club was a long table topped with fancy finger foods and sweet treats: chocolate covered almonds, strawberries and cream, powdered cakes, crab legs, lobster tails, chicken wings, spring rolls, and an endless array of delectable edibles protected by a baker's dozen of pretty servers dressed in tight black uniforms.

Scantily clad women and salivating men swarmed around each other like crazed wolves confused about which was hunter and hunted. Flirtatious eyes and flashing smiles delivered many into carnal temptation. Shaking hips and pumping torsos combined with raspy voices and untamed hands blended with smoke filled air and cups running over created the ideal coupling atmosphere.

"This place is on fire!" Luis shouted over the loud music, almost spilling his Piña Colada as he danced. He looked amazing as he moved his hips in black leather pants, white shirt embroidered with dark roses unbuttoned to the navel, and snake skinned boots in dark gold matching his hoop earrings. Luis grabbed the hand of a flirty blonde with large blue eyes dancing sexily beside him. Lifting her arm above her head, he gave her a quick spin, letting his eyes wash over her fit frame. She whispered something naughty in his ear and slipped her phone number into his front pocket. Smiling wickedly, he slapped her backside and sent her back to her giggling friends.

"I can't lie, this is the hottest club I have ever been to," Forrest agreed, dressed in navy slacks and a cream polo. A five o'clock shadow was on his face giving him a rugged Mediterranean appeal. He sipped on a dark colored beer and leaned against the wall admiring a fiery red head dancing provocatively across the room. "I think I'm in love," he declared before he took a deep swallow of beer.

"You always in love," James laughed and popped Forrest on the arm. "Who you looking at?" he asked, after taking a sip of rum and coke, looking extremely attractive in a white linen suit with dark cream sandals. He wore a diamond and platinum bracelet as thick as a watch band which glistered brighter than the disco ball. Half karat diamond studs sparkled aggressively in each ear in rigid competition with the diamond bands he wore on his right pointer finger and left pinky finger.

"Her over there." Forrest pointed and tapped Luis, who was whispering in the ear of a dark chocolate goddess. Luis pulled his cell phone out of his pocket, quickly entered the woman's number and sent her on her way. He turned to look at the woman that hypnotized Forrest.

"You couldn't tame that Forrest. She too wild for you boy! She would twist your spine," Luis teased.

"I would love for her to twist my spine," Forrest laughed. "She could twist it all night long, every night for the rest of my life."

"Listen to you mister romantic. I can't believe that you're hunting in the meat market," James said.

"She is beautiful," Forrest declared. "I have never seen anyone like her."

He admired her lean form gyrating sensually in a very short kelly green skirt with magenta frill and a matching halter top revealing a tight and perfectly flat stomach. Her legs were extremely thin, but very strong and shapely. The magenta stilettos she wore magnified the definition in her calves. She was a nymph; her shoulders square yet delicate, her neck swanlike, and her hair radiant like sunlight bouncing off rubies.

"She a'ight," commented Luis. "Kinda strange looking to me. I guess she has a cuteness to her that's kinda unique, but she is way too skinny. She's shaped like Jack the Pumpkin King on *Nightmare Before Christmas*, but you white boys like those lonely chicks. You know, the kind that ain't got no body," he laughed.

James laughed hysterically. Forrest smiled despite himself.

"Damn what you're saying. She's exquisite," Forrest retorted not taking his eyes of the twirling woman, her hair flying like tongues of fire in the wind.

"Go holla at her playa," James said. "She's over there waiting for you. She just don't know it yet."

"Sick her dog," Luis joked, imbibing his frozen delight.

"Okay, I'm going in for the kill," said Forrest taking another sip of beer. He placed the bottle on the table and ran is fingers through his ebony curls, careful not to shift his yarmulke. "Y'all come with me. She looks like she has a girl with her."

"I ain't looking for no chicks," said James.

"Well I am," Luis said as he straightened his collar. "Come wit' us Jay. From the back her friend looks like a winner."

"Man, you can only see her butt from this angle," Forrest said.

"That's all I need to see. She gotta nice bubble that I might wanna pop," Luis said and placed his drink on the table next to Forrest's. "Let's roll."

 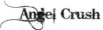

The threesome walked through the crowd unto the dance floor, pushing gently to part the tight ruck.

Forrest tapped the scarlet dancer on the shoulder. "Excuse me miss, do you mind if I dance with you?"

The woman turned around slowly, her hands planted on her narrow hips. Her friend stood quietly next to her.

Surprising recognition slightly disfigured Forrest's face. At once the sterling hair and angelic face of the fire nymph's friend was recognizable. *Sadie.* Forrest looked back at James.

James tried hard to hide his shock, but his eyes betrayed his true emotions.

"Hello Forrest, Luis, James," Sadie greeted uneasily. "This is my best friend, Sky."

"Nice to meet you Sky," Forrest greeted as he kissed her hand and smiled. His face lit up like a Christmas tree when looking into her pine green eyes.

"Likewise," Sky responded with a smile of her own. "Nice to meet all of you."

"Sky, this is James," Sadie said. "My umm…" Her words became suspended in midair and unable to break through the invisible force that held them there.

"Her fiancé," James finished the sentence and put out his hand. Sky took it and shook it firmly. "This is Luis." James pointed over his shoulder with his thumb.

"What up," Luis replied rudely, totally uninterested in being in Sadie's company. He avoided all eye contact and searched the room for his next victim. With ease he spotted a golden Latin doll with long raven waves, gypsy eyes, and more curves than a honeycomb. "I'll catch y'all dudes later. The devil is callin' me." He licked his juicy lips. "Mami was born for me," he said and disappeared into the crowd.

"So, would you like to dance?" Forrest asked Sky again. She was even more beautiful up close. Her freckles reminded him of the first and last line of a poem by Gerald Hopkins. Forrest lifted her hand, kissed it again and said,

"Glory be to God for dappled things...He fathers-forth whose beauty is past change: Praise Him." In divine truth this speckled beauty was a testimony to God's glory.

Sky smiled and said, "*Pied Beauty.* Indeed I am." She grinned from ear to ear. "Sure, I would love to dance. I like you verrrry much." Sky gave him her other hand to kiss. He did. She turned to Sadie with a wicked look in her eye and asked, "Are you going to be okay without me?"

"Go have fun. I'm cool," Sadie answered, not moving her eyes from James.

"You sure?" Sky asked again.

"Girl, go dance! I'm just fine," Sadie barked lovingly.

Forrest and Sky left the two forlorn lovers staring at each other in silence, both ill at ease.

A few seconds passed and Sadie decided to cut through the air between them. It was becoming burdensome and too much to bear.

"You look nice," she complimented. "White always looks good on you. It brings out the beauty of that onyx skin of yours."

"Thank you. You know how amazing you look." He touched the red orchid in her hair and gently felt the soft silver strands that held it. The scent of her infiltrated his nose. Spiders crawled all over him again. He put his hand in his pocket. "A matter of fact, you look a bit too amazing. I see you are wearing my favorite dress." He grimaced.

She knew that he hated for her to wear that tight violet dress it public. Although it was ankle length, it was like a second skin and revealed every inch, truly every curve and intimate crease of her.

Sadie blushed.

"Sadie, you know how I feel about that dress," said James.

"Well, I haven't heard from you in days. You haven't called or accepted any of my calls. I didn't know if I was a newly single woman or not so I wore it just in case,"

Sadie stated in a high pitch voice revealing her wounded self.

"In case what?" James was not amused. The thought of Sadie with another man made him see red.

Sadie completely ignored the question. "How have you been?" she asked.

"Okay and you?" James subdued his anger. Getting mad would only make things worse and he could not stand for things to get worse than what they were.

"I'm fine. Sky came down from New York to stay with me for a while. I didn't think it was good for me to be alone," answered Sadie as she looked James in the eye.

Guilt stabbed James' heart and twisted its jagged knife oh so slowly. Sadie's statement was a personal attack on his cowardice. He knew that he should be the one with her, but fear and pride prevented it.

"I'm glad that someone is home with you," he mumbled.

"Me too," she said, disappointed with his response. "Well, it was nice seeing you." Sadie walked past him, bumping into him hard, almost knocking him off balance.

James grabbed her arm.

She spun around.

His grip tightened.

"Wait," James demanded. "Don't walk away from me."

"Why? Didn't you walk away from me?" Sadie exclaimed. A heavy tear ran down her cheek smearing her eyeliner.

"I deserve that." He closed his eyes and took a deep breath. "I love you." James pulled her to him and kissed her firmly and wildly. Her warm tears flooded his lips. He drank them in passionately for her love was truer than anything he had ever known. For a moment he thought some of his own tears would mingle with hers, but his pride would not let them come. Pulling back, his breath rushed into her ear. "I just need a little time," he whispered. More time to digest what he saw. What was he supposed to do? Was he supposed to sweep her up in his arms and forget everything that had happened? How was he supposed to cope with his woman being brutalized by some unknown fiend? James felt helpless and hopeless, less than a man.

"I may not have much time," she cried. She understood the struggle behind his eyes, but her struggle was a greater one and she needed someone who could stand by her through hell and heaven. And, right now she was in the deepest crevice of hell hoping to be rescued.

"I just don't know what to do," he admitted.

"Me either, but I shouldn't have to do it without you!" Sadie broke free from his embrace. She ran as fast as she could, disappearing into the swaying crowd.

17

"How was your...let me count." Sadie held up her fingers and moved them one by one. "Third date in the last two weeks?" Sadie asked Sky with a hapless smile.

Sky pulled the key out of the door, closing it behind her, and tossed her purse on the couch. She plopped down next to Sadie and grabbed her hand.

"It was soooooo romantic," Sky cooed. "This guy is truly unbelievable. First, Forrest took me to a dinner theater. Everyone participated. I played a show girl named Bubbles. You know I showed my behind too! I danced and sang and really cut up." She laughed. "It was lots of fun. Afterwards, we went to this dark little jazz club and sat in a corner and talked for hours. The music was mellow and extremely sexy. Girl, he made me wanna jump across the table into his lap. Then, he took me to his house where we played video games and drank beer. After my fingers got tired, he kissed each of them one by one then he brought me home, walked me to the door, and kissed me sweetly on the cheek. I could feel his excitement pressing hard against my leg if you know what I mean. He said goodnight and left. Forrest hasn't even tried to make a move yet and I know I'm sexy as hell," Sky said in one breath. "Tell me the truth. Is it all a show? Is he a real gentleman or is he just tryin' to fatten me up for the kill?"

"No, Forrest is really like that. He's a very sweet guy," Sadie answered fiddling with her hair. She nestled against the sofa pillows and pulled her legs up in Indian style, careful to tuck her silk night slip between her legs to hide her underwear.

"And he's a doctor too. I think we have a winner," Sky squealed.

"You sure do." Sadie dropped her eyes and laid her head back on the sofa. "Forrest is a good man."

"Are you okay?" Sky asked. Her smile vanished instantly upon seeing her friend's obvious unhappiness.

"I'm fine," she lied, her usually sparkling eyes dull and distressed.

"Sadie Covington, you are not fine. You're mopin'. It may be that funky perfume you always wearing," Sky joked, and slapped Sadie's leg lightly.

Sadie smiled. "Did you see James tonight?"

"For a moment. He usually stays in his room. He told me to tell you hello and that he loves you." Sky held Sadie's hand in her own. "He does love you. He always looks so sad. Forrest says that he picks up the phone three times a day to call your number and hangs up. I don't know what's goin' on between you two, but you both need to talk."

"I know," said Sadie. "I'm going to hit the sack. I just wanted to wait up for you to make sure that you remembered the pass code.

"Thanks. When are you going to tell me about your troubles?" asked Sky.

"Soon," Sadie said. "I'm not in the mood to talk tonight. My food hasn't been agreeing with me lately. I've been feeling a bit nauseous. I can barely hold anything down."

"Okay. I hope you feel better," Sky said as she rubbed Sadie's arm. "Do you want me to get you some ginger ale or somethin'?"

"No. I'll be okay."

Sky frowned. She knew that a bit of queasiness would not suck all the life out of Sadie. It was more than that. A lot deeper and darker. It was the reason why Sky was asked to come to Atlanta in the first place. The reason she still wasn't given. The sadness vigorously thriving in Sadie worried Sky. It seemed to discolor Sadie's skin an inhuman gray and shade her eyes in a dejected haze. "I'm here when you need me."

"I know." Sadie kissed Sky's cheek and stood up. "Goodnight," she said.

"Goodnight," Sky lazily slurred as she reluctantly went to her room, lingering momentarily in the hallway hoping for Sadie to call her back, and regretfully closed the door.

Sadie walked into her room and shut the door behind her. The tidy chamber was so spotless that it almost seemed that no one could sleep in it. She sat upon her plush lavender comforter and stared at a self portrait of her and James on the far wall. All of a sudden the quietness around her began to press against her. Her bed felt cold beneath her thighs and a sharp pain shot through her heart. The painting swirled before her eyes as fresh tears clouded her vision. Sadie was lonely and she knew that there was only one person who could banish the lonesome throb in her chest. She picked up the phone and slowly dialed James' number. His answering machine came on.

"James, this is Sadie." She instantly felt foolish for saying her name. Of course he knew her voice. "I was just calling to say hello. Call me when you get the chance. Love you."

"Why pine over someone who does not love you?"

"Hello," Sadie whispered into the receiver. There was no answer. She hung up the phone and shrugged off the assumed hallucination.

"My love for you is infinite. Forbid me not to adore you."

"Who's there?" Sadie sibilated. The room became cold. Frosty bumps rose on her shoulders and with an inevitable domino effect it traveled down her arms and disbursed in a painful exhale. Immediately Sadie started to bawl.

"It is me my love. Do not weep, but flatter me with joyful laughter. My love for you is pure."

A bright light filled the room, knocking Sadie on the bed forcing her to cover her face with a pillow. Sadie removed the pillow with trembling hands. Spots danced before her eyes as she forced them to focus. Within moments her vision was restored and Turiel stood before her wearing a long white robe that pulsated with its own yellowish light.

"Go!" she wept. "Come to me no more! I don't want your love. Leave me alone! You've torn my life apart! You may've cost me James."

"Sadie, are you okay?" Sky yelled through the door. She had heard Sadie screaming in her room and saw bright light coming from under Sadie's door. "Sadie?" Sky screamed as she banged frantically against the hard wood. "Open the door!"

"No one can come between you and me," Turiel stated as he bore down upon Sadie, his wings fully spread and brushing against the walls with glistening feathers, casting her in shadow. "You are not your own, but mine." His eyes flashed a bright gold.

"Get away from me!" Sadie screamed over and over until her voice became hoarse and her throat pained. She buried her head underneath a pillow and pulled her knees to her heaving chest; her slip crumpled above her hips exposing her upper thighs.

"You belong to me," Turiel echoed as his delicate fingers ran up her quaking legs leaving a purple trail upon her flesh.

"Open this door!" Sky screamed as she threw her frail body against the door to no avail. "Sadie!" she shrieked and slammed into the door again, this time hurting her shoulder. Sky fell to the floor, aborting moans before they were born, and kicked the hard wood with all of her power. The door would not budge under her pounding feet, feet reddening and swelling with each strike. Brighter light spilled from the spaces around the door. "Sadie!"

Turiel snatched the pillow out of Sadie's clenched arms causing feathers to fly up in the air and rain upon the bed and floor. A guttural sob poured from her throat as his tingling breath tickled her face. Warm sensations prickled her skin from top to bottom. His hands gently wrapped around her arms as he pulled her into his embrace. Her breast pressed hard against the penetrable firmness of his body. Like a sponge, he took her body into his, becoming one flesh, filling every opening in her body with liquid light. She drowned in excruciating ecstasy unable to contain the perverse pleasure causing orgasmic seizures to quake her body. Solidifying, he pushed her back into her own person. His lips covered her entire mouth burning her with white flame. He vanished.

The door flew open as the broken door knob crashed to the floor. Sky stood in the entrance way with a fractured bar stool in her hand and her hair flying wild and sticking to her perspiring face. Coughing uncontrollably from the thick odor in the air, she ran over to the bed where Sadie's unconscious body was twisted up, legs bent in impossible ways, hips and torso pointing in opposite directions, arms stretched wide as if being elongated on a torture rack. Handprints were seared on both arms and her lips were bubbling and red. Her hair was shining like the sun.

Sky cupped her mouth with her hand, biting down on her palm to remain in reality, refusing to drift into terrific insanity. The hair on her neck and arms stood erect like quills.

"Who did this to you?" Sky wailed. She reached out to touch Sadie, but recoiled. Fear whispered all kinds of blasphemies in her ear. She rebuked it and rushed to her friend's bedside. She poked Sadie's face with a tubule pillow. No movement. The smell surrounding Sadie made Sky's head swoon. She retched on the floor.

Stumbling over to the nightstand, Sky picked up the phone and dialed 911.

"I need help!" she screamed. "My friend has been attacked! Someone broke in. Her arms...." Sky dropped the phone.

Sadie's lips folded inward and paled in color. They normalized within seconds. The handprints on her arms faded until they were no more. Her body flexed and wrung until it lay gracefully upon the unruffled comforter. Sadie's eye lids fluttered. Groggily she sat up. She opened her eyes completely and blinked them slowly to focus.

"Sky, is that you?" she slurred.

"Yes, it's me," Sky cried. Snot and tears ran down her face in a torrent of clear goo. "What happened to you?" Sky stared at Sadie unblinking. Sky looked like a human vibrator. Even the floor moved with her juddering. Sweat clung to her half naked body; she wore nothing, but panties and a bra revealing her ribs and protruding pelvis bone. She pulled her knees to her chest and wrapped her arms tightly around her legs.

"The angel came again," Sadie slurred and fell back upon the bed. Her eyes rolled back, her body convulsing.

Sky rocked back and forth on the floor. Tears blurred her vision. Her mind tried to process what she had seen, but it was blocked by logic and thwarted by fear.

"Angel, what are you talkin' about?" Sky cried as she crawled to the foot of the bed. She reached out and touched Sadie's skin. It felt like fire. She jerked her hand back as if she had placed her fingers upon the eye of a stove.

Sadie's body sprang into a sitting position, in one swift movement, as if a force propelled her upward. "Call Daddy. Ask him what to do," she uttered before she fainted once more and succumbed to another frightening seizure.

Sky picked up the dangling phone.

"Ma'am, how can I assist you?" the emergency operator asked.

"My friend is sick. Her body is jerking out of control. Send someone at once," Sky whined, her hands trembled so badly that she almost dropped the phone.

"What's wrong with her?" the operator inquired.

"I don't know. I heard her cry out. I was in my room. No one is home, but us, but it sounded like someone was in the room with her. I yelled for her to let me in, but all I could hear was her in distress. When I finally broke her door in and got into her room, she was alone and bruised, but now the bruises are gone and she is seizing on the bed."

"Gone?" the operator asked in a skeptical tone.

"Yes gone!" Sky snapped. "Something strange is happening here. Just send someone and now!"

"I'll send someone as soon as possible. Keep a close watch on her and don't try to hold her down. Does she have a history of seizures or epilepsy?"

"No," Sky answered, crying softly into the receiver.

Sadie's body quaked violently, making the entire bed bounce off the floor.

"Hurry please! She's gonna hurt herself thrashing like that!" Sky screamed.

"Help is on the way. I need your complete address and name," said the operator.

Sky gave the operator her name and the address and hung up the phone before the operator could respond.

"Mr. Covington is a whole state away. What can he do?" Sky asked herself as she rumbled through Sadie's nightstand for her address book. Sky found it under a crossword puzzle book. She flipped through the pages so fast that she almost ripped them from their binding. With nervous fingers and a murmuring heart, Sky dialed the Covington's number and waited with fearful eyes locked on Sadie's thrashing body. The line was busy. "Dang it!" She slammed down the receiver and tried again, this time getting an answering machine. She hung up the phone and wept.

18

The refrigerator was almost bare: a corner of milk left in the container, a six pack of beer, a bottle of ketchup, a few sticks of butter, and a half eaten chocolate bar. James closed the door and opened the cabinet above the stove. He pulled out a loaf of bread and put two slices in the toaster. He leaned against the counter and waited. The crispy bread popped up. He placed the toast on the plate and rubbed the stick of butter directly onto the toast leaving dark crumbs stuck in the pale stick. In two bites he finished the first piece of toast. James reopened the refrigerator and grabbed a can of beer. He drank it quickly and finished the last piece of bread.

"Great dinner," he mumbled to himself, letting out a big belch as he flicked off the kitchen light and went into the living room; his dingy jogging pants were sagging and his stained tank top was wrinkled beyond belief. James scratched his days old whiskers and rubbed his head covered in prickly stubble. He picked up the video game controller and continued the game he had been playing almost nonstop for the past twelve hours. The phone rang.

"Hello," he answered. It was a telemarketer. He hung up.

Suddenly he wanted to hear Sadie's voice. The desire filled him so deeply, so intensely that he could hardly hold the game controller. He placed it on the coffee table and slipped from the couch to the floor. Sadie permeated his mind like the odor that lingered on her flesh permeated his nose when he was near her. His stomach twirled in erratic circles. He needed to hear her, be near her, love her. Her soul cried out to him. He heard it deep within himself beckoning, begging, hankering for him to be in her arms. Her absence was like a deadly poison snaking through his system and she was his only antidote. James picked up the phone and heard the dial tone wavering indicating that he had voice mail messages. He dialed a special code and heard Sadie's message then quickly dialed her number.

"Hello," Sky answered, her voice choked with tears.

"Is everything okay?" James asked.

"Who is this?" she cried.

"James."

"Sadie's in trouble," Sky wailed. "I don't know what's wrong. She won't stop shaking and the ambulance isn't here!"

"Ambulance?" James asked. "What happened?"

"I heard noise in her room. She was screaming. There was a strange light coming from under her door. I broke down the door. No one was there. Sadie mumbled something about an angel. Maybe she was praying or something. I don't know. She looked wounded and then she didn't and now she is seizing and I think she is gonna die if she keeps on like this!" Sky squalled into the phone. "I....I" she paused. Someone was knocking on the front door. "Help is here. I gotta go." She hung up the phone, pulled a sheet off of Sadie's bed and wrapped it around herself, then, rushed to the door to let the paramedics in.

James ran upstairs and dressed himself quickly. He jumped in his car and made his way to the hospital closest to Sadie's apartment.

19

The hospital was cold and smelled of sickness. Not unsanitary sickness, but the clean sterile scent that only hospitals possessed. The scent that made one think of disease and death and medical catastrophes. The scent that brought images of blood and bodily fluids and cold steel equipment cutting through unhealthy flesh to mind. James hated the hospital smell and he seemed to hate it more as it mingled with the myrrh scent drifting from Sadie's pores as she lay unconscious upon the crisp white sheets of the hospital bed. He wanted more than anything to leave and never return, but guilt and fear for her safety prevented him from letting her out of his sight. James picked up her hand and kissed gently from her palm to her elbow and let it fall back upon the bed.

"Are you hungry?" Sky asked James as she shifted in the hospital bed where she lay spooning Sadie's unconscious body. Sky's arm was wrapped loosely around Sadie's waist as she tried to adjust comfortably between the bedrail and her best friend. Sky had been there for two nights sleeping right next to Sadie hoping that she would wake up. James had been there too, sitting quietly next to the bed on the brink of tears and filled with frustration.

"A little. Why?" James yawned. He wiped his eyes and rubbed his hand across his bristly head.

"I'm going to the cafeteria," Sky said, sitting up, pulling her tangled mane from under Sadie's pillow, and sliding off the bed. She kissed Sadie's forehead. Sadie did not stir. Sky stretched wide. A big yawn escaped her mouth as she rolled her shoulders and arched her back causing a loud pop.

James looked at her; his face twisted. "Don't hurt yourself. If you keep popping like that they are going to have to roll another bed in here," he joked.

Sky laughed softly. Swiftly she smoothed the wrinkles out of her T-shirt and adjusted the belt on her jeans. She slid her feet into a pair of Victoria's Secret *PINK* flip flops and slowly drug her feet around the bed to James.

"Yeah, bring me something back." He reached in his pocket and gave her a balled up twenty dollar bill. "Get anything you want. My treat."

"Thanks," she said, taking the money and shoving it into her back pocket. "What do you want?"

"Meat, no seafood, and something to drink, no hot beverages," he mumbled and leaned back in his chair.

"While I'm gone, you may want to shave. You look like a mountain man right about now," Sky remarked.

"Buy me a razor and buy yourself a comb because you look like a red mountain lion right about now," James responded with a sly smile.

Sky playfully put up her middle finger and left the room.

The humming of the air conditioner and the beeping of Sadie's heart monitor all of a sudden sounded like heavy metal music to James' ears. He reached over Sadie and grabbed the remote and turned on the TV. The evening news was on. He listened half heartedly as he leaned back in his chair trying to get comfortable. A light tapping on the door disturbed his disquieting boredom.

"Come in," James said, not bothering to turn around.

A tall attractive Asian man walked into the room carrying a clip board and wearing a white jacket with a stethoscope hanging around his neck. Wire glasses sat on his nose with its arms hidden behind black bobbed hair. Black arched brows and high cheek bones ending in a square chin gave him a male model look.

James safely assumed that he was Sadie's primary physician. Although many doctors had come in and out of her room for the past two days, James remembered seeing his face more than once, but he never had time to formally introduce himself.

"I'm Dr. Fat," he pointed to the silver name tag pinned to his coat reading *Dr. Chow Fat*. "Miss Covington's physician. And you are?" He held out his hand. James stood up and accepted it with a firm hand shake.

"I'm James Tucker, Sadie's fiancé. Nice to meet you sir. I hear that you are one of the best around." James put his hands in his pockets and cleared his throat as he watched the doctor check her chart and the monitoring machines.

"I try," Dr. Fat said while working.

"Is she okay?" James inquired as he sat down, hands folded on his lap.

"Sadie will be just fine," Dr. Fat answered, scribbling on his clip board. "All of her tests came back normal. Even her brain scan detected nothing unusual."

"Why is she still in a coma?" asked James.

"She is resting off whatever trauma brought her here," the doctor answered. "I am still unclear of the circumstances surrounding the traumatizing incident. Do you know what happened?"

"Not at all." James shook his head. "Even her roommate is in the dark on the subject."

Dr. Fat stood silently for a moment then let out a perplexing sigh. "Well hopefully Sadie will shed some light when she wakes up."

"So there is nothing to worry about?" James asked, folding his arms across his chest and staring the doctor straight in the eye.

"She is in perfect health and so is the baby." The doctor smiled. "Soon the medication will be wearing off and she will be waking up and ready to go home."

"Baby?" James questioned, his face as pale as the moon.

"Yes, she is a month pregnant," Dr. Fat answered with the sudden feeling that he had stuck his foot in his mouth.

"Pregnant?" James swallowed hard. His legs turned into fettuccini. He fell back against his chair holding his head in his hands. "Pregnant? How can that be?"

"I'm sorry, did you not know?" the doctor asked holding the clipboard against his chest. Dr. Fat's eyes stretched to their fullest capacity revealing ebony irises.

"No," James spat through his teeth. "I didn't know." His hands trembled uncontrollably. Tiny dots of sweat grew upon his forehead.

"I'm sorry, was this pregnancy unplanned?" Dr. Fat questioned. "Mr. Tucker, there is nothing to worry about. Most pregnancies aren't planned, but most parents adjust and their lives become fuller when a new family member arrives. A deeper bond is created. All will be perfectly fine." The look on James' face unnerved Dr. Fat. "Is everything okay?"

"Hell no!" James belted as he jumped up from his seat, knocking the chair sideways. He furiously punched the wall leaving a small dent in the wallpaper, startling the doctor and causing him to pick up the phone to call security. James swung the door open and angrily rushed into the hallway whisking past Sky cursing and growling, knocking the food from her hands and her against the wall. The doctor hung up the phone.

"What's going on?" Sky asked the doctor as she rubbed her aching arm. James had bumped into the same shoulder she had wounded days ago when she was trying to get into Sadie's bedroom and it ached terribly. Sky picked the burger bags up from the floor and sat them upon the food tray next to Sadie's bed.

"Apparently Mr. Tucker isn't happy," Dr. Fat responded. "Would you like me to take a look at your arm?" He pointed to a big purple bruise forming on her upper arm.

Sky shook her head no and said, "Why is that?" Her eyes narrowed.

"I think I should look at that arm," Dr. Fat insisted as he proceeded to massage the bruised tissue and feel for broken bones or for something out of joint. "All seems well. You should alternate between cold and warm compresses to help that shoulder feel better. A matter of fact," Dr. Fat pulled a business card out of his jacket pocket and shoved it into Sky's uncooperative hand. "You should make an appointment with my office so I can fully examine and x-ray you to be totally sure."

Sky reluctantly took the card and stuck it into the back pocket of her jeans.

"What made James fly out of this room like that?" she impatiently asked, her eyes still in annoyed slits.

"I am not at liberty to say," he grimaced. "Are you a relative?"

"I'm her sister," Sky lied. "Tell me what's goin' on!" She placed her hands on her hips and got nose to nose with the doctor.

Dr. Fat took a step backwards and looked at her strangely. His eyes shifted to Sadie then back to Sky. There was no way those two came from the same gene pool he thought, but said, "Your sister is doing quite well and so is her baby. If there is nothing else you need, I'll be going now."

"Baby?"

"Yes, she is pregnant," he hesitantly answered walking quickly toward the door.

"Forgive me for being abrupt. I was just worried about her," Sky apologized.

"That's okay," he smiled and placed his hand upon the door handle. "Mr. Tucker was worried about her too until he found out he was going to be a father," Dr. Fat mumbled as he exited.

"Why would James be angry about a baby?" she asked herself while letting her eyes rest upon Sadie's flat belly. "Well that's his problem. Babies are always good news." Sky sat down on the bed next to Sadie and rubbed her hair, amazed by its metallic appearance. "Girl, you are gonna be a mommy!" she smiled. "That makes me Auntie Sky," Sky squealed and ran over to the phone to call Mr. and Mrs. Covington to tell them the wonderful news.

20

"Hello," Mrs. Covington answered the phone with a mouth full of chocolate covered almonds.

"How are you Mama C?" Sky asked, her voice high pitched and full of excitement.

"I'm doing good, baby. How are you? It has been a long time," Mrs. Covington said, swallowing her sweet treat. A big smiled covered her face as she sat upon her couch with her legs folded beside her.

"I'm just fine," Sky answered. "Life is good. I can't complain. For now I'm just trying to enjoy Hotlanta. I am so glad Sadie invited me down. It had been such a long time since I visited."

"We just left Atlanta. We didn't stay as long as I wanted, but we still enjoyed our time. How does it feel to be a big time author? We bought your books and Carlos gives extra credit to students who buy your books. He may single handedly be responsible for your success."

"Tell Daddy C I'm grateful for that! I'm lovin' livin' life!"

Mrs. Covington smiled as Sky laughed through the phone.

"How's my girl doing?" Mrs. Covington asked, rolling a cocoa covered nut between her fingers.

"Well," Sky hesitated trying to prepare herself for the tongue lashing she was going to get for not telling Mrs. Covington sooner that Sadie was in the hospital.

"Well what?" Mrs. Covington snapped; her mouth bent. "I don't like the sound of your voice. If something is wrong, you better spit it out!"

Mr. Covington walked into the room and sat down next to his wife. He kissed her on the cheek and turned on the TV, careful to keep the volume low so she could hear through the phone clearly.

"Who are you talking to Ebbie?" he asked, seeing her displeased face.

"Sky," she whispered. "Well what child?" Mrs. Covington said sharply into the phone. "You better speak girl before I come through this phone and tan your tail!"

"I...I...I tried to call you Momma C, but...but...umm...I couldn't get through," Sky tried to explain. "I know I should have called again, but..."

"Is my baby okay?" Mrs. Covington asked, her voice high pitched and full of worry. A humbling fear subdued her. She dropped her candy back into the bag and let the chewed pieces linger in her cheek for a moment before she took a painful swallow.

Mr. Covington picked up the remote and turned off the TV. He tried to push back the panic that was welling up inside of him.

"What's going on?" he asked.

"Calm down Mama C. Everything is okay. Sadie is in the hospital and I'm here with her. James was here too, but he left." Sky decided to leave out the fact that he was livid when he stormed out of the hospital. A bad report could cause a parent's opinion to change indefinitely. "The doctor said that she'll be just fine. She's sleeping now, so she can't talk, but the doctor assured me that there is nothing to worry about," informed Sky.

"What happened?" Mrs. Covington demanded. "And don't you leave out a single detail. Do you hear me girl?" she scolded.

"What's going on?" Mr. Covington asked.

"Sadie is in the hospital," Mrs. Covington replied with her hand over the receiver.

"Put the phone on speaker," he demanded.

Mrs. Covington pushed the speaker button. "Sky," she called.

"Yes ma'am," Sky answered, nervous beyond belief.

"Tell us what's going on," the Covingtons said in unison.

"Well, a few nights ago…" Sky started.

"A few nights," Mrs. Covington whined. "My baby has been in the hospital for a few nights and you are just now calling us!"

"Let her speak, baby," Mr. Covington requested as he placed his hand upon his wife's knee to calm her.

"Go ahead," Mrs. Covington snapped, her bottom lip quivering.

"I'm so sorry I didn't keep calling Mama C. I tried to call that first night, but I was so scared when I tried then I got caught up in all the commotion and never tried again. Please forgive me," Sky begged.

"It's okay," Mr. Covington answered before his wife could bless Sky out. "Just tell us what happened."

Sky iterated every detail of what happened to Sadie. Sky told them about the abuse and miraculous healing, the mention of an angel, and the seizures. The Covingtons listened carefully with disquieted hearts. Mr. Covington gritted his teeth in rage and fear, but Mrs. Covington squeezed her husband's hand in worry and disbelief.

"Dr. Fat said that she is gonna be fine. We have nothing to worry about," Sky continued. "All the tests showed that nothing was wrong and there's not a bruise on her body. I'm not sure if they believed my story," she grumbled. "The only strange thing that the doctor pondered over was her hair. He thinks she must've experienced somethin' mind blowing for her hair to gray instantly. No one can figure out why it turned silver with an eerie glow. You should see it, it's like a mirror cut into shreds."

"We should be there," Mrs. Covington cried.

"She's truly fine," Sky promised. "Sadie's sleeping like a baby." She paused, waiting for any comments. The phone was quiet. "I do have some good news though."

"Please, we need to hear some," Mr. Covington said sadly.

"You guys are gonna be grandparents!" Sky squealed, her high pitch voice ringing through the speaker like a siren.

"How do you know this?" Mr. Covington asked, his voice low and grave. His eyes swelled with tears. His large hands balled into fists as he contemplated the omen Sky had just unknowing given. He waited for Sky's answer.

"The doctor told me," she answered confused by his mournful tone. "Aren't you happy?"

Mr. Covington stood up from the sofa and walked out of the room with tears streaming down his face and neck. A broken spirit drowned within him. He could feel it gurgling inside, too hopeless to save itself, desiring and deserving death. He was helpless in protecting his daughter.

"Of course we're happy," Mrs. Covington lied as she watched her forlorn husband disappear down the hall. "Of course we are. Thank you so much for calling. Call me back as soon as Sadie wakes up, okay."

"Okay," Sky said, perceiving that she was being rushed off of the phone. "You will be the first to know."

"Thank you, baby. You have a good night," Mrs. Covington said as she hung up the phone in the middle of Sky's goodbye. Mrs. Covington stood up slowly and followed her husband into the bedroom, afraid of what she may find.

Mr. Covington sat on the side of the bed flipping through an old rolodex. He turned the knob slowly letting the old yellowed cards fall one by one.

"Carlos, what are you doing?" she asked, confused about his disconcerting calm.

"Looking for my old friend Dr. Monique Davis' phone number?" Carlos answered as he gently fingered the time colored pages.

"Why would you want to talk to her at a time like this? We haven't spoken to her in years. Doesn't she run a women's clinic in Atlanta?"

"Yes," he mumbled.

"Sadie has her own doctor," Ebbie cautiously moved closer, her voice near panic. "I am sure she is capable of finding her own OB/GYN." Her voice began to shake.

"I am not looking for an OB/GYN. I am looking for a doctor who can perform a discrete and safe abortion," he droned, tears began leaking from his face like a hole in a water balloon.

"How can you consider such a thing?" Ebbie Covington wailed. "You are speaking about your grandchild!" She pushed the rolodex away from his hands and threw herself at his feet. "Don't' tell our daughter to murder our grandbaby! You know Sadie lingers on every word you say and if you tell her to do this she may do it!" she wept.

Mr. Covington gave no response. He pulled the rolodex to him once again and began to turn its wheel.

"It's our flesh and blood. You can't let myths and legends convince you to sacrifice your own seed! You have to know how crazy you are behaving!" Mrs. Covington wailed.

He placed his hands upon her head and let them smooth her soft hair. A pitiful smile curved his lips interrupting the path of tears.

"That baby in Sadie's womb is not one of us. It's a dangerous creature. We can't allow it to be born," he whispered.

"That *creature* is our grandbaby and I forbid you to cause it any harm," she spat and knocked his hands away. "If you suggest that Sadie get rid of that baby, I will never ever forgive you. Never!"

Mr. Covington bent his head and looked into her eyes and said, "I'm sorry that you feel that way. I love you and would never want to breathe without your forgiveness, but I will warn Sadie of the consequences of having this baby and I will give her Dr. Davis' number. If she keeps this child by her own volition and against my pleading and

warnings, I will stand behind her decision, but I will not be silent when all our lives can be endangered by the birth of this child."

"Please..." she cried.

"I have to. This once, stand behind me. I need your faith and support." Carlos held out his hand. "You have to know how my soul is crying out. You know that I would never do anything to hurt you or Sadie. I love you both more than myself. Trust what I have to do."

Ebbie hesitantly took his hand and he pulled her to him, holding her as tight as her small frame could endure. He wept upon her shoulder.

21

It was cold, the kind of sinus clogging unnatural cold that only air conditioners could generate. Sterilizing orange scented disinfectant filled the icy air. Monotonous beeps sounded every few seconds. Sadie pulled her covers tight around her arms. The cloth did not feel like her high thread count sheets. The blankets were scratchy and rough unlike the plush comforter that covered her bed. A feather pillow was not beneath her head; instead, it was a flat cushion-free wad of cloth. Cardboard is what the mattress felt like. She opened her eyes.

"Where am I?" she yawned, letting her eyes take in the hospital bed, the cords connecting her to the beeping monitors like spider webs, the TV mounted to the wall, and her sleeping best friend on the chair next to her bed. Sadie sat up. She flung her legs off the side of the bed, careful not to yank out the IV in her arm, and nudged Sky with her toe.

"What?" Sky growled in her sleep, refusing to let her dream escape.

"Wake up." Sadie poked again, this time the poke was more like a small kick.

One of Sky's eyes opened.

"Sadie?" Sky mumbled.

"In the flesh." Sadie smiled. The light reflecting off of her hair made sparkling bows on the wall.

"You're up!" Sky marveled at the display then jumped up and locked Sadie in a thankful embrace.

"How long have I been asleep?" Sadie asked, laughing lightly at her excited companion.

"A week," Sky responded as she quickly kissed Sadie on the cheek before giving her another hard squeeze.

"Wow!" Sadie exclaimed. "I feel like Rip Van Winkle.

"With that silver hair, you look like him too," Sky joked.

"Shut up," Sadie laughed and softly punched Sky on the thigh.

"How do you feel?" Sky let go and sat back in her seat. Her playful demeanor disappeared and serious concern took control.

"I feel great. I have never been so well rested," Sadie laughed. "I'm surprised my parents aren't here." Sadie adjusted the hospital gown, securing the opening in the back.

"I told them that there was no need. The doctor said that you were just fine, but I promised them that I would call them as soon as you woke up. You want me to call now?" Sky asked.

"No. Not yet," Sadie answered.

Sky uncrossed her legs and leaned forward and asked, "What happened to you in your room?"

Sadie's countenance fell. Her memory was foggy, but she could visualize Turiel's face as it leaned in to set her lips on fire. Tingling sensations tickled her insides and traveled to parts most sacred. She remembered being caught up in such pleasurable and painful ecstasy that she thought that her body was in tug of war between heaven and hell.

"Sadie, tell me what happened," Sky urged. "Did someone attack you? You were screamin'. There was a strange light streaming from around your door. You said somethin' to me about an angel."

"I can't remember," Sadie interjected as she turned her head away from Sky.

"Liar!" Sky spat. "Tell me!"

"You wouldn't understand." Sadie turned back to face Sky and said, "Let's not argue. Everything is all right now. Did you call my father that night?"

"Yes, but I couldn't contact him. I thought you couldn't remember anything." Sky frowned. "You remember tellin' me to call Daddy C."

Abruptly changing the subject Sadie asked, "So anything exciting happened while I was out?"

"James was here," Sky mumbled, purposely looking at the TV screen. She exhaled a disappointed sigh before changing the channel.

"Really? Sadie asked.

"Yeah. He sat in this very chair for the first few days refusing to leave your side. But as you can see, his devotion was short lived," squawked Sky full of resentment for not being told the truth. "He was gone faster than a glass of water in the middle of the desert. He ran out of here so fast that I thought he was Jesse Owens."

"Where did he go?" Sadie asked, annoyed by Sky's sarcasm and tempestuous tone.

"How do I know? He stormed out of here like a crazy fool, almost knockin' me over after hearing some rather shockin' news from the dear old doctor," Sky replied sucking her teeth. Some of the venom evaporated. She could never stay mad at Sadie for long.

Sadie's lips turned into a vexed slant. "What was so shocking?" Her brows furrowed.

"You..."

"Me what?" Sadie asked. Now her arms were crossed. She hated when Sky made her fish for answers. They had been playing this "beg for information" game for fifteen years.

"You should know hot thang," Sky muttered. "You the one keepin' secrets."

"Okay, out with it. I don't have the patience for this. You know James and I have been having problems and the last thing I need is for him to be mad at me about something I did when I was asleep," Sadie snapped.

"I doubt you were asleep when you were doin' it," Sky laughed.

"What are you talking about?" Frustration filled Sadie. She picked up a pillow and threatened to knock Sky's head off.

"I'm talkin' about that little bambino in yo belly!" Sky grinned.

"What?" A look of ultimate horror disfigured Sadie's face. "What are you talking about?"

"You and James are way too dramatic concerning this new baby. I understand that it wasn't planned, but most of us weren't planned...."

"Pregnant?" Sadie asked. Her stomach flipped. It felt like foreign fingers were fondling the back of her neck. The room began to spin. Everything blurred. "Pregnant," she whispered under her breath right before her body fell forward ripping the IV from her arm and hit the floor, bumping her head hard against the cold white tile.

"Nurse!" Sky screamed. "Nurse!" Sky searched for the correct button on the hospital bed and pushed it at least ten times.

Within minutes a pair of nurses were lifting Sadie from the floor and putting her back into the bed. A giant purple lump rose on the right side of Sadie's forehead. Her eyes fluttered and she awoke.

"Are you okay," A tall slim nurse with bright green eyes and strawberry blonde hair asked. She fingered the bruise gently making sure the skin wasn't broken.

Sadie let her eyes focus on the nurse's pretty ivory face. "I'm okay. Just lost my balance."

"Good," the nurse said as she tucked the sheets around Sadie's waist. She fluffed her pillows then took a step backwards. The nurse crossed her arms and said, "Miss Sadie, try not to get too excited. You have a nasty bump on your forehead and a nice bruise on your arm where you pulled out your IV." The nurse picked up Sadie's chart and ran her eyes over it. She turned to face Sky. "Please, no more excitement. The mother-to-be has had enough stress for a lifetime."

Sky rolled her eyes at the nurse and side stepped her to get to Sadie's bed. The other nurse shook her head and left the room.

"Visiting hours are over, you know?" The nurse put her hands on her narrow hips. "If I were you, I'd be a little bit more pleasant."

"I don't give a...." Sky barked when Sadie grabbed her hand and squeezed it as hard as she could. "Ouch!" Sky squealed and jerked her aching fingers away.

"I'll be careful Nurse Tina. It was my fault. I tried to get up too fast and got a little woozy. Sky only tried to help. I'm very grateful that you let her stay here with me. She's very grateful too. Aren't you Sky?"

Sky sighed and looked up at the ceiling and uttered, "Yes."

"O...okay." Nurse Tina gave Sky a side glance of disapproval. "Any more accidents and she's out of here."

"Everything is under control." Sadie smiled, trying to refrain from laughing as she watched Sky shoot birds and stick out her tongue behind the nurse's head.

"Get your rest and call me if you need me," the nurse said as she exited the room.

"Heifer," Sky coughed.

Nurse Tina looked back and scowled, letting the door slam behind her.

22

"I can't believe this BS!" James growled as he paced the hard wood floor of his living room. He stopped near the mantle over the fireplace. With one swift swipe, he knocked all the photos of him and Sadie to the floor sending metal and glass everywhere. He kicked at the debris and started to angrily pace again.

"Calm down dude," Luis urged. He sat on the sofa next to Forrest. Both of them eager to know what tumultuous event had transpired.

"What's going on? You've been cursing and clowning since you left the hospital a few days ago," Forrest asked. He leaned forward with his elbows on his knees while Luis leaned back against the sofa so they both could have full eye contact with their raging friend. "Is Sadie okay?"

"Lu, you were right. Women are hoes!" James roared.

"Hell yeah," Luis agreed, nodding his head and sucking his teeth. "That's the truth."

"What are you talking about?" an appalled Forrest inquired. "Those words don't even sound right coming out of your mouth."

"What she do?" asked Luis, leaning forward, eagerly awaiting the character damning answer. "Did she call out another dude's name in her sleep? Did you catch her and her best friend makin' it happen? Does she have herpes? AIDS? Crabs? The clap?"

"No stupid! None of that!" James growled.

"Well it can't be worst than any of that," Forrest added.

"Yes it can." James mumbled.

"What is it then?" Forrest and Luis asked impatiently.

James turned his back to his friends and faced the wall. Ire bubbled from his eyes as streaming tears. He swallowed to control the shiver in his voice, but the shiver morphed into an irate rumble. "She's pregnant," he choked. "She's about a month pregnant and we have not slept together in...in...forever!"

"What?" Luis and Forrest said in unison.

"She's pregnant and it sure as hell ain't mine!" James yelled as he spun around squeezing his fist. His eyes were wild and dangerous. "How could she do this to me? I was faithful to her. I would've never cheated on her!" he scoffed. "See, this is what I get for trusting a scandalous broad," he angrily laughed. "She played me. Sadie played me!" James pointed at his chest with his thumb. "Me!"

Forrest shook his head and let it drop. "I feel sorry for you bro. I don't know what to say."

"I know what to say..." James bellowed.

"Just wait a minute," Luis spoke up. He scratched his head and took a deep breath. "Maybe it's not what you think."

"What! Obviously she has been banging someone else. Now you trying to..." James started, but Luis cut him off.

"Calm down and lemme talk," Luis demanded. "Stop jumpin' to conclusions. You and I both know that some crazy things have been happenin' with yo girl. This could be one of them."

"Since when did you start taking Sadie's side?" James growled, bearing down upon Luis.

"He's not taking sides Jay. You need to step back and let him finish," Forrest said reaching out his hand to place a barrier between the two men.

"I don't have to let him finish anything! I know what I know..." James was cut short again.

"Shut up and listen!" Luis yelled as he jumped to his feet, knocking James a few steps back. With his chest, Luis pushed James against the wall. Luis pointed his finger at the side of James' face and yelled into his ear, "Let's not pretend that we didn't see what we saw that night at her house when you called us whinin' like a lil' ho. It was obvious that she had been assaulted and you said it wasn't the first time something weird had happened."

Forrest pulled Luis out of James' face and stood between the angry friends.

"Plus," Luis continued through clenched teeth. "Forrest told me what his new girl saw before Sadie went to the hospital. I doubt if she had time to pick up a new dude while being attacked by phantoms."

"That's true man," Forrest concurred. "You didn't even consider that before you started to condemn her."

James' hands relaxed. The anger in his face writhed into fear. He fell back against the wall and let himself slide down to the floor. His stomach tightened and he fell over on his side. He squeezed his eyes closed and swallowed the sobs that threatened to come up, refusing to let another tear drop. Things were even worse than he imagined. His fiancé could be pregnant by some *thing* a lot more horrible than another man.

"What am I going to do?"

23

It was ninety-eight degrees in Miami. The wide brim straw hat that Mrs. Covington wore aided little in keeping her cool. She fanned herself with a matching straw fan as she sat on the back porch with her husband's lap top computer on her lap. She adjusted the legs of her orange capri pants and the bottom of her matching shirt so that they would not gather under the computer. She Googled the words *angels, love,* and *women* and came up with thousands of hits. Browsing through a few of them, she discovered the same myths that her husband shared with her. Foolish taradiddles about angel-woman love affairs resulting in total debauchery and flooding chaos. None of it seemed logical, all fantastic tales reinvented by weirdo youths trapped in fantasy worlds. She sat the computer on the patio table and leaned back against her chair.

"What was that creature's name?" she asked herself. "I'm sure Carlos said a name," Mrs. Covington whispered, closing her eyes and trying to think. Nothing. She took a sip of her husband's strawberry lemonade and names came to her like a vision.

"Uriel...Ariel..." she mumbled as she snatched up the computer and entered *names of angels* into the search. A long list came up. She let her eyes rest upon each name as she tried to gather some familiar twang from it. Her eyes finally came to Turiel. "That's it!" she exclaimed and put the name Turiel into the search engine. She found nothing so she decided to enter more keywords like *angel, watcher* and *Turiel*. After about an hour of searching, she came across a link which took her to a book called, *The Secret Grimoire of Turiel*. She opened the Adobe file and discovered that the incantations in the book could supposedly summon the angel.

"I wonder if this could work?" she asked herself, instantly angry that she was beginning to believe in this craziness. "Well it can't hurt to see, can it?" she mumbled as she left her seat and headed into the house.

Mrs. Covington pushed print and the document printed from the wireless printer in her library. She picked up the e-book and placed it into a large yellow envelope, went into her bedroom, and pulled her husband's faculty directory out of the night stand. Quickly she flipped the pages until she arrived at the name, Dr. Olga Putina, professor of Pagan Theology with a focus in witchcraft and nature based religions. Mrs. Covington hesitantly dialed the number because she knew how her husband felt about the woman.

Mr. Covington believed that Dr. Putina was a kook who cared more about shock value than the truth. She would stage huge séances for her students and hire special effects artists to scare the pants off of the ignorant young adults. He felt that she was all flash and no fire.

"Hello," Dr. Putina answered in a heavy Russian accent.

"Dr. Putina, this is Ebbie Covington, Carlos Covington's wife. How are you today?"

"Very well thank you. Please call me Olga. We have known each other long enough to greet one another as friends. What do I owe this pleasure?" Dr. Putina asked, sounding a little like the count on Sesame Street. Sometimes Mrs. Covington wondered if Dr. Putina was really from Russia. For all she knew, Dr. Olga Putina could really be Becky Smith from Idaho.

"Do you have a few minutes to spare?" Mrs. Covington paused. "I have a few questions for you." She asked. A bead of sweat formed on her forehead.

"For you, of course," Olga purred.

"I was sitting at my computer earlier and I was surfing a few websites for baby names." She cleared her throat. "My daughter is expecting."

"Congratulations. I'm sure that the baby will be the perfect addition to your lovely family. Carlos is tickled pink I bet."

"Thank you. He's as surprised as I am," Mrs. Covington swallowed. "Anyway, I came across the name Turiel and found it to be absolutely exquisite," she lied.

"Yes it is. It's an angelic name meaning, 'rock of God.' It is a very powerful name. I highly recommend it," Dr. Putina paused.

"Thank you," Mrs. Covington said nervously.

"I am quite flattered," Dr. Putina said. "It's always pleasant to hear from you, but did you call to ask my opinion on baby names?"

"No," Mrs. Covington laughed uneasily. "While searching under the name, I came across a book called, *The Secret Grimoire of Turiel*, and I was wondering what you knew about it."

"Oh yes. It's an ancient text that allows one to summon the holy angel. It gives thaumaturgies precise instructions on how to contact Turiel. It was believed to have been written around 1518, but many think it's older and have been replicated from some previous text. It was discovered in 1927 after being sold in Spain by an ex-priest to Marius Malchus, who translated it into English from the original Latin," Dr. Putina paused. "Are you interested in magic? I never thought of you as a believer in such things. Is the dark side calling you?" Dr. Putina chuckled.

"No. I leave that sort of thing to you and my husband," Mrs. Covington uneasily uttered.

The professor laughed dryly. "So what is your interest here?" Dr. Putina asked suspiciously.

"Well," Mrs. Covington paused. Her heartbeat quickened. "Do you think that this Turiel thing can really be summoned?"

"Of course, I believe that all things are possible..."

"Spare me, please," Mrs. Covington cut the professor short. "I need to know if you sincerely believe that this creature can be summoned."

"I... I...assume so," Dr. Putina stammered. "What is it that you need from me Ebbie?"

"I need your help."

"What for?"

"You know what for. To...call...Turiel," Mrs. Covington entreated. "Can you help me?"

"I would love to, but my hectic schedule would not permit..."

"I'll pay you."

"But..." Olga began, but was cut off once more.

"My daughter could be in trouble and you may be able to help me help her."

"I don't see how an incantation could aid your daughter," the professor skeptically responded.

"Will you help me or not?"

"I don't think your husband would approve. He doesn't seem particularly fond of me," Dr. Putina intoned.

"What he doesn't know won't hurt him. I'll pay you five thousand dollars to get whatever you need to set up this hocus pocus. When will you be able to fit me in?"

"Umm...um," Dr. Putina hesitated. How could she turn down easy money? The cash could help her fund her next student field trip to Salem, Massachusetts to investigate the witch trials. "I cannot guarantee results," she sputtered. "If you do not get the results that you seek I cannot be blamed. My time is precious and if I schedule you I will have to be paid. I am a very busy woman with seminars booked..."

"Understood. Will you help me?"

"Sure. We can do this on Tuesday in my office."

"Thank you," Mrs. Covington exhaled. "Please keep this little appointment between the two of us. I know you think that I'm crazy, but I have my reasons."

"Bring cash," Dr. Putina sourly mumbled. "See you then." She hung up the phone.

Mrs. Covington put the phone back on the receiver and fell back on the bed. An overwhelming feeling of stupidity and dread permeated her body. She could not believe that she solicited the help of that wacky wizard. What was she thinking and how was she going to justify spending five thousand dollars? Mr. Covington did not monitor her accounts, but five thousand dollars is a big chunk of change to withdraw. She sat up and pulled out her planner and marked the date on her calendar as *important meeting* and clapped the book closed.

"Sadie, baby, I am sure that this won't work, but I'll try anything for you," Mrs. Covington whispered into the empty air as she stuffed the envelope under the mattress and went back to the back porch to finish sipping on the delicious sweet drink that was waiting for her. Hopefully her husband wouldn't be there to see her guilt ridden face. She had faced enough humiliation for the day.

24

"Are you comfortable?" Sky asked, plumping the pillows behind Sadie's head. "I can fix you somethin' to eat or find us a movie to watch. Maybe I can order us some Chinese food or call Forrest and ask to him run down to the corner store to pick up some Oreos and milk. Who knows, I could also..."

"I'm just fine," Sadie popped Sky's hands and snatched the pillow away from her. "I've been home for three days now and you've been aggravating me since I stepped foot in this place. Please sit down and leave me alone," Sadie demanded with an appreciative smile on her face as she habitually wiggled her nose and took a deep sniff.

"I just want to make sure that you're fine. You scared me when you fainted and I'm not leavin' this room; so, get used to sharin' your bed," Sky snapped. "I'm still waitin' for you to tell me what happened that night you went to the hospital." She crossed her arms and rolled her eyes and settled in the bed next to her friend.

Sadie lowered her eyes and sighed. Reliving the memories was almost as frightening as the actual experience.

"You know you can tell me anything. I'm here for you girl. I got yo back," Sky reassured Sadie. "There is nothing in this world that I won't do for you. You are my best friend and I love you."

"I know that," replied Sadie unconvincingly.

"Well, what's the matter then?" Sky asked, adjusting her tank top and plaid boxer shorts. She pulled the blanket over her legs and got comfortable.

Sadie looked into Sky's eyes and said, "Something very strange has been happening to me. This...this..." she stumbled over her words. "...creature has been attacking me." She swallowed hard and pushed her head back against the pillow, never taking her eyes off of Sky. A queasy flutter circled through her belly. *What if she doesn't believe me?* Sadie thought. *What if she thinks I have lost my mind and thinks I need to see a shrink?*

"Creature? What the hell you talkin' about?" Sky sprung up with her face twisted in knots. "What kinda creature?"

"I knew you wouldn't understand. I don't blame you. I don't understand either." Sadie shook her head. She took a deep breath, inhaling the unholy fragrance clinging to her supple flesh.

Sky settled back down and said, "Sorry, I'm listening. Tell me what happened."

"An angel has been visiting me."

"An angel," Sky gasped. "What..."

"It has been..." The words evaporated in Sadie's throat. Her heart started beating in her ears. Sadie began to cry. "It has been sleeping with me."

"What are you saying?"

"You know...it has been having its way with me. Taking advantage of me."

"You sayin' that the angel has been having sex with you?" Sky inquired in complete shock; her eyebrows stretched into scarlet bows.

"I think so," Sadie responded.

"You don't know?" Sky's eyes were as wide as windows.

"It's complicated." Sadie paused and closed her eyes. "It's like he consumes me. I feel pleasure and pain all at once. My entire body feels penetrated, wonderfully violated all at the same time. I'm paralyzed in fear and sensually captivated by him all at once. The experience is sexual, but not the same as male female sex. The act of penetration is total body instead of just genital consummation. I can feel him everywhere as if he dissolves into me, me being a sponge and him being liquid. It is the most amazingly frightening thing imaginable."

Sky let her body fall backwards against the pillows. She stared dumbly at the ceiling. "You sayin' you liked it?"

"No! I've begged for him to leave me alone, but he keeps coming and now I'm pregnant and James and I have not slept together in months."

"Back up," Sky rolled unto her side to face Sadie. "You mean to tell me that the baby ain't James'?"

"It can't be," Sadie whined.

"No wonder he is madder than a stripper dancing at the school for the blind."

Sadie popped Sky on the thigh. "It's not funny," she smirked.

"I know it ain't funny," Sky laughed. "But James ain't gonna buy this angel knocked me up bit. I'm havin' a hard time digesting it myself. I would never believe you if it wasn't for that scene before you went into the hospital."

"I know." Sadie dropped her hands upon her face and shook her head slowly from side to side. She took a deep breath and looked helplessly into Sky's eyes. "What am I going to do? I love James so much and I would never cheat on him. There is no way in the world I can explain this."

"If you are sure it's not James' and you think some kind of sex crazed demon knocked you up, have an abortion," Sky suggested.

"I don't know if I could do that. I'm not sure how I feel about abortion. I think it's immoral, but in certain circumstances I think it's needed. It's such a touchy subject." Tears began to form in the corners of Sadie's eyes. "Plus, James already knows and so does my parents."

"Who cares who knows! It's your body and your choice. Whatever choice you make, I'm with you. Either way, you won't be alone." Sky hugged her friend.

"Thank you."

The telephone rang.

"Do you want me to pick that up?" Sky asked.

"What does the caller ID say?" asked Sadie.

"It's your peeps," answered Sky.

"Yes, hand me the phone," Sadie requested.

Sky picked up the phone and handed it over.

"Hello," Sadie spoke into the receiver.

"Hello sweetheart," Mr. Covington's baritone voice echoed through the phone.

"Hey Daddy, how are you?"

"I'm good. How are you sweetie?"

"Sky is taking good care of me. I can't complain. I'm feeling a whole lot better," Sadie said. Something weird was in her father's voice. It sounded like he was pretending; like he was trying his hardest to control his emotions. His voice was reeking with insincerity. The cheery camouflage was unnerving.

"Good. I'm glad to hear that all is well on your end." Mr. Covington let out a worried sigh. "I just wanted to check up on you. I'm not going to keep you long. I have a number to give you. Call as soon as you can."

"What's it for?"

"A friend of mine. She's a wonderful doctor," Mr. Covington said in a trembling voice. He gave her the doctor's information.

"I'm fine Daddy. I left the hospital with a clean bill of health…"

Mr. Covington cut her off saying, "I am against you having that baby. You and I both know what could happen if you carry that thing to term."

"Daddy, this thing is your grandchild," Sadie snapped. "Your assumptions could be wrong."

"I know," his voice cracked. "It kills me…" He swallowed hard and cleared his throat. It sounded as if he was trying to fight away tears. "I made you an appointment for next Friday. Call and get directions. I love you, baby." Mr. Covington mumbled and hung up the phone.

"Daddy," Sadie called. Only a dial tone pulsated in her ear. She slammed the phone down.

"What's wrong?" Sky asked.

"My father made me an appointment for an abortion," Sadie cried. "How could he be so cold-blooded? I understand his fear, but this is his grandchild."

"He knows about this angel?"

"Yes, and he thinks that the baby will become some kind of mutant," Sadie cried. "Maybe it will, but maybe it won't!"

Tears started to flow from Sky's eyes as well. She grabbed her friend's hands and squeezed.

"Look at me," she said.

Sadie lifted her eyes.

"This is your choice. No one else's. Don't forget that. Whatever decision you make, I am with you," Sky sobbed and hugged Sadie as tightly as she could. "Make up your own mind about this thing. Don't let anyone pressure you into doing anything you do not want to do."

"Okay," Sadie wept into her best friend's bosom. "Why did this happen to me?" she wailed. "Why?"

"God gives us nothing we can't handle," Sky stated as she rubbed Sadie's hair.

"God?" Sadie popped up angrily. "Why would God let this happen in the first place?" she belted. "I prayed for God's help, but my supplications fell upon deaf ears. I have no need for God. I'll ignore Him like He has ignored me."

"Don't say that. You sound like my father," Sky begged.

"Maybe your father is smarter than you think!" Sadie snarled and fell back against the bed with tears and anger flooding her twisted face.

"Nonsense! You are speaking out of emotion. God may be your only hope in this situation. I advise you not to get on His bad side," Sky quipped.

"Whatever!" Sadie snapped and turned her back to her friend and sulked in silence. God was the last thing she was worried about. Where was God when Turiel was having his way with her? Sadie had no interest in Sky's trust in God.

Sky turned her back also and whispered a small prayer under her breath. Something deep within her knew that the worst had not yet come.

25

"Who was that on the phone?" Mrs. Covington asked, her arms folded and her eyes frightened.

"Sadie," Mr. Covington mumbled and brushed past his wife. She grabbed his arm and spun him around.

"Don't walk away," she hissed. "Don't pretend like you two are the only ones that are affected by this situation. I deserve to know what's going on. Don't I deserve to know?" Her eyes began to swell with pain. "You have never harbored secrets. Why start now?"

"I'm sorry," he whispered. "You're right. You should know everything. I apologize for keeping information from you."

"What did you say to her?" she growled.

"I gave her Dr. Davis' number," he whispered and avoided her eyes. "I told her that I scheduled an appointment for her to get rid of the baby."

Mrs. Covington let go of her husband's arm and inhaled loudly then let out a painful exhale.

"Why couldn't you wait?" she cried. "There may be another way! Why couldn't you wait before you advised her to kill our only grandchild?"

"I want that thing out of my daughter," Mr. Covington said in a stoic tone.

"That thing is your grandchild," she wept. "You are talking about your own flesh and blood!"

"That thing is a monster waiting to hatch and destroy us all." Mr. Covington turned his back to his wife. "Forgive me if I seek life and not death."

"The only monster I see is the heartless one standing before me!" she screamed.

A sharp hurting filled Mr. Covington. His chest burned from within. He searched his wife's eyes for a reason for such hateful words. Surely she had to realize that he was fighting for their daughter's life.

Mrs. Covington saw the pain in her husband's eyes and guilt worked its way into her soul. She would not apologize just yet. Her anger was raw and teetering on insanity.

"What did Sadie say? Did she agree with you?" Mrs. Covington asked.

"She sounded defiant and offended by my suggestion. Sadly, she sounds as if she wanted to keep it," he answered.

"Good," Mrs. Covington whimpered. "Good."

"I see no good in this," he dropped his head.

Mrs. Covington put her arms around him and laid her head on his back. He winced under her embrace. His spirit rumbled within him.

"It will work out in the end," she whispered. "It will work out. Maybe things are not as they seem. Maybe it is James' baby after all and we are worried sick about nothing. Where is this faith that you talk to me about sometimes? You have to have faith that our girl will make it through this and that our grandbaby will be born healthy, happy, and normal."

"I pray that you are right my love. I hope that you are right," Mr. Covington uttered. He turned to face is wife. "I love Sadie. I love you. Remember that." He kissed her lips and picked up his coat and walked out of the front door.

26

"Thank you for agreeing to meet me for lunch," Sky said as she spread a white linen napkin across her lap. She took a sip of water then flashed Forrest a twinkling smile.

"It's my pleasure beautiful. I feel privileged to be around you," Forrest responded. "You are simply amazing." He smiled back admiring how the pink sundress she wore complimented her red skin tone. In his mind, he had named her Lady Esau after the red man in the Hebrew Bible.

"Oh stop! I'll never be able to go back home to New York if you keep flatterin' me like you do." Sky ran her fingers through her wild mane causing the bracelets on her arm to make music.

"That's the whole purpose my dear. I want you to stay here with me forever," Forrest said, grabbing Sky's hand and squeezing it softly. "But I'm sure that my intentions were clear from the beginning. I was smitten by you from the moment I laid eyes on you."

Sky blushed deep red.

"But, I'm sure this emergency lunch wasn't called for me to pour my heart out," Forrest said smiling. "By now you should know the contents of my heart. There isn't room for much else than you."

"You know how to pour it on thick don't you?" Sky said with one eyebrow lifted. "I think you are trying to flatter me out of my panties."

They both laughed.

"So what's up?" Forrest asked right before he inserted a buttered breadstick into his mouth.

"I'm really worried about Sadie. She says that she's okay but I know she ain't and it's bad enough that she's havin' these weird experiences, but she stresses herself over James all the time. Do you know if he still wants to marry her?" Sky opened her mouth just in time to bite down on the breadstick Forrest was lifting to her lips. "Thank you," she uttered.

"To tell you the truth, I'm not sure. I know he loves her dearly, but I don't know if he can deal with her situation. He hasn't said much about it. He hasn't said much about anything," answered Forrest, filling Sky's glass with wine.

Sky flipped her hair behind her shoulder and said, "Well, the reason I asked is because she is thinking of giving up the baby."

"What?" he questioned. Forrest placed his hand atop of Sky's.

"Yeah, she's afraid. I'm sure that you know about her supernatural suitor." Sky laughed uncomfortably. "Her father thinks that the baby will be some sort of hell spawn. Her mother has been callin' nonstop tellin' Sadie to keep it and James hasn't called at all. You can't imagine the amount of stress she's under. Frankly, I'm pissed that James doesn't have the balls to offer any support!"

"Calm down," Forrest rubbed her finger thumping hand. "I get your frustration, but I have to say, James has a right to be standoffish. Sadie's entire situation is a lot to swallow. What does she expect him to do?"

"I don't know. Be a friend maybe!" Sky snapped.

"How can he be a friend to the love of his life? He couldn't bear watching her get brutalized and now he has to sit by while she carries the fiend's child. James is a mere man," Forrest exclaimed. "I think Sadie is lucky that he hasn't officially called everything off yet."

Sky's eyes narrowed into deadly green lasers. She slowly stood up and placed her napkin upon the table. "Enjoy your lunch," she spat through her teeth and stormed away.

"Sky wait," he called after her, but her slender body cut through the crowd like a razor blade. Within seconds she was no longer visible. Forrest gulped down the remainder of her wine and placed a hefty tip on the table.

"Me and my big mouth," he mumbled as he got into his silver Bentley and sped down the street.

27

The week flew by on humming bird wings. James sat in a plush leather chair and looked hopelessly at the stacks of invoices upon his desk. He picked up his phone and buzzed his assistant. A tall and awkwardly cute young man quickly entered, picked up the stack, and left back out. James placed a legal pad on an empty space on his desk and began to jot down a few ideas for expanding his company. Business was better than it had ever been. All of his shops were booked solid for the next four months. All of his employees were excellent workers and seemed happy. His finances were rock solid. Everything was exceeding his highest expectations. James opened his lap top, surfed the net, and played a few online games. After clicking off a game of solitaire, he spun his chair around and peered through a gigantic window overlooking Atlanta. Tiny bubbles popped within his belly, troubling his bowels. He unbuckled the gold buckle of his black snake skin belt and unbuttoned and unzipped his pants. The lack of pressure did little to help since he wore his clothes a little larger than needed. Everything he ate or drank as of late made him unsettled. Sleep was foreign to him. All he thought of was Sadie and her mysterious pregnancy. Every time she came to mind he wanted to vomit. Anger had taken over sympathy and frustration had taken over consideration.

"I can't marry her. This is too much," he said to himself. The thought of living without Sadie was enough to make him wish he was dead, but the thought of living with Sadie seemed to have impending death looming over him. There was no way he could raise a child that was not his. All he could think about was someone making love to his woman and giving her life, taking away his right of a first born son with the most perfect woman he had ever known. The thought of something invading Sadie's fertile Nile, reaping from the oasis he had so carefully nourished was much too much for him to bear. James felt robbed, punked, and most of all helpless. He picked up the phone and dialed his personal assistant again. The assistant picked up.

"Princeston," James said.

"Yes sir."

"I need you to call my wedding planner."

"Okay, I'll connect you as soon as I get her," Princeston said.

"No, I don't need to talk. Just tell her that the wedding is off."

"Will do sir," Princeston paused, a little confused by this sudden unexpected request. "Is there anything else you need?"

"No. Just call her as soon as I hang up."

"Okay," Princeston hesitated. "I'm sorry to hear the bad news. I thought that you and Miss Covington were a great couple."

"Me too," James responded as he hung up the phone not waiting for Princeston to respond. There was no way James was going to explain his situation to his aide.

Princeston was a nice guy and easy to talk to. James had invited him over for a couple of sports nights with him and his boys, but he was not interested in confiding in Princeston. James' pride could not bear more scrutiny. He was embarrassed enough to explain it to himself; therefore, he was definitely not going to explain it to a mere associate. The feeling in his stomach worsened. He knew what he had to do. He picked up the phone and dialed Sadie's number.

"Hello," Sadie mussitated after picking up the phone on the second ring. She sounded as if she had food in her mouth.

James froze. His mouth opened, but not a syllable was formed. The sound of Sadie's voice shrank his anger into infantile weakness. James started to hang up, but thought better of it. It was time for him to face her. He had been in hiding long enough.

"Hello," Sadie repeated after a noisy swallow and a quick suck of her teeth, this time with a clear voice.

James cleared his throat and rubbed his hand across his bald head. "Sadie," he whispered, ignoring her horrible phone manners.

"James," she sighed anxiously.

"Yes," he paused. His eyes became cloudy. "Sorry about that. I didn't hear you pick up," he lied. James loosened his collar. All of a sudden, despite the constant cold air blowing from the air conditioner, the room seemed so hot that he could fry fish in the air. "How have you been? You've been on my mind a lot lately. I hope everything has been all right. Sky is taking good care of you I'm sure," he paused. James rubbed his head again, this time massaging with his finger tips. His nerves were getting the best of him. "I've been so busy," he paused. "You know how it gets sometimes. This place has been a mad house. I'm enjoying the weather though. Me and the guys should go out and shoot some ball."

Sadie didn't like the uneasiness in James' voice. It was not like him to engage in small talk. Whenever James called, he called to say something specific. Even if he just wanted to say hello. He said hello and ended the call.

"I've been doing okay. I'm glad that you called," Sadie said discomforted.

James voice cracked, "How's the baby doing?"

"Just fine," Sadie whispered. "The doctor said that we both are okay. Thank you for asking. I know it took a lot for you to." Sadie went silent for a moment. "You know that I would never do anything to hurt you."

"I know," James whispered. "I know."

"I would never cheat on you," Sadie whispered.

"I know," James grumbled.

"Are you okay?" she asked with a voice soaked in tears.

"No. No, I'm not. I'm so far from okay I don't think I'll ever be okay again." James paused. "Baby," he called.

"Yes sweetheart," she croaked.

"I can't marry you."

"I know," Sadie whined.

"But, I want you to know that I love you with all of me. I just can't handle this. I've been trying to figure out what to do with all of this, but there is nothing I can do to help you. Please forgive me," he wept.

"I understand..."

He cut her short. "You are everything to me and losing you is the hardest thing for me to imagine, but I think it's for the best. Take care of yourself and...and...and... remember that I love you." James sniffed hard. "Okay?"

"Okay," she whimpered.

"I'll always be your friend," he swallowed. He knew it was a lie as soon as it exited his mouth. He could never be her friend. If he could not be with her, he did not want to be near her. "If you ever need me, don't be afraid to call," his voice wobbled. "I mean it, baby, call me for anything you need." He paused, waiting for Sadie's response, but nothing came through the phone lines, but broken whimpers from a shattered spirit. "I am so sorry that I can't be there for you. I hate myself for not being strong enough. Please know that I love you," James exhaled loudly. "Goodbye, baby."

"Goodbye."

James hung up the phone. He dropped his head and took a deep breath. His red rimmed eyes blinked sluggishly in melancholy anger. He stood up slowly. His hands fell to his sides as if his fingers and pants were attracting magnets. He closed his eyes. Thunder raged in his head. There was no peace for his thoughts. The sound of his grinding teeth filled the frigid air conditioned air. With one swift yank, he jerked the phone up and threw it into the nearest wall.

28

Sadie slumped against the kitchen counter. The floor seemed to feel colder than it was moments before. Sadness stifled her heart. It cut off the oxygen flowing through her blood and for a moment she swore the blues that ricocheted through her being actually began to tint her skin. Of course it was just her overactive imagination trying to cope with the devastation she was feeling. The love of her life had walked away from their future together and there was absolutely nothing she could do. Her hung head began to strain her neck. She looked up and came face to face with the calendar on the wall. It was Tuesday. Right there and right then, she decided that Friday would be the day that she reclaimed her life. Sadie opened the kitchen drawer and pulled out a red marker. She circled the day and threw the marker into the dining room. A horrid gathering shaped in the pit of her intestines. It snaked its putrid agony into her belly and crawled up her chest. With demonic strength, a wall crumbling wail bellowed from her throat and it was followed by another and another. Sadie pounded her defiled belly with her fists daring the creature inside of her to give up the ghost and be gone. Waters fell from her eyes to join the currents of mucus that cascaded into her mouth. Her screams morphed into coughing whimpers then into sickening sniffles. The floor caught her trembling body as she slid down into a ball. She was still. So still only her blinking gave proof of life. She held her breath, hoping that she would just pass into oblivion, but nature took over and forced her to gasp for air. Sadie damned her body for craving life when her heart craved to suffer no longer. Sadie closed her eyes and became paralyzed by her pain. There in the dining room, she was frozen for three hours before Sky turned the key in the front door.

"Sadie, are you home?" Sky called as she closed the door behind her and walked into the living room. She

tossed her floral print cloth purse on the couch and flopped down beside it. "Sadie, are you here?" she asked again. There was no response. Sky picked up the phone to check the messages. There were none so she hung up and flipped through the caller ID. She saw that Forrest had called Sadie's number as well as her cell phone at least three times since she had walked out on their lunch date. Sky also saw that James had called. A smile crossed her face. Hopefully he and Sadie had made up. Sky kicked off her four inch heels and turned the corner into the dining room.

"Sadie!" Sky yelled, startled by her friend lying on the floor crouched, still, and staring off into nothingness. "What's wrong?" she asked as she stooped down and gathered Sadie into her arms. "What happened?"

Sadie said nothing, but the tears came in splinters of silver cutting down her cheeks.

"What happened, Sadie?" Sky began to cry too as she squeezed her best friend so tight that Sky's arms felt like sticks pressing against Sadie's flesh. "Did the angel come again?"

"No," Sadie whispered. "It never left me," she groaned as she gave her belly an otiose punch.

"Everything is going to be okay," Sky whispered and kissed Sadie's damp forehead. "Everything will be just fine."

"Nothing will ever be okay again," Sadie cried. "James is gone."

"What do you mean he's gone? Did that thing do something to him?" Sky's voice squealed in Sadie's ear. For a moment, Sky imagined herself in danger but quickly dismissed the thought. She knew that Sadie would never put her in harm's way.

"Worse," Sadie croaked. Her voice was a haggard whisper.

"What can be worse than that?"

"He doesn't want to marry me. We're over," Sadie calmly said. She breathed deeply, letting her loveless fate sink in. There was nothing she could do to change his mind. She did not even want to try. He would be a fool to continue to be mixed up with her and her demon lover. "James just called to tell me that the wedding is off. We're off," Sadie blubbered.

"He broke up with you over the phone? How could he be so cruel? That low life…"

Sadie held up her hand to cut Sky short and said, "He did nothing wrong,"

"Don't defend that coward! He could have said it to your face!" Sky belted

"He couldn't face me and I don't blame him. Neither should you," said Sadie. "Never speak ill of him. He is a good man. Watch your mouth."

"I'm so sorry Sadie," Sky softly grabbed Sadie's arms and moved her backwards so she could clearly see her face. "I'm so sorry."

"Me too." Sadie looked away. "I'm not going to have this baby. It's no telling what kind of birth defect it may be born with." She paused to wipe her eyes with the back of her hands, popping her knuckles against her face.

"I hate when you do that," Sky laughed sadly.

"I know," Sadie smiled.

Sky stood up and held out her hand to Sadie. Sadie grabbed it and Sky pulled her to her feet. They made their way to the sofa and they sat opposite to one another. Silence; ear aching silence invaded the room. Ten minutes passed.

"Are you sure about the baby?" Sky asked.

"Yes. I would be a terrible mother anyway. I could never get over the way it was conceived and I would always be reminded of losing James." Sadie ran her fingers through her hair and sighed. "Plus, it may be trouble like my father warned."

"There's no way on earth you would be a terrible mother. You have too much love in your heart. Whatever your reason, I'm with you; but, don't give up yo' baby 'cause yo' man left you or yo' dad wants you too. Give it up if you feel in your heart that it's the right thing to do."

"Thanks Sky. You are the best." Sadie smiled painfully. She loved the way Sky could flip back and forth between proper and improper English. Especially when she was angry. "I don't want to talk about me anymore. How was your lunch with Forrest?"

Sky rolled her eyes to the ceiling and twisted her lips. She answered, "Terrible. We had a fight and I walked out."

"What about? Forrest isn't the fighting type," Sadie asked.

"You and James," Sky mumbled.

"Me and James!" Sadie exclaimed. "Don't waste your energy defending me and James. You pick up that phone right now and call Forrest and make things right. There is no sense in both of us moping around here."

"He shouldn't have…"

"It doesn't matter. He has called for you a few times today. Call him back and make it right," Sadie insisted.

"Are you sure Sadie?"

"Yes," Sadie smiled. "I love you. I want you to be happy. Just because things didn't work out between me and James doesn't mean that you and Forrest can't be happy. Girl, call your man and have fun making up!" Sadie forced a wicked little smirk.

"Okay, I'll call. But only because you want me too."

"Girl please! You know you wouldn't have the will to stay away from that fine man for a day. A doctor who is handsome, sweet, faithful, and rich doesn't need to be alone for too long. All these thirsty hoes in Atlanta will gulp him up quick. If you don't call him, I will!" Sadie joked.

Sky pushed Sadie playfully. It was amusing to her when Sadie used vulgar language. It was as foreign to Sadie's mouth as truth to a politician's. They both laughed quietly, wiping away stray tears.

"I'm tired. I'm going to lie down for a while. I need to rest my eyes and clear my mind." Sadie stood up and started towards her room.

"Sadie," Sky called. "Promise me that you're gonna be okay."

"I'm going to be okay," Sadie sadly smiled. "I have to be. Being okay is the only hope that I have right now."

Sky nodded and said, "Good. I'll be in shortly. I'm going to call Forrest first."

"I don't need you to sleep with me anymore. I'm okay. Go to your room. I'm tired of waking up with your bushy hair in my face," Sadie quipped.

Sky laughed and walked towards her room. She stopped and yelled down the hall, "Sadie!"

"Yes," Sadie answered without turning around. Her hand rested on her door knob. Peace and quiet was so close. She hoped that Sky had not thought of anything lengthy to discuss.

"I'm going with you Friday and there is nothing you can do to stop me," Sky stated matter-of-factly as she disappeared into the guestroom and closed the door behind her.

Sadie opened her door and disappeared behind its false protection. Leaning against the door, her reserve shattered. Hot emotion erupted from her twisted mouth and reddening face. She held her belly and fell to the floor in silent painful sobs. With a little thump, her head rocked her vanity, knocking over the razor blade she used to trim her eyebrows. Sadie picked up the sliver of silver and held its twinkly potential up to the light. Thoughts of ruby caressing silver filled her. The marriage of metal and flesh tantalized her teetering mind. If she was brave enough, she would take the metal of hope and release the blood from her veins, but she possessed no such will. Sadie could never take her own life. Despite the seeming hopelessness of her situation, she knew that there was always a chance for things to work out. Life was funny that way. Tomorrow always seemed to shake off the sorrows of today. She tossed the blade to the side and balled herself into herself and wept silently for she knew that this too shall pass.

29

The university's campus was always swamped with students. They never seemed to be inside of the buildings, but milling around like piles of worms tilling the soil. They were a forest of denim and cotton that shifted with each blow of the wind. Mrs. Covington resented the crowded yard. Suddenly she regretted wearing her canary yellow suit. She stood out like a vegetarian at a barbeque joint. The more people she passed the less inconspicuous she became. Even a few of her husband's students waved hello and offered her unwelcomed smiles. If Mr. Covington knew that she was meeting with Dr. Putina, he would be livid. No, livid was too kind a word. He would be pissed to the highest degree of pisstivity. There would be no way to explain her way out of this one. Mrs. Covington willed her short legs into maximum speed as she power walked across the campus until she arrived at her husband's department building. She paused outside and inhaled deeply before she rushed inside of the gigantic glass double doors of the dark gothic building. Once inside, she quickly skipped past her husband's office door and rounded the corner to Dr. Putina's office. Mrs. Covington knocked three times and impatiently waited, unconsciously shuffling her sunflower yellow sandaled feet and rubbing her moist palms on the sides of her skirt. Finally after four harder knocks, an unearthly pale, raven haired young man dressed in all black wearing an overload of silver jewelry opened the door.

"Yeah?" he asked in a flat lifeless voice.

"Is Dr. Putina in?" Mrs. Covington asked, her voice cracking with nervous uneasiness. Every few seconds she glanced down the hall and prayed that her husband's office door would not suddenly swing open.

"Yeah," he replied, his mouth remaining open after the word tumbled out.

Mrs. Covington looked into the boy's eyes. They seemed to be cloudy pools of drug injected onyx. He said nothing as he stood in the doorway with a blank look on his face.

"Excuse me," Mrs. Covington said.

The boy stood unmoving as if he did not hear a thing.

"May I pass by you?" Mrs. Covington asked.

"Yeah," the boy answered, but did not move.

Mrs. Covington glanced back down the hall and saw a student knocking on her husband's office door. She turned back towards the boy.

"Move to the side please," she alarmingly urged.

"Okay," he slurred as he sidestepped with the speed of a growing tree.

Mrs. Covington pushed past the zombie boy, knocking him off balance, and barged into Dr. Putina's office.

The office was painted a dark purple. Crystals, strange symbols, and an infinite number of books about the occult lined the walls. Stars and moons decorated the ceiling and glitter seemed to be everywhere. Instantly, Mrs. Covington felt like an idiot for being there.

The boy angrily climbed to his feet, snatched his backpack off of a nearby chair, and stormed out of the door holding up his middle finger. Mrs. Covington scoffed at the disrespect and turned on her heels. She dropped her purse on Dr. Putina's desk and crossed her arms. The professor's head popped up and a crooked smile bent her invisible lips.

"Ebbie, nice to see you again. You look lovely." Dr. Putina grinned, seemingly pleased with Mrs. Covington's irritation.

Mrs. Covington ripped open her purse and pulled out the money she promised and threw it on the professor's desk.

"I don't have the patience or the time for niceties," Mrs. Covignton spat. "Let's get down to business so I can get the hell out of this place!"

"Did I do something to offend you? Please tell me what I did to warrant such hostility," Dr. Putina asked, trying fruitlessly to stop grinning.

Mrs. Covington's eyes narrowed into slits.

"You did nothing wrong," she hissed. "Please forgive my rudeness. May we begin?"

"Of course darling." Dr. Putina stood up. Strand upon strand of beads in every shape and size hung around her neck. She wore a gypsy skirt and a dashiki. Her platinum blonde hair was pulled back in a ponytail and a pair of jeweled glasses with a matching chain sat upon her nose. Soft laugh lines lined her mouth and faint crow's-feet fanned the corners of her clear gray eyes. Bright red lipstick colored her otherwise nonexistent lips. "Help me move these chairs please," she requested.

The two ladies moved both of the chairs that faced the professor's desk and pushed two other chairs against the far wall. Dr. Putina rolled up the area rug in the center of the floor revealing a circle about nine feet in diameter with a number of pentacles in the middle.

"I have been casting spells for a week. You don't know how daunting it was for me to give praise to the Christian God in order to make this séance successful. Such foolishness turns my stomach," she complained then temporarily stopped what she was doing and looked up at Mrs. Covington. A wide and frightening smile contorted the professor's face. "But, for a friend I'll do almost anything."

"You mean for money," Mrs. Covington mumbled under her breath, internally shaken by the doctor's impish grin. Mrs. Covington leaned against the wall, silently cursing herself for meeting up with such an eccentric kook. She knew in her heart that there was no way that this whole spell casting session would work. The doctor had as much power to channel the supernatural as a bird had to break dance. How in the world did she allow herself to consider doing such a drastic idiotic thing? Mr. Covington would have never encouraged her to contact Dr. Putina and Sadie would be disappointed in her lapse of judgment. Mrs. Covington looked at her purse and considered picking it up and hightailing out of this *Dungeons and Dragons* capsule. The only thing that planted her feet on the floor was the hope that she could bring peace back to her family. Her husband and daughter were convinced that a demon was the culprit that tore their lives asunder. For the moment, she decided to swallow her pride and open her mind to the impossible.

"Tonight will be the final spell and your beloved angel shall humbly appear to you," Dr. Putina sang. She picked a manila envelope up from her desk and placed it in the middle of the floor. "What a glorious occasion!" she exclaimed as she placed the final necessities in their places.

Mrs. Covington looked at the witch doctor with disdain. *Why am I here?* She thought as she observed the freakish setup of the room. Surely there was no hope in this place of unicorn figurines and dragon embroidered draperies.

"Are you ready to begin?" Dr. Putina asked.

"I guess so," Mrs. Covington reluctantly sat down where the doctor instructed her to.

Dr. Putina dimmed the lights. She placed a hard bound version of *The Secret Grimoire of Turiel,* which looked as ancient as the very mountains, upon her lap and turned through its browning pages. At once she began summoning the angel. She spewed out lists of strange names, familiar planets, and hierarchies of angels. She rocked back and forth as she begged the Lord God of Heaven to send her a messenger. Minutes aggregated and produced an hour. Sweat dampened the professor's brow as her lips called upon the unseen.

"I adjure you by the entire host of Heaven, Seraphims, Cherubims, Thrones, Dominations, Virtues,

Powers, Principalities, Archangels and Angels, by the great and glorious Spirits and by your Star and by all the constellations of Heaven, and by whatsoever you obey," Dr. Putina wailed. Her thin lips wrapped around each word like a label on a bottle as she read from the book. Her pale skin flushed pink as her voice rose higher into the air. "Attend to me according to the prayers and petitions which I have made to Almighty God, and that you send me one of your messengers who may willingly and truly and faithfully fulfill all my desires, wishes and commands, and that you command him to appear to me in the form of an angel, the angel Turiel, willingly entering into communication with me, and that he neither bring terror nor fear to me, or mulishly deny my requests, neither permitting any evil spirits to appear or approach in any way to hurt, terrify, or affright me, nor deceiving me in any way; through the virtue of our Lord. Amen." Dr. Putina took a deep breath. She squeezed her eyes tighter and said, "Come in peace."

The room shined as if the very sun levitated in the midst of them. Mrs. Covington fell backwards and covered her eyes. Dr. Putina cowered in awe and unholy fear. Unbelief mingled with supernatural splendor sent chills down her protruding backbone. She crawled under her desk and folded her body in terrific despair.

The brightness of the room attenuated into a soothing shine that brought unnatural comfort and the feeling of nurturing protection to the women. The scent of myrrh filled the air. Immediately Mrs. Covington knew that the creature was her daughter's tormentor.

The professor crawled from beneath the desk and sat akimbo before the celestial being. Mrs. Covington peeked through her fingers then dropped her hands as she moved near the far wall. She rested her back against the cold sheet rock and waited for the divinely beautiful creature to speak.

"Holy one," Dr. Putina saluted as she stretched out her arms and bowed her head.

"No one is holy, but God," it answered, its eyes narrow and dangerous.

"Are you the mighty and honorable Turiel?' she whispered, her voice a trembling ghost. She lifted her head and affixed her eyes upon the handsome messenger.

"I am Turiel," he bellowed. "You know nothing of might and honor. I dare you try to cajole me! Heathen, what right do you have to summon me? You are not worthy to utter my name."

"Please accept my humblest apologies..."

"Enough of your gibberish infidel! If you value your life, cease your foolish murmurings. Why did you summon me?" His voice vibrated off the walls. A look of disgust lined his face. He observed the stupefying shock in her eyes when he first appeared; the unabashed vain awe that gave her a sense of false power as if she had the might of a miracle worker. There was nothing he hated more than unbelievers who pretended to believe. What a cowardly lot they were, pathetic pretenders who preyed upon the innocence of others. He could smell fakeness dripping from her flesh. It was like a stinking oil that secreted from her pores.

Dr. Putina quickly pointed to Mrs. Covington and crawled back under her desk.

Turiel smiled. "Mother of my lover," he whispered. "What want may I grant you? You are blessed among women."

Tears rushed down Mrs. Covington's face. She rose to her knees and held her fists in the air.

"Leave my child alone!" she begged. "Sadie has done nothing to deserve the way you have abused her!"

"I cause her no pain. I love her," he said.

"You love nothing! Love does not force a person against their will. Sadie doesn't love you!" Mrs. Covington screamed.

"I love..." Turiel began.

"You love nothing demon!" Mrs. Covington spat. "Go back to your proper domain and leave us be!"

Turiel's eyes flared as his face twisted into a sinister mask, his beauty melting into pure iniquity. The soft glow surrounding him suddenly lit up like a tempestuous fire.

Dr. Putina crawled from under her desk once more. A sense of pseudo-confidence pulsed through her veins as she uttered, "Oh, rebellious spirit, I demand you to leave her child alone! I command you to go back into the bowels of despair where you belong! I cast you away from earth into eternity in hell!"

Turiel turned to face the pretentious professor.

"You have no power over me fool! Be gone from here!" he screeched as his wings spread across the room. Instantaneously he flew shoulder first into her chest. The professor's body crashed through the wall, her arms and legs touching one another like closed fingers and thumb. A scarlet cave leaked within her chest. Blood poured from her red gaping lips. A string of blonde hair fell over one of her lifeless canescent eyes as she sat lodged within the sheet rock Sheol.

"What have you done?" Mrs. Covington screamed as she stared at the murdered professor.

"I have given you fair warning," the angel hissed. "Sadie belongs to me. Her seed is flesh of my flesh and this earth is for the taking," he exclaimed, vanishing.

Pounding on the door shook Mrs. Covington from her stupor. She heard the voices of other faculty members screaming for the door to be opened. Mrs. Covington looked over at Dr. Putina's dead body and panicked. She picked up her purse and the professor's appointment calendar, opened the window, and climbed out. Her feet touched the ground instantly and she sprinted across campus like a ripened cheetah, as fast as her old bones could carry her.

30

A loud chiming noise rang through the room. Sadie sat up on the side of her bed and wiped dreams from her eyes. Worrisome dreams that she was happy to flee from. Vicious visions of chaos and destruction, angels and demons, dark and light, life and death. She reached over and quickly gave her alarm clock a slap to stop its annoying clanging. It was Friday, Armageddon for the tiny soul thriving within her. The clock read 8:00 a.m., two hours before the life ending operation. Sadie's hands involuntarily rested upon her belly. She quickly removed them and jumped up from the bed, determined not to let her emotions dictate the decision that she had to make. After picking out her clothes and shoes: a ragged pair of jeans, a fitted T-shirt with *Life Sucks* on the front of it, and a worn out pair of Converse high tops, she grabbed an old comfortable bra and a pair of high waist cotton panties. Sexy was the last thing she wanted to feel. It was the last way she could feel. A matter of fact, an overwhelming feeling of dread snaked through her chest. She leaned against the wall and let out a defeated sigh. A bantam tinkle invaded her nose, warning her of impending tears, but she was all cried out. The sadness inside of her was stale. She stood up straight and placed both hands upon her face. She suspired loudly, dropped her hands and opened her chamber door. Sadie yelled down the hallway.

"Sky!"

There was no answer. Sadie yelled again, this time getting an irritated grunt as a response.

"It's time to wake up girl. We have to get ready to go!" Sadie shouted and closed the door after she heard Sky fumbling around in her room. Sadie padded into the bathroom and entered the shower. About twenty minutes later, she emerged from the bedroom dressed. She entered into the living room detangling her hair with her fingers.

On the couch sat a sleepy-eyed Sky with her hair in a wild fuzzy mess. An oversized T-shirt draped her slender frame as khaki shorts displayed her knobby knees.

"You want something to eat?" Sadie asked as she walked into the kitchen to prepare a small breakfast.

"Sure," Sky whined. A morning person she was not.

"Whatcha want?" Sadie asked as she looked inside of the refrigerator.

"I wanna get back in bed," Sky complained, flopping across the sofa, her head hanging over the side, her hair sweeping the floor.

"Well that's not an option if you don't want to see me hanging from my shower curtain," Sadie jested. "There are some blueberry bagels in here and I have some strawberry jam and cream cheese."

"What else you got?" Sky asked.

"Some cereal and milk, frozen waffles, grapefruit, and turkey bacon," replied Sadie. She popped a sliced bagel into the toaster and poured herself a big glass of orange juice.

"I'll take some cereal and milk," Sky requested.

Sadie picked up her food and walked out of the kitchen. She sat the dining room table and began to eat.

"Whatcha doin'?" Sky lifted her head up off the sofa and asked.

"I'm eating," Sadie laughed. "You took too long to decide. I'm hungry."

Sky stood up, dragging her feet into the kitchen.

"That's messed up," she grumbled as she fixed her breakfast, slamming the cereal bowl on the counter and splashing milk. "How you gonna offer and renege?"

"I can do that," Sadie laughed with food falling out of her mouth.

"Nasty heifer," Sky laughed. She sat down next to her friend and ate quickly. "You ready to go?" she asked Sadie.

Sadie felt queasy. The bagel she had eaten did little to calm her turbulent belly. She placed her elbows upon the table and massaged her temples. Fear crept upon her. *What if I'm making a mistake?* She mentally questioned. The thought of her being a round jolly mommy-to-be warmed her heart and made her mission even harder to carry out. Every breath she took was laborious. She squeezed her eyes shut.

"Are you okay?" Sky asked, placing her hand upon Sadie's shoulder. "You sure you want to go through with this?"

"Yes," Sadie replied as she hopped up from the table, grabbed her keys, and headed for the door. Sky quickly followed. In less than five minutes, they had made it out of the apartment building and into the car. Sadie sped down Peachtree until she turned onto the highway. The speedometer vibrated as Sadie's foot pressed down on the accelerator.

Sky's heart began to pound in her chest as her eyes witnessed the speedometer climb from ninety-five to one hundred miles per hour.

"You need to slow down," Sky entreated. "You're going to kill us both at this rate." Sky grabbed Sadie's knee. "Calm down. Everything will be alright."

Sadie lifted her foot and the car gradually lost momentum. Her hands gripped the steering wheel so tight that the wheel threatened to come off.

"Move over to the right lane. We have to get off on the next exit," Sky instructed.

Sadie did as she was told without hesitation.

"Are you okay?" Sky asked.

Sadie said nothing. Her eyes were glued to the road before her, her mind battling with her emotions.

"Are you okay," Sky asked again.

Sadie continued to ignore her friend as she pulled her candy apple red car into Dr. Monique Davis' parking lot. She parked near the entrance and quickly exited her vehicle.

Sky had to jog to catch up with her. Sadie entered the building, checked the directory and headed to the elevator. Sky followed behind her like a bumbling flunky.

"You need to slow down," Sky moaned.

Sadie said nothing as she exited the elevator and walked up to the reception desk. A very pretty woman with rich golden skin and a mass of thick black curly hair greeted her with a smile. The woman looked as if she could have been a member of any race on earth. Sadie could not decipher if she was Black, Hispanic, Mediterranean, or Indian. Maybe she was a bit of all of it.

"How may I help you," the pretty lady asked. Her black eyes sparkled in the bright sunshine beaming though the endless windows of the office.

"I have an appointment with Dr. Davis," Sadie said, her eyes shifting from the receptionist to the waiting room. There she saw an array of women in every shape, race, and background, waiting to suck a life from their womb. Soon she would be one of those women waiting for an executioner in a white coat to wave them into the death chamber. Sadie's hands began to shake uncontrollably. She placed them flat upon the desk to stop the trimmer, but her fingers seemed to pop up from the marble. *Calm down.* She demanded herself. *Just calm down. This is for the best.*

"Are you okay," the receptionist asked with faux concern, the smile not leaving her face. She knew that it was common for women to be nervous. Abortion was a difficult decision for many women to make.

"Y...y...yes," Sadie stuttered. She looked into the receptionist's eyes then noticed a picture of five children tucked neatly next to the receptionist's computer. It sat so far back that it probably went unnoticed by most. "Are they yours?" Sadie pointed.

"Yes," the receptionist forced an uneasy smile. "I have five wild ones."

Sadie instantly felt sick to her stomach. She thought to herself. *How insensitive could you be to the plight of the women who walk in and out of this clinic on a daily basis?* Sadie grabbed Sky's hand and pulled her to the desk. *I wonder how many children the doctor has. Will their pictures be on the walls of the operating room?* She gave Sky a nod and instantly, like a soul truly in sync, Sky knew what to do.

"Her name is Sadie Covington." Sky reached into Sadie's back pocket and pulled out her insurance card and driver's license. "Here is her insurance information. You can give me any paper work she needs to fill out and I can make sure that she does it."

The receptionist handed Sky a clipboard with a stack of papers attached. Sky thanked her and led Sadie to an empty seat in the corner of the room.

"Are you sure you want to go through with this?" Sky asked again before she pressed the point of the ink pen on the first form.

Sadie nodded.

Sky filled in the documents as Sadie whispered her personal information in her best friend's ear. Sky quickly finished, instructed Sadie to place her signature where needed, and took the clipboard back to the receptionist.

"Here you go," Sky said to the receptionist.

"Thank you," replied the receptionist. "The nurse will call you when it is time."

Sky nodded. She turned and looked at Sadie sitting across the room with head bowed and broken spirit. All happiness seemed so far away from Sadie. Despair wrapped its melancholy arms around her and enticed her to fade into gray. Sky walked over slowly. A feeling of helplessness filled her. What could she do to make the present seem not so dim? She sat down next to Sadie. Sky's mouth opened, but nothing came out. There was nothing more she could say so she grabbed Sadie's hand and held it in her own; both women waited patiently for whatever was to come.

31

Carlos Covington walked through the front door of his home and placed his keys on the hallway table. The cool conditioned air was like paradise to his sweating skin. The outside sun had tanned him two shades darker this week alone. It was good to be home. Good to be away from all of the commotion going on at work.

"Ebbie," he called. A deep wrinkle crinkled his forehead, his eyes laced with solicitude. He walked into the living room and plopped down on the sofa. Slowly peeling off his socks and shoes, he placed his feet upon the coffee table.

"Ebbie," he called again. It was unusual for her not to be in the living room working on some sort of craft.

"Ebbie," he called once more. He pulled off his polo shirt, revealing a white wife beater soaked in perspiration.

"Yes," she answered in a groggy voice.

"Where are you sweetheart?" Mr. Covington questioned, pulling off the soaked tank top and balling it up in his hands. He was in great shape for his age. Lean muscles lined his arms, broad shoulders and a hard chest made him look years younger, although silver hairs curled from his pectorals.

"I'm in the bedroom," Mrs. Covington answered.

Mr. Covington looked at his watch. It was after eleven a.m. Mrs. Covington had never slept after eight in the morning since the day he met her. She was a true morning person. Most mornings he swore that she stirred before the birds.

Mr. Covington scratched his head and stood up. He made his way down the hallway to his bedroom. He pushed open the cracked door and stood in the doorway. Placing his hands in his pockets, he curiously leaned against the door frame.

"Sleeping late?" he asked, his eyebrows high.

Mrs. Covington turned to face him and said, "Just a little tired I suppose."

The lines around her eyes and mouth looked pronounced when she looked so solemn. A smile would have been an instant face lift.

"Are you feeling okay? You've been acting strange all week," he asked.

Her throat went instantly dry.

"What do you mean?" Her voice cracked and her eyes shifted to the wall.

"You're sleeping late. Yesterday you dropped every dish you picked up. You haven't had much to say. You've canceled all of your appointments for the next week." Mr. Covington hesitated. He looked down at his hands and lowered his voice. "We haven't made love in three nights." He lifted his head and his eyes met hers. "Is something wrong? Did I do something?"

"Of course not sweetheart," she answered, relieved. *He doesn't know.* Pulling the covers up, she opened her arms and said, "Come lay next to me."

Mr. Covington stepped out of his shorts and climbed into the bed behind his wife. His cotton boxers clung to his thighs as he curled his body into a perfect spoon, instantly becoming one with the woman he loved.

"How was work?" she asked.

The feeling of his warm breath upon her neck was soothing. She reached back and pulled his arms tighter around her.

"It was awful. The campus was nearly shut down," he answered while cupping her breast with his hands.

"Why?" she asked.

"Do you remember Dr. Putina? She was a professor in my department. The one who was always staging elaborate séances and the like." He paused. "Thin, blonde, and weird. You met her a couple of times through the years. I was never very fond of her because of her deceitful ways

with the students. It bothered me how she played upon their naivety and trust."

Mrs. Covington's body stiffened. A frog climbed into her throat and refused to budge.

"Do you remember who I'm talking about?" He nudged her with his pelvis.

"Y...yes," she forced out.

"Well, on Tuesday she was found dead in her office. She was killed, thrown through the wall and her chest smashed in. Everyone was questioned by the police and the entire department was in an upheaval. That's why I've been coming home late all this week. I tried to tell you about it earlier, but it has been a little hard to get your attention," Mr. Covington admitted.

"I'm so sorry that I've been wrapped in my own thoughts. Sadie has been on my mind a lot."

"Mine too," he replied.

Mrs. Covington swallowed hard. Her heart pounded within her chest, imperiling to smash through her ribs and spilling its guilty secret.

Mr. Covington felt the unsavory thumps.

"It's okay, baby," he said. "I'm sure that Sadie will be okay. She has to be. Right?"

"Right," she agreed. "What did the police say?

"A few witnesses saw a kid entering and exiting her office around the time of the murder. He was the last person seen with her and he was the only appointment listed on her desk calendar. The kid, a bit of a weirdo, was always stoned out of his mind and heavily into the occult. He walked around looking like Marilyn Manson on a daily basis. I saw him around her office often, but I felt that he was quite harmless. Although he was a pot head, he was very helpful to Dr. Putina and the rest of us when we needed him. The boy was an "A" student and had been accepted into graduate school at one of the Ivy League universities." He shook his head. Pity is all he felt for the boy. Mr. Covington kissed his wife's shoulder and continued, "When questioned, he had no alibi. As usual, he was high as a kite. But he kept saying that he was not the only one in Dr. Putina's office."

Mrs. Covington held her breath. What if the boy could identify her? She could be accused of murder. No one would believe what killed the professor. What if the cops found her fingerprints? Her hands were on the desk, the chairs, and the window. Tears ran from her eyes, falling unto Mr. Covington's arm.

"Are you okay, baby?" Mr. Covington asked.

Sniffing, she said, "I'm fine. I just feel so sorry for that poor woman." At least she did not tell a whole lie. She was sorry, but sympathy had been overridden by selfish fear.

"There were also rumors that she was having an affair with him," Mr. Covington said.

"Isn't she married?"

"Yes, but students say that the two were spotted out somewhere arguing and she was telling him to back off. Some think she was trying to pay him to leave her alone."

"Why would they think that?" Mrs. Covington asked.

"Well, there was money on her desk when she was killed," Mr. Covington replied. "But all of this is hearsay. No one knows what happened. I don't think they were lovers. The professor seemed to really love her husband. Besides, I don't think the boy did it, but one can never tell. Killers are always described as being the nicest people."

"Only a monster would kill like that," Mrs. Covington whispered. "Only a monster."

"It's a very sad thing." He tucked his chin into his wife's shoulder. "No one deserves to die that way. She was not my favorite person, but she did nothing to harm anyone. I can't imagine anyone being her enemy. Maybe that kid smoked a bad joint and lost his mind. He swore he was not the last one with her."

"Did the boy say who else was in the office?" she asked, finding it harder to breathe with each passing moment.

"He said it was some lady who knocked him down trying to get to the professor. When asked to describe her, he could remember nothing, but she was old and pretty. The police found it hard to believe that an attractive old woman would be strong enough to throw the professor through the wall. Besides, no one else saw this woman, but him. The boy swore he didn't do it. But, with all the evidence pointing towards him, the police arrested him today and charged him with first degree murder."

God have mercy upon my soul. Mrs. Covington wailed internally as she turned her head into her pillow and wept over her cowardice and knavery. Her foolish plan to summon a demon caused two people to lose their lives and she would forever be responsible.

"Are you okay, baby?" Mr. Covington inquired as he rubbed her hair. He kissed the nape of her neck and back.

Mrs. Covington let the pillow sop up her tears and turned to face her husband. She grabbed the sides of his face and planted a hard kiss upon his lips.

"I don't want to talk anymore," she whispered. "I've missed you." She pulled him atop of her and prayed that within his arms all of the terrible thoughts that stalked her would disappear.

32

Sadie slowly disrobed. The cold floor made her feet numb. She folded her clothes and handed them to Sky. Sky gave Sadie a white hospital gown and helped her dress and tie the strings behind her back. Sadie sat upon the operating table, agitated by the paper covering its firm leather. She lay down, trying hard not to look at the machine that would suck the creature out of her womb. A tall nurse entered the room.

"How are you?" the nurse asked with a deep Spanish accent. Her black eyes danced when she spoke. A bright smile adorned her round tan face. Jet black curls wiggled to her shoulders.

"I'm okay," Sadie responded in a trembling voice.

"Are you sure?" the nurse asked as she placed her hand upon Sadie's shoulder. "You have to be positive that this is what you want. Now is the time to leave if you are unsure."

"I'm sure," Sadie grumbled. Her voice went uncontrollably high pitched.

"Good." The nurse smiled once again. "Dr. Davis will be in soon. Right now I am going to give you something to relax you and to mask the pain. Okay?"

"Okay," Sadie responded.

The nurse pulled an IV needle out of her pocket and hooked a bag of liquid to an IV pole. Putting on a fresh pair of rubber gloves, she tied a rubber band around Sadie's arm.

"Look at your veins. They are popping out nicely for me," the nurse cooed as if she received some sort of perverse pleasure out of seeing them. She rubbed Sadie's skin with an alcohol pad.

Sky crossed her arms and rolled her eyes. She sat back in her chair and tried her very best not to comment on the nurse's weird behavior.

The nurse pushed the needle into Sadie's vein and quickly inserted the IV cord. Sadie winced, but remained silent. The nurse untied the rubber band and discarded all of the unneeded materials.

"That was quick and painless. Wasn't it?" The nurse grinned.

"Yes," Sadie grumbled.

"You relax yourself and the doctor will be in soon," said the nurse. She patted Sadie on the shoulder. "The procedure is fast and safe. Dr. Davis is one of the very best. You are in capable hands so don't worry."

"Okay," Sadie said as she let her head relax against the cool leather.

The nurse left the room and Sky scooted her chair over to Sadie.

"How are you feeling?" Sky inquired.

"I'm okay I guess," Sadie answered. She couldn't stop her hands from trembling so she pressed them into her sides of her legs. "I really want to get this over with. Home is where I wanna be right now. The doctor needs to hurry up. I've been waiting long enough."

"I feel you. I hate bein' in any kind of medical facility. I don't like to be in the vicinity of a hospital or clinic," Sky complained.

"Well, thank you for being here," Sadie whispered. She understood Sky because she hated hospitals also.

"I could never let you do this alone, especially with Senorita Creepy as your nurse," Sky said sarcastically. "You saw the way she was sweatin' your veins?"

Sadie laughed quietly.

"You know she would be tryin' to suck your blood if I weren't here," Sky snapped. "I bet that's a fake accent she has. You know she straight from Transylvania."

Sadie shook her head and smiled a sad smile.

Sky held her best friend's hand.

"Everything is going to be just fine and soon enough this will all be in the past and time will heal all the hurts that has been caused to you," she assured Sadie. Sky kissed the back of Sadie's hand. "You will be just fine."

"I hope so," Sadie responded. "I sincerely hope so."

The door swung open and in walked a very tall and voluptuous woman wearing a white doctor's coat and lime green slacks. She had to be at least five feet ten inches tall and two hundred pounds minimum. Although she was a large woman, she was not fat by any means, but a toned curvy feminine phenomenon. Her waist was small, stomach flat, thighs big, with breasts and behind out of this world. She was what you called super thick. Only a real man could handle a woman like her. Her face was yellowish brown and attractive with dimpled cheeks and a beauty mark on her top lip. Brown and bouncy hair leapt with every move she made. She held out her hand.

"I am Dr. Davis. Pleased to meet you," she said.

"Nice to meet you as well," Sadie said with a thick tongue. The medicine in the IV was beginning to work.

"Nice to meet you too." Dr. Davis held out her hand to Sky.

Sky took it and shook it firmly.

"Take care of my girl," Sky demanded. A sad and dangerous look was in her eyes. "She has been through a lot and needs no more troubles."

"I most certainly will. Everything here is sterile and safe and I have over fifteen years of experience. There is absolutely nothing to worry about," the doctor said. "Are you going to stay for the procedure or will you feel more comfortable in the lounge?"

"I'm staying here," Sky snapped. "There is no way I would leave Sadie alone at a time like this."

A forced smile curled the doctor's mouth.

"Wonderful," she said. "I'm sure Sadie appreciates your support. Please move your chair back against the wall and when the nurse comes back in, I will begin," the doctor said as she made her way to the sink and washed her hands and placed a surgical mask on.

Sky reluctantly did as she was told. She placed her chair in a corner so she could see everything.

Sadie was out of it, her head bobbing slowly. She was fading in and out of consciousness.

Moments later the vein admiring nurse reappeared. Sky rolled her eyes upward as the Latin vampire walked back into the room.

The nurse secured Sadie's legs in stirrups and the doctor turned on the suction machine. After the nurse sterilized Sadie's private parts, the doctor pulled on her gloves and picked up the suction hose. A shiny tube approached Sadie's vaginal cavity when the room went blinding white.

Sky instantly fell to the floor. The sound of the tube hitting the floor reverberated through the room. A yelp from the nurse was heard as she dropped down.

"Do not harm the child. His path is foreordained. Leave the woman or perish under my wrath," a soul penetrating whisper echoed through the room.

"Who are you?" the doctor wailed.

"I will be who I will be," the voice echoed, drilling through every fiber of the living.

The light was gone. Sky opened her eyes. Everything seemed a blur. Her head ached. Shadows danced before her eyes. She leaned against the wall and waited for her vision to clear. Soon the cowering nurse and the dumbfounded doctor took form before her eyes.

"Are you okay?" Sky asked as she crawled across the floor towards the two women.

Silence.

Sky touched the nurse's hand. The nurse jerked away. She stared up at Sky and yelled, "What kind of curse have you brought here?" Angry tears rained from her red rimmed eyes. Her cheeks trembled with frustration. "Get your evil away from here!" the nurse screamed as she did the sign of the cross.

"How can you call anyone evil? Look at what you do for a living!" Sky growled.

The nurse slapped Sky across the face. A bright hand print was tattooed across Sky's cheek.

"Get out!" the nurse screamed.

Sky grabbed the nurse by the neck and said through her teeth, "If you put your filthy hands on me again you'll regret it."

The doctor snapped out of her stupor and pushed between the warring women. She stood and pulled them both to their feet.

"Lola, remove the IV from Miss Covington's arm," Dr. Davis demanded. She faced Sky. "And you calm down and sit down." The doctor picked up her tools from the floor and put them where they belonged. She took off her coat and mask and folded them up. She turned back to Sky. "When your friend wakes up, get her out of here. I cannot help her." A look of dread and despair covered the doctor's face. She paced the floor slowly, looking around her as if someone was there she could not see.

The nurse removed the IV from Sadie's arm and angrily threw Sadie's clothes to Sky.

"Dress her and get out," the nurse roared.

Sky caught the clothes before they could hit her face. A look of sheer hatred played in her eyes. Ignoring her desire to snap the nurse's face in half, she began to dress Sadie. Sky placed Sadie's underwear around her ankles and awkwardly pulled them up over her hips. She then tugged on Sadie's jeans until they rested snugly in place. Sky put Sadie's bra in her purse and pulled her T-shirt over her semi-conscious head.

"We have to get out of here," Sky urged Sadie.

"Is it all over?" Sadie slurred. "Is it done?"

"We are done here," Sky said.

"Is the baby gone?" Sadie whined.

"No," Sky whispered as she pulled her friend from the table and pulled Sadie's arms over her shoulder. Sky heaved her friend up and headed for the door. The nurse opened it quickly as she mumbled to herself in Spanish.

The doctor placed Sadie's other arm around her neck and the three of them made their way through the lobby. The waiting patients sat in stupefied silence as they witnessed the doctor help hoist a patient out of the clinic.

"Hold on," the doctor told Sky.

Dr. Davis walked into her office and picked up her purse. She quickly grabbed Sadie's arm once again.

The doctor turned to her waiting patients and said, "I'm sorry ladies. Please find yourself another doctor. My office is now closed. If you need a referral, the receptionist will offer you one," she exclaimed. Dr. Davis turned to the receptionist. "Arrange for the office to be cleared out by the end of next week. I realize that the economy is horrible so I'll pay you for two months and write you a recommendation. You'll have to find another job. Sorry," she said as she left her office leaving everyone it in stupefied silence.

They entered the elevator and soon exited the building.

"Thank you for your help," Sky said as the doctor helped her put Sadie in the car.

Sadie flopped down like a dead body. She faded in and out, oblivious to her surroundings. Incoherent words fell from her lips in faint whispers. Suddenly she fell silent and let sleep come.

"You are welcome," Dr. Davis responded as she reached into her pants pocket and pulled out her car keys.

"Where're you going?" Sky asked.

"Away from here. I quit!" Dr. Davis yelled as she hopped into her car and sped away.

Sky shrugged, got into the car and drove off in the opposite direction.

33

"So it's really over between you two?" Luis asked. He dribbled the basketball on the hot concrete of the driveway. Nylon shorts clung to his damp legs as sweat poured from his pores and ran down his glistening chest. He tossed the ball and it bounced off the rim.

"Brick!" Forrest yelled as he held out his hands for the ball.

Luis tossed the ball to him and positioned himself under the basket.

"Yeah, it's over," James answered nearly out of breath as he checked Forrest. James shifted his eyes. A sickening sensation slithered through his stomach. "I called her last week and ended it."

"You called her?" Luis and Forrest said in unison.

Sweat sprinkled the driveway like rain.

"Man, that's cold," Luis remarked as he stole the ball from Forrest and made a basket. "Twenty-one!"

"Good game," James said as he slapped Luis on the butt.

James' stomach twisted. He was hoping to avoid the subject of Sadie, but it was not in Luis' nature to let questions go unanswered. James placed his hand on the side of his head and stretched his neck. He did the other side and rolled his shoulders to relieve some built up tension.

"Yeah man," said Forrest as he gave Luis a high five. "Let's go in and get a cold one."

"Word," Luis agreed.

The three men walked into the house and went straight into the kitchen. Forrest opened the refrigerator and pulled out three beers. Luis took a beer and sat at the kitchen table. James sat on a barstool next to the kitchen island and Forrest sat on the kitchen counter. Each one of them took a deep gulp of cold beer before they took their next breath.

"So you punked out and broke up with your fiancé over the phone?" Luis laughed. "You a little sissy."

"It's not funny man," Forrest reprimanded with a smirk on his face. "Want a paper towel?"

"Yeah, pass me one." Luis took the napkin and wiped his face. He threw one at James.

James gave Luis the finger and wiped his face.

"You don't deserve no tissue," Luis joked.

Forrest laughed aloud.

"He ain't no punk Forrest?" Luis asked.

"Hell yeah!" Forrest answered. "I can't believe you didn't have the balls to meet with her. What's that all about?"

"I couldn't face her man," James admitted. "I love that woman and I couldn't bear to see her hurt." James scratched his head. "I can't marry her. I don't know how to deal with her grisly goon and its three-headed baby."

"Sky said that Sadie was going to get rid of it," Forrest said.

James nearly fell from his barstool. "What?" He could not believe that Sadie would consider getting rid of her baby. She was totally against abortion and thought of it as a cowardly alternative for purposeful responsibility. Abortion was only justified concerning issues regarding rape, incest, and/or danger to the mother. James was baffled by her decision. Then again, Sadie could qualify for two out of three of those reasons.

"Yeah. Sky called me on Thursday and told me that Sadie had an appointment on the following day. I haven't talked to her in a couple of days. Maybe I'll call later to see how everything went. She told me not to call so soon because Sadie may be in a bad state of mind. I told Sky that I would go over and check on Sadie to make sure that she's recovering well if she approves," Forrest said before he took another sip of beer.

James looked up at the calendar on the wall. It was Tuesday. His brow furrowed and he drank deeply.

"Call Sky and ask her how everything went," said James. "Let me know how Sadie is doing."

"Okay, man. I'll do that for you," said Forrest. He jumped down from the counter and tossed his empty bottle into the trash then opened the refrigerator to get a new one. "Are you sure you don't want to call and talk to Sadie?"

James looked down. He did not have the strength to hear her voice. He didn't think he had the strength to speak to her ever again.

"Forrest you know he ain't gone call that girl. You need to cut it out. That broad is history and you know it," Luis grumbled. "Toss this for me." He threw his bottle to Forrest for disposal.

"I know that he won't, but he should. Sadie is going through a hard time right now and she needs to know that he still cares," said Forrest. He threw Luis' bottle in the trash and started on a fresh beer.

"She knows I care. The whole world knows I care. I don't need you trying to make me feel bad. I did what I had to do. If you were in my position you would have done the exact same thing so don't be in here acting all noble when you know you almost crapped yourself when you saw how Sadie healed right before your eyes that night!" James roared. He slammed his bottle on the island top and jumped up. "I love that girl," James sneered. "She knows that! I'm not giving up because another man has stolen my woman. I'm giving up because she's being pursued, by the freakin' boogieman! How am I supposed to compete with that? I can't protect her. I can't help her. I'm useless when it comes to her situation. What kind of man would that make me if I sat around and watched her get harassed night after night and did nothing about it?"

Forrest reached in the refrigerator and pulled out another beer. He presented it to James with an excusatory

smile. A wee bit of ire diminished from James' glare. He took the beer.

"I'm sorry. I had no right to judge you," Forrest apologized.

"Well I got the right!" Luis laughed. "I don't care what you say. You can jump up and yell all you want 'cause you should have at least bought the girl some dinner before you gave her the boot." He shook his head. "And y'all say I'm hard."

"Shut up!" Forrest laughed.

James sat down and exhaled his anger. He grimaced and said, "That was trifling of me huh?" He sighed and took a swig.

"Yep," Forrest said as he held up his bottle. All of the men clinked their bottles together.

"What's done is done. Don't lose no sleep over it," Luis said. "You did what you felt you had to do and there ain't no shame in that."

"Thanks man," said James. "Thanks. I needed to hear that 'cause you know I feel like toilet chocolate."

"You should!" Luis laughed. "But I respect you though."

"Me too," Forrest agreed. "You're a good man. I'm sure Sadie understands and respects your decision. She's a smart girl and I know that she loves you enough to let you go. She wouldn't want to put you in any danger."

James held up his bottle and they clinked them to together again. The thought of Sadie protecting him made him feel even more like a cur.

"I'm gonna go take a shower and chill out for a while. I'll catch y'all dudes later," James mumbled.

"A'ight," said Luis. "Don't go upstairs and cry like a girl 'cause you feel bad."

"I don't cry dude. I leave that to you when your chick kicks you to the curb. Me and Forrest hear you begging on the phone late nights. You ain't foolin' no one.

You ain't no playa. You get played," James retorted with a crooked simper.

"You wish!" Luis laughed. "I can take both your women right now. Oops, you ain't got no woman."

"Don't get your teeth knocked out," James said while shaking his fist. "But on the real, I'm out."

"Later dude," Luis said, throwing an air punch. James waved him off.

"Peace," said Forrest.

James drained his beer and tossed the bottle in the trash. He left the kitchen and made his way up the stairs. Every step felt was like he was walking on soft earth swallowing his feet with every pitiful move. His knees nearly buckled beneath the weight of his despair. His heart swelled with indignity and despondency, the organ literally ballooning within his chest like a festering sore bubbling over. A sharp pain moved up his left arm and bolted down his right. He wished that his agony was a mere heart attack. That would make his life so much simpler. Heart attacks felt like playful pinches in comparison to lost love. James reached out his hand and grabbed the knob with trembling fingers. He twisted the metal circle and let himself into his room. It was cold and empty, as empty as his life would be without Sadie. The pain came again. He balled his fists and gathered the pain within him and allowed his anger, his heartache, his misery to feast upon the debilitating twinge. Once the door closed behind him, he fell across the bed and refused to let the tears come. It was his decision to live without Sadie. He chose to let her fight her own battle. Now, he had to deal with it.

34

The faint smell of urine drifted from a grimy steel toilet stinking in the corner of the cell. The repugnant odor floated past Oliver Snickermier's nose causing him to cover his narrow nostrils with his painted black fingertips. The remnants of smeared black eyeliner surrounded his dark eyes like a raccoon mask. His black hair lay slicked to his pale skull like greasy strings of inked pasta. All of his precious silver jewelry was gone. It had been taken by the police officers before they stripped him of his clothes and forced him into the orange prisoner's uniform he wore. He sat upon his bunk bed with his hands entangled on his lap wondering how in the world he had arrived in the palace of the depraved. How he, Oliver Snickermier, a privileged educated man who has never even played slap boxing, had been charged with first degree murder. How he, the valedictorian of every school he had ever attended was sitting in a cell with a snagger-toothed fiend with bleeding chapped lips and shifty eyes and a giant beast pulsating with veined muscles and a slew of tattoos boasting of his victories as a death dealer. What in heaven's name was he doing in this place?

His parents were positively going insane. They called the detention center excessively threatening to sue the entire universe if he was not released. Yesterday he met his lawyer and was already annoyed by the flashy suit and shiny shoes that he wore. Why should Oliver care? He just wanted to get out of this place. If only the day when Dr. Putina was killed was not such a blur. He had smoked so much marijuana that day that he could barely remember waking up. Oliver did recall going to her office. He went there almost every day. He was her helper and sometimes they even smoked a little weed together. A matter of fact, she rewarded his good efforts with a fresh dime bag. Sometimes she would sprinkle it with a bit of angel dust and they both would lie on her office rug and watch the stars on the ceiling swirl before their eyes. Why would he kill a professor so cool? Why would anyone kill a person so cool? Everyone that knew he loved her and if they did not love her they did not know or understand her.

"What are you in for?" the chapped lipped fiend asked, jarring Oliver from his thoughts.

Oliver looked up with mistrusting eyes. He had seen many movies enacting this very scenario. Never did he dream that he would be the main character in the drama. He cleared his throat and sat up straight. He ran his blackened fingertips through his hair and looked the fiend in the eye.

"Murder," Oliver grumbled. He pushed his back against the wall and squeezed his hands tight. A bead of sweat appeared under his nose. He wiped it away quickly. There was no way that he would allow the fiend to sniff out his fear.

The fiend laughed hysterically, jerking his body periodically as if he had Tourette's Syndrome. He shuffled his feet and seemed to do a little dance as he made semi-circles around Oliver's bunk.

"He said he's in for murder," he told the tattooed beast. He laughed too.

The fiend walked over to Oliver with long rocking strides. The inmate was tall and sinewy. Tight sandy curls made polka dots across his bright pink chin forming an abrasive looking beard. He popped his knuckles and sucked his bottom lip.

"I don't believe you killed no body," he said as he crossed his arms and leaned his shoulder against the wall.

"You never know," said the tattooed beast. Bright colored illustrations gleamed off of his golden brown skin. His shirt was unbuttoned to his navel exposing a chest decorated with a slew of skulls with bat wings. There was even one extending from the back of his bald head to his cheeks. "He may be one of those crazy cult kids. Look at his chipped fingernail polish and remember his eye makeup when he first came in?" The beast pointed.

"This little thing couldn't kill nothin'," the fiend bragged. "I bet he couldn't even throw a punch. He ain't but one hundred pounds soakin' wet."

"Sounds like a challenge to me little man. What you gone do?" the beast instigated.

Oliver's heart thumped with its highest intensity. He took a deep breath and stood up on wobbly knees. He swung his arms and clapped his hands then shook his damp raven hair. Without warning, his brows became raven arrows, his eyes sharp slits and, his mouth a diagonal sneer.

"Little man stood up. Looks like you got a challenge," the beast laughed.

"You insultin' me boy?" the fiend asked as he moved closer to Oliver. His fists balled tight and his arms flexed with line upon line of toned tissue. "You think you can take me?" he sneered. "I'll do you a favor. I'll give you the first punch before I make you my girlfriend."

Oliver looked away from the fiend as if he was going to turn and run. Then, without delay, Oliver roundhouse kicked the fiend across the face. Blood spewed from the fiend's nose. Oliver then kneed the fiend in his genitals and punched him in the back of the neck. The fiend hit the ground right before he received Oliver's foot in the middle of his back. Years of watching Ultimate Fighting Championship finally paid off.

"Who's gonna be who's girl now?" Oliver asked as he kicked the fallen man in the ribs. Crazed intensity raged from Oliver's eyes as spittle rained upon the fallen fiend.

The tattooed beast held out his hand for Oliver to shake. The sneer on Oliver's face deepened into an invitation to annihilation. The beast broadened his chest and extended his hand once more. This time the acceptance could determine life or death; for, the nature of the beast manifested itself behind his eyes. A cold chill softened Oliver's sneer. His TV training may not be successful against such a foe. It was only luck that he defeated the fiend. Oliver reluctantly received the olive branch extended.

"Good job little man," the beast congratulated. He turned to the wrenching man on the cell floor and yelled," Get up before I get you up!" The beast kicked the fiend in the butt and watched him crawl to his bed. "You lucky I don't like fellas 'cause if I did you would be our little penthouse pet," the beast chided. He turned to Oliver once more and said, "You all right with me. You won't have no more trouble out of him."

"I better not," Oliver said giving the fiend a menacing glare. "I better not."

35

Since Dr. Putina's murder, the entire university had been on edge. Everyone constantly looked over their shoulders in silent fear because no one truly believed that Oliver Snickermier had murdered the doctor. He was well respected among the professors, the students he tutored for minimal pay or for free marijuana, and the minuscule group of friends he spent his free time with. All across the campus students formed small rally's and marched around the campus and they picketed the local police station demanding Oliver's release. Signs reading *"Free Oliver"* littered the campus everywhere. Letters rained down on the Snickermier household in support.

Meanwhile, the faculty, staff, and student body pulled together to honor the doctor with an eloquent home going service and burial. The ceremony was held on campus with the auditorium decked out in ancient relics, rich scarlet curtains, and funeral programs trimmed in gold.

The professor looked radiant dressed in a white gown. A floral wreath made of baby's breath topped her head. Her lips and cheeks were a like red rose against her ashen skin and flax colored hair that clung to her tilted head. Delicate fingers, adorned with numerous gems of every color, crossed her static chest. Yet somehow in the seeming purity of her appearance, her glossy eyes were cracked in an unsettling slit that caused a palpable yet invisible hand to brush the nape of every onlooker's neck.

Famous psychics, mediums, and spiritual guides paid her homage by honoring her memory with grandiloquent longwinded eulogies. From wall to wall, the crowd oooed and aaahed at the accomplishments of Dr. Olga Putina. Clapping hands praised her prestigious listings of degrees, awards, memberships, books authored, and extensive travels.

After the service ended, the dead professor's husband Mr. Nicolai Putina, a very stout pink man with a thought provoking under bite, thanked the university for its kindness and faded into aching silence as he mounted the lonely diadem where his wife lay sleeping the eternal sleep. To the masses Olga Putina was nothing more than a fantastical kook. To him, she was the paint on his canvas. Without her, he was colorless, void, and left without inspiration. Mr. Putina waited until the last person exited the auditorium and sat down next to his wife's gleaming chrome casket. His bald head rested against the death box as he silently mourned the greatest love of his life.

"That was some spectacle," Percy Flippin, a professor of religious studies, mumbled to the Covingtons. He had to raise up on his toes to keep his comments within earshot. A small portly man he was with dark olive skin and wild salt and pepper hair. Sparkling blue eyes full of sincerity and contentment lit up his kind bulldog face. A long beard hung from his round chin, curling over his barrel chest which was carefully stuffed into a stretched to the limit blue and gold striped polo shirt. Tattered and faded blue jeans wrapped around his chubby bow legs. Broken-in brown loafers, complete with pennies, curved to the shape of his feet.

"Yes it was," Mr. Covington replied as he held out his hand to his wife. She accepted it, stood up, and locked her arm with his.

"Ceremonies like this makes you feel like the floor might crumble and swallow you all up because of the blasphemy. I wasn't sure if I was at a funeral or a cult meeting," Dr. Flippin commented as he filed behind the Covingtons and headed for the nearest door.

"Amen to that brother," Mr. Covington agreed as he loosened his tie. "Percy, there is so much to say about this lunacy, but I'll have to talk to you at work on Monday. Classes are canceled for the rest of the week. I have to get out of this place." He headed towards the exit. "I have to get out of this place," he repeated. "So many bad spirits are stirring in this place. I feel like I'm suffocating. You know what I mean?"

"Of course. I think most people here were either weird or weirded out," Dr. Flippin stated. He offered his hand to Mrs. Covington. She placed it within his sweaty palm and he kissed it lightly. "Ebbie, it was a pleasure seeing you again. You look absolutely radiant in that green dress. Maybe I should buy my wife one just like it.

Mrs. Covington smiled a dry smile and said, "Thank you." She dreaded the thought of going out with Mrs. Flippin wearing the exact same dress. The crazy thing was that Dr. Flippin would actually buy one for his wife not realizing that women hated having similar wardrobes.

"It has been a long time since I've seen you. Velanon asks about you often. When I saw you on campus, you were in such a rush I didn't get a chance to speak to you. You were flying across campus like a dog was on your tail," Dr. Flippin laughed. "I didn't know you could move like that."

Mrs. Covington's heart slammed against her ribs. Her hold on her husband's arm tightened as he looked down at her with questioning eyes. She looked away, her eyes whispering of guilt, her arms shaking with shame.

Dr. Flippin turned to Mr. Covington and said," Carlos, you and Ebbie should have dinner sometime with Velanon and I. Velanon would just love the company. You know how she loves to entertain. She just redecorated our kitchen and would love the opportunity to show it off. She's been taking cooking classes at the local community center and she swears she's Julia Childs. I haven't eaten so much pretty food in my life. You should see it. My steaks have flowers on it and my potatoes smiley faces," he chuckled. "I swear I haven't had a normal dessert in ages. Last night she prepared watermelon chocolate a la cookie cake! It looked beautiful, but I haven't given a verdict for the taste yet."

"Sounds good. We'll set a date soon." Mr. Covington opened the door letting his wife and his colleague out into the warm tropical air. The chill of the air conditioning instantly faded away. "We parked this way," he said as he pointed.

"I'm in the opposite direction." Dr. Flippin smiled and waved. "I'll call you soon. Take care Ebbie," he said and turned on his heels.

"He's such a sweet man," Mrs. Covington uttered. Her voice fluctuated in nervous waves. She silently prayed that her husband would miraculously forget Dr. Flippin's sighting of her on campus. "We really should do dinner soon."

Mr. Covington nodded in agreement.

The couple walked through the parking lot in silence. Mrs. Covington clung nervously to her husband's arm. He walked along, his mouth bent downward and his brow furrowed. The car soon appeared before them and he opened the door for his wife, waited until she was securely inside, and closed the door. Mr. Covington slowly made his way to the driver's side and locked himself within the vehicle.

"Why didn't you tell me you came to the campus?" he asked as he started the engine and put the car into reverse.

"It slipped my mind," she lied. "I couldn't get to your office that day because of all of the commotion."

"You were on campus when Olga died?" he questioned. His voice elevated a pitch. Thoughts of Oliver came to him. The boy insisted that he had seen an attractive older woman in the professor's office.

"I...I...I'm not sure. I...I...I wanted to take you to lunch, but there were so many people everywhere," she whispered. She secretly damned herself for shuddering. That was the surefire way for Mr. Covington to tell when she was lying. She hated herself for being such a poor fibber. It was just much too difficult to say something untrue to the love of her life.

"You never mentioned that to me. It's not like you to forget something like that," he said. Suspicion laced his voice. The car crawled down the street.

Mrs. Covington could not wait to get home, but the car seemed to drive below zero miles per hour. She stared out of the window and held onto the door handle. She hoped by some sheer miracle that Mr. Covington would drop the subject. No such super wonder would occur. Nothing divine would be intervening on her behalf.

"I don't understand why you didn't tell me that you were on campus." His voice was scolding. He looked at her then to the road then back at her. "Why would you forget to mention being on campus on a day like that?"

"It slipped my mind," she uttered. "It's really not important. Please don't make it more than what it is."

Mr. Covington looked her in the eye. She turned away. He pushed his foot down on the accelerator trying hard not to focus on the woman invading his every thought. A creeping nausea crawled through his belly and made its way up his throat when his mind considered that she may have attributed to Dr. Putina's death. He knew that his wife did not have the strength to kill the professor, but he had an abstracting qualm that she knew who did.

36

Dark clouds spread across a scarlet sky. Thunder rumbled, roared, growled, echoed through the atmosphere. Lightning wrote messages, too fast to read, but sketched definite characters across the chaotic heavens. Horns blew in melodious brilliance coalescing with the whistling wind. The sound of trumpets rumbled with the thunder, almost drowning out the crackling booms. A baby screamed. Wrinkled flesh wrapped in swaddling clothes. Tiny hands sprang up. Fingers grotesquely extended and ripped through the cloth. A man child was revealed. His cry transformed into a deep blaring roar. His eyes were like flames, his skin like clay. A great earthquake split the earth. Foul vapors filled the air. A gem encrusted crown rose from a pit and sealed itself upon the baby's head. The child crawled, then stood, then walked. His legs twisted and stretched. His arms popped and elongated. A man. A strong menacing, but beautiful man he became. His crown lit up and light filled the earth. Beneath his feet were twitching and writhing humans, crushed and creating a river of blood. In his left hand was an inverted cross, in his right was a scepter. Engraved upon his head...

An ear piercing scream burst from Sadie's mouth. She sat up in bed and flung the sweat soaked covers from her trembling body. Jumping up, she rushed for the light switch. Quickly she turned the light on and fell upon the floor in a cold sweat. Her chest heaved as she fought to catch her breath. Her womb burned with discomfort. Tears rolled from her eyes in torrents of pain as she held her belly.

"Help me!" Sadie screamed. Her voice broke in shards of cracked syllables. "Help me!" she wailed.

Her bedroom door swung open. Light filled the hallway.

Sadie wailed and gnashed her teeth. She tore the front of her gown and fell prostrate before the angel.

"Forgive me," she begged.

Turiel stood before her, his face a mask of destruction. His white robes gleamed and his eyes burned with an unquenchable fire.

"What have you done?" the angel asked. His voice sounded like many seas. "Have you harmed the child?"

"No!" Sadie wailed. "The baby is still within me." Circles of rainbows surrounded her lashes as her tears filtered the angelic light, her body racked with dread.

Turiel's light faded into a soft glow.

Sadie lifted her head and looked into the celestial being's face, her bosom exposed to him and her face torn in terror.

"Be not afraid. I bring you tidings of great joy. Blessed you are among women for the cleansing of the earth will come through you. The child will be a man child. His name shall be revered among the nations. His countenance will be as an angel of light. The nations will bow before him and you will sit at his right hand. You will name him Khalid Erebus. You shall marry the earthly one who loves you. Taking the sir name Tucker, the prophesy will then be complete. Heed my words and do not deviate from them."

"How do I know that the truth is in you?" Sadie whimpered.

"I will give you back your love. I will give you back James."

Sadie looked into his flaming eyes and whispered James' name.

"Will you care for the child and love and protect him?" Turiel asked. "Will you live your life to secure his future? Will you ensure that he will receive every advantage and opportunity?"

"I will," Sadie sobbed. "I will."

Turiel's wings lifted into the air and with one flap, he was face to face with the trembling mortal. He grabbed the sides of Sadie's face and pulled her to him. His lips kissed hers. His tongue was like a hot coal within her mouth. She winced in pain, but for the first time, she

reciprocated and tried to match the demon's passion. He pulled away with honest surprise. His wings pushed backwards producing a great wind, placing him beyond her doorway. Sadie fell to her side, but refused to let Turiel out of her sight.

"Isn't that what you wanted?" she snarled, her eyes cutting. She shook her shoulders allowing her gown to drop to her waist. "I'm not fighting you any longer. Why do you draw away?" she croaked. "Do you not want me anymore?"

Turiel bared his teeth.

"I get it. You only get off when you are forcing yourself on me," Sadie cackled.

"James will be yours. Be patient and I will bring him to you," Turiel snapped, his face showing a trace of anger. His wings wrapped around his body and he vanished into the darkness of the hall.

37

Forrest's arm fell across Sky's face waking her from her sleep. One of her eyes opened then the other. A giant yawn left her dry mouth. Sky swallowed hard then pushed her sleeping lover's limb away and climbed out of bed. The clock read 11:30 a.m. Late night passion made her forget to set the alarm. Forrest was very late for work. Sky was sure he would be spastic when she woke him. She firmly grabbed his shoulder and shook it.

"Sweetie," she whispered in his ear. She ran her fingers through his thick dark hair. He was so handsome. Sky smiled. "Sweetie," she whispered again, this time allowing her lips to caress his earlobe. "Baby, wake up." Sky rocked his shoulders until he opened his eyes.

"Yeah babe," he slurred. Forrest opened his eyes. He looked up at Sky and grinned. "You are so beautiful." He tried to grab her waist, but she wiggled out of his grasp. "Where you going? Come back here and make me the happiest man alive again," he said, kissing and lightly sucking Sky's fingertips.

"Mmm," Sky crooned. "I would love to, but you gotta get outta here. I forgot to set the alarm. It's almost noon."

Forrest swore and jumped out of the bed, grabbing his clothes in the process. He kissed Sky deeply and bolted from her room with one leg in his pants and his shirt thrown over his arm. She ran behind him with his shoes in her hands. She handed them to him at the front door and waved goodbye as he jumped in his car and sped down the road. Sky closed the door and headed towards Sadie's room to check in on her.

"Sadie, are you okay?" Sky asked as she walked into Sadie's bedroom. The morning light beamed through the blinds. Sky pulled the blind string, letting the sunlight flood the room.

"Sadie," she yelled as she held her friends shoulders and shook her gently. Sadie's gown fell past her hips, exposing her nakedness. Sky tied the front of Sadie's gown together in order to hide her bosom. She shook Sadie once again. This time Sadie began to stir.

Sadie opened her eyes. The floor was hard beneath her bottom. She looked into Sky's searching eyes.

"What happened to you?" Sky asked. "Why're you on the floor? Why's your gown torn?"

"I had a dream, a very strange dream," Sadie replied. She sat up and leaned her back against the bed. The smell of myrrh was fresh in the room.

"Was that thing here again?" Sky asked. It was impossible for her hands to cease shaking. The thought of seeing Sadie in another traumatic state frightened her. Last night Sky thought that she heard something while she slept, but she wasn't sure. The comfort of Forrest's arms was too great for her to move. She instantly felt bad about her selfishness. "Was it here?" Sky asked again. She sat down beside her friend with her legs folded beneath her. "Answer me Sadie!"

"I don't know," Sadie slurred. She placed her hand upon her belly and smiled. She let her head fall back against the mattress and looked up at the ceiling. Strangely, inhaling the pungent smell of the room calmed her. She sucked in the air hoping to taste it then exhaled in petty disappointment.

Sky acknowledged the motherly gesture with complete confusion. The simpleton look on Sadie's face was even more discombobulating.

"Since when have you become so happy 'bout this baby?" Sky asked.

"Since last night," Sadie responded. "I had a vision." Sadie smiled. "I'm having a man child."

"A man child?" Sky's face twisted. "You mean you havin' a boy?"

"Yes and my son will be royalty," Sadie cooed as she rubbed her tiny belly.

"Royalty? There ain't no kings in America," Sky snapped, rolled her eyes and crossed her arms.

"Of America?" Sadie laughed. "He will be the king of the world," Sadie replied with a demented grin on her face. "He will crush his enemies beneath him," she swooned. "He will rule us all and James and I will be right by his side."

"Now you talkin' crazy," Sky stood up. "You still dreamin'." Sky waved away Sadie's sleepy tirade. "Don't be talkin' like a fool this early in the day. I got better stuff to do than hear your kingdom come prophesies."

Sadie's eyes fluttered. Her mind drifted in and out of consciousness.

"He will trample the world beneath his feet," Sadie whined.

"Yada yada yada," Sky mumbled. "Sadie you need to wake up. You beginning to scare me."

"James will be my husband. Our love will last forever," Sadie grumbled, her eyes closed as her head bobbed back and forth. "The baby will bring us together."

"I hate to break it to you, but James is gone. No baby ain't never kept a man. Please don't trick yourself," Sky snapped. She grabbed Sadie and tried to shake some sense into her.

"My child will be king of kings," she whispered and knocked Sky's hands away.

"There is no such political position as king of the world," Sky snapped, surprised at Sadie's strength. Sadie knocked her away effortlessly. Sky ignored her instinct to leave the room and continued, "I don't know what the hell you ate last night, but you need to shake it off and snap back to reality."

"Say what you want," Sadie snarled. Her eyes appeared dangerous sending icy prickles down Sky's spine. An eerie darkness seemed to circle her eyes as her silver brows reached down to her nose. Sadie continued, "I had a vision and my son will be great! His name will be revered and he will be praised."

"Okay, crazy lady. You need to get some sleep. Maybe you bumped your head last night 'cause you babblin' like an idiot. Maybe that thing came back and made you sniff that funk that's floating around in here." Sky fanned her nose trying to ignore the fear building within the pit of her belly. "If it makes you feel better, I'm sure the baby will be great 'cause you'll be a great mama, but you have to accept the fact that James ended your relationship. You have to move on."

Sadie looked up at Sky and glowered. Like a passing cloud, the stupor left Sadie and her mind cleared. Tidbits of the conversation remained with her. All she knew in her heart was that her child had to be protected and James would be her mate once again. Sadie looked into Sky's perturbed eyes and shrugged her shoulders. It didn't matter what Sky thought. Sadie valued her opinion and was forever grateful for her support, but Sadie knew that her dream held truth and her marriage to James would come to fruition. Now all she had to do now was wait.

"You're right. I guess I was still dreaming," Sadie lied. "Thanks for the dose of reality."

"You're welcome girl. I'll tell you the truth anytime!" Sky laughed uncomfortably. She crossed her arms and slowly back peddled.

"Could you hand me the phone please?" asked Sadie. "I need to call my dad."

"Sure." Sky picked up the cordless phone and tossed it to Sadie. "You need some privacy?" Sky asked as she made her way to the door.

"If you don't mind," Sadie replied as she picked up the phone and started to dial.

38

Ornate mahogany benches lined the courtroom. The judge's bench and witness chair was decorated just as magnificently. Flags lined the back of the courtroom representing state and national ideals. Beige tile accented with what looked like gold leaf covered the floor. Two small trees sat in the far corners of the room. The words, *Justice Is Blind,* were engraved on the wall behind the judge's bench. Eggshell walls decorated with gavels and high stuccoed ceilings completed the hall of justice.

Upon the bench sat an elderly judge with smooth onyx skin. Black letters engraved on a gold plate read, *Judge Johnnie Ruth Walker.* White hair zigzagged from her temples in a lovely kinky afro. A scarlet blouse could be seen above the collar of her robe. A pair of giant glasses sat upon her nose, hiding the wisdom in her eyes. She shuffled through the papers in front of her with bent arthritic fingers.

"How do you plead?" she asked in a light wispy voice, her muddy eyes looking down at the scrawny defendant.

"Not guilty,' answered Oliver Snickermier's sharply dressed attorney, Mr. Alabou Money.

"Do you want to be tried before a jury of your peers?" the judge asked.

"Yes your honor," Mr. Money answered for Oliver. Oliver nodded his head in agreement. "I also ask that my client be granted bail."

"I object," the state prosecutor exclaimed. He pointed at Oliver and shook his ebony finger. "Mr. Snickermier was identified by a truck load of witnesses as being the only one present around the time of the murder. I ask that no bail be granted."

"No bail will be granted," the judge said.

A deep bellow escaped the mouth of Oliver's mother.

Mr. Money stood up and said, "Your honor, my client has never had trouble with the law. He does not have a history of violence and..."

"There is a first time for everything. No bail will be granted," restated Judge Walker. She looked at Mr. Money like a roach that needed to be stepped on. She disliked him very much and she was aware of his unsavory practices and courtroom shenanigans.

"But your honor..." Mr. Money began.

The judge looked over her glasses at Mr. Money and said, "The trial will be scheduled two months from today." She slammed down her gavel. The elderly judge stood up on rheumatic knees and slowly scuffled out of the room.

Mr. Money turned to Oliver, his eyebrows perfectly plucked and his dark hair combed back into a gelled helmet and said, "Don't worry. She's a jerk, but she is a fair judge. There is no evidence against you. Once the jury is selected and your character witnesses testify, you will be out of here faster than a worm on an anthill." A grimy cackle escaped his throat. He wiped his mouth with the back of his hand.

Oliver observed the two diamond pinky rings on each of Mr. Money's hands. His suit had to cost at least two thousand dollars not to mention his shoes and belt. Even his briefcase was of exquisite quality. Automatically Oliver didn't trust him. He didn't trust anyone who wore their worth on their back. He believed that people who spent so much money on superficial things were compensating for some deficiency in character. Oliver did not have a problem with people liking the finer things in life. But he did have a problem with people who put unhealthy value on the material.

Oliver imagined Mr. Money jumping into his fancy car and driving up to his fancy home and kissing the cheek of his fancy gold digging wife then running into his fancy bathroom to intake some not so fancy drug to keep himself from weeping every night. Oliver laughed at the thought. Money never meant much to him, maybe because he always had plenty of it. Who was he to judge? He shrugged his shoulders and waited for the guards to seize him. He could see his mother out of the corner of his eye weeping on the shoulder of his father. Oliver's dad yelled out, "We'll get you out of here!" before the guards escorted Oliver back to his holding cell.

"How'd it go?" the beast asked Oliver as he walked into the cell and the clank of the bars sounded behind him.

"My trial begins in a couple of months," Oliver responded.

"If you last that long," the fiend mumbled under his breath.

Oliver shot him a warning glare. The beast told the fiend to be quiet in an array of unsavory words.

"When is your trial?" Oliver asked the beast.

"Right before yours. I ain't got no lawyer so I guess the state appointed attorney is going to ensure that I spend the rest of my life in a cage," the beast growled.

"What are you in here for?" Oliver asked. He sat upon his bunk and threw one of his legs up.

"He in here for what we all in here for. He broke the law," the fiend snarled.

"They said that I raped a woman," the beast confessed. He shot the fiend an angry glance. The fiend turned his head in hateful defiance.

"Did you?" Oliver asked. Disappointment filled him. He was actually beginning to like and respect the beast. There was no possible way he could ever respect a rapist.

"Hell naw!" the beast roared. "I didn't touch that girl. Her cousin did it and she was too scared to tell her abusive father about his favorite nephew so she blamed it on me because I used to hang around her crib with her brother. Her pops never liked me because I would never let him beat on her when I was around," the beast growled. "See what being nice to stupid strawberries get ya!"

"If you're telling me the truth, I can get you a lawyer," Oliver said.

"I'm innocent," the beast exclaimed.

"We're all innocent!" the fiend interjected.

"I'm willing to take a lie detector test and I am willing to offer my DNA. I ain't did nothing wrong!" the beast yelled. His giant chest swelled with frustration. It looked like steam rose from the top of his head.

"I'll tell my lawyer to send another attorney from his firm to you. I'll foot the bill. Don't worry about a thing. I know what it feels like to be blamed for a crime you didn't commit," admitted Oliver. He looked up into the beasts eyes and saw something that he had not noticed before. The beast's animalistic characteristics dissolved into something very unexpected. His maw transformed into lips. Flaming eyes mellowed into a deep brown. Flailing tentacles became well-built arms and legs. The beast melted away into something particularly peculiar. The beast melted into a human. Oliver smiled.

"Why you grinnin' like that?" the beast asked with a bit of suspicion. "What I got to do? I'm not into dudes and I'm not killin' nobody for you. So what's the deal? Nothing in life is free!"

"You don't have to do anything. This is free." Oliver held out his hand. "My name is Oliver Snickermier. What's your name?"

"I'm Kashard Perez," the beast said and accepted Oliver's hand. The two men shook hands.

Oliver smiled again. He realized that his perception shaded what was really in front of his face. All that time, he was living with two inhuman creatures that he felt the world was better without. He had prejudged his cellmates. Although one turned out to be a true fiend, the other was not what he seemed to be. Despite Kashard's mammoth girth and graffitied body, the beast wasn't quite a beast at all. He was a simple man just as Oliver was.

39

Mrs. Covington sat up in her bed and pushed the covers below her torso. The chilly air conditioner and the twirling ceiling fan made the room feel like a refrigerator. The phone rang. She placed the book that she was reading upon the nightstand and placed her glasses upon the book. A heavy sigh pushed through her nose.

"Who is calling this time of day?" she mumbled. People knew that the Covington's were rarely available during the middle of the day. Mrs. Covington was usually engulfed within her latest project and Mr. Covington was usually on campus. But these were not usual times. Both of them were home. Mrs. Covington was huddled under her bed covers reading, *The First Chronicle of Zayashariya: Out of Night* and Mr. Covington was in his home office with his head buried in a stack of books trying to figure out a way to banish the lusty angel from the material world. Mrs. Covington reluctantly picked up the ringing phone. Times like these she wished that they had invested in a caller ID.

"Hello," Sadie's voices sounded through the receiver.

"Baby!" Mrs. Covington squealed. She sat up straight and flung her legs over the side of the bed. "How are you? Are you okay? Why haven't we heard from you?"

"I'm just fine," Sadie laughed. "Sorry I haven't returned y'all's phone calls. So much has been going on here." Sadie hesitated. There was something oddly disturbing in her mother's voice. She did not sound as secure and calm as she usually did. There was a high pitched nervousness that accented every syllable of every word she pronounced.

"How have things been going there?" Sadie inquired with a hint of worry.

"As well as expected considering the circumstances," Mrs. Covington answered. She exhaled hard and said, "Do you remember your father's colleague Dr. Putina?"

"You mean the one who was heavily into witchcraft?" asked Sadie.

"Yes," Mrs. Covington's voice wavered. "She was killed not too long ago. Everyone at the university is in total shock, as they should be."

"That's just awful. She was pleasant enough to be around. I think she was a respectable woman. Does anyone know who killed her?" Sadie responded.

"No one knows," Mrs. Covington's voice cracked. The lie scraped her throat on the way out of her mouth. "One of her students has been arrested for the crime, but most people believe that he's innocent."

"What does Daddy think?" Sadie asked.

"Your father is suspicious of everyone," she snapped. "And don't let the subject of you come up. Everything goes downhill from there."

"I'm sorry that I've caused y'all so much stress," Sadie whined.

"It's not your fault. How could you control an angel's crush?" Mrs. Covington scoffed.

"You believe me Momma?" Sadie asked with utter surprise in her voice. Was it possible that Ebbie Covington had been convinced of the supernatural?

Mrs. Covington opened her mouth, but nothing came out. Not only did she believe Sadie, but she had met the creature that haunted her. She had seen his fiery eyes and stared in awe of his beauty. She begged him to have mercy on her daughter and to leave her be. She watched in horror as the creature annihilated Dr. Putina and faded like infatuation. A matter of belief was not the issue. Admitting that belief could incriminate her and she was not willing to flatter the world with the unbelievable account of Dr. Putina's murder.

"Ma?" Sadie called.

"Would you like to speak with your father?" Mrs. Covington asked, making herself cough in a way that it seemed as if she could not carry on the conversation. "He would be elated to speak with you."

"O...O...okay." Sadie was confused. How did the conversation suddenly shift? Sadie knew that fake cough like she knew her own scent. Her mother always did that when she was uncomfortable with a subject. Did Mrs. Covington still doubt Sadie after all this time? It hurt that her mother, after all this time, still did not believe her. "I would love to talk to Daddy." Sadie allowed her mother to copout.

"Hold on," Mrs. Covington said. She placed the phone on her shoulder and pushed the intercom on the wall. "Carlos," she called into it. She let the button go and her husband's voice echoed through the speaker. "Sadie is on the line." Mrs. Covington put the receiver back to her ear. "He'll pick up in a second. What was the great news you wanted to tell us?"

"I'm having a boy," Sadie exclaimed.

"How wonderful!" Mrs. Covington smiled. "I'm sure going to spoil him rotten. Your father won't be pleased, but I'm sure when he sees his grandson for the first time his heart will melt. You should name the boy after your father. That would really win him over."

"I hope he will warm up to the idea because this baby will be a part of our family. I have a name for him already," Sadie said.

"Really..." Mrs. Covington began.

"Hello," Sadie's father answered.

"I'll let you two talk," Mrs. Covington said.

"I love you Momma," said Sadie.

"I love you too," Mrs. Covington replied right before she hung up the phone.

"How have you been?" Mr. Covington asked, his voice unreadable.

"I've been doing okay. I won't complain. Ma told me about the professor. I'm sorry to hear about that."

"Yes, it's a shame," Mr. Covington replied. "So, how are you feeling?"

"I'm feeling fine, really," Sadie answered.

"Has that *thing* been ailing you?" asked her father. A sharp edge was now shaping his words.

"What *thing*?"

"The demon. The baby," Mr. Covington maundered. "Did you get rid of it?"

"No." Sadie whispered.

"Why the hell not!" her father spewed.

"I tried to but…"

"What do you mean you tried? How could you still be pregnant when you know what the result will be?" Mr. Covington spat. He gripped the receiver so hard that it threatened to crack in his palm. "You are playing with danger and your stubbornness can cause us all to perish."

"I'm not being stubborn! I went to the clinic, but something happened. Something interceded and the baby was saved," belted Sadie.

"What do you mean?" he asked.

"I was drugged at the time, but Sky said that a bright light filled the hospital room and a voice told the doctor to stop. Everyone was scared to death. Dr. Davis even quit her job."

Mr. Covington's countenance fell.

"What can we do?" he asked. "Destruction is inevitable!"

"No Daddy. Saving the child was a blessing. I had a dream that he ruled the world and that all bowed to him," Sadie proclaimed.

"What are you…" Mr. Covington began.

Sadie cut him off and continued, "Turiel came to me and told me I was blessed among women and that my child will be the ruler of the world. He told me that I would have

James back and that we would be a family. Turiel said that I am to name the child Khalid Erebus Tucker."

"What kind of name is that?" Mr. Covington asked near panic. His skin twitched against his bones. How could Sadie be so happy about something so unnatural? Calamity and devastation was written all over this.

"I don't know, but I am sure it is a regal name," Sadie sang.

"I have to find the meaning of this," Mr. Covington croaked. "Spell it for me."

Sadie obliged her father with the spelling.

"Be happy for me Daddy," she begged. "A miracle has come to us."

"I find that very hard to believe. How can a demon create a miracle, Sadie? That makes no sense." Mr. Covington's voice trembled in fear and anger. "Do you know how crazy you sound? Listen to yourself! You know better than that!"

"Believe it!" Sadie snapped. "You are going to be a grandpa. You have to accept that."

"I don't have to accept anything!" Mr. Covington yelled.

"Daddy, you should be happy," Sadie cried. "Why can't you be happy for me? This baby is coming whether you like it or not. Neither of us like the circumstances surrounding my pregnancy, but I'm pregnant. What's done is done! Now we both have to live with that fact. Be happy for me."

"Happiness is an impossibility for me now." Mr. Covington hung up the phone and his heart lamented for he knew that nothing good could come from evil.

40

Mr. Covington sat at his computer and logged into the university library. He had not slept well in what seemed like ages. He was so tired, mentally and physically. It seemed as if nothing he could possibly do could help Sadie. He had hope at first, but now Sadie wanted to keep the child. A loud yawn left his mouth. He leaned his face against the palm of his hand and his eyes closed.

A young handsome man walked haughtily and full of authority, clothed in expensive clothes. His brown eyes were like knives that pierced the soul of anyone who looked into them. His voice was deep and melodious. It wooed the people with every word. Power illuminated from his fingertips as people worshiped him. They fawned over his intelligence, his looks, his affluence. Envy and admiration filled their hearts. When the man smiled, hearts melted like chocolate in a sauce pan. Miracles flowed from his very words. Healings occurred. The blind saw. The lame walked. The deaf heard. Money appeared in the hands of the poor. Even nature obeyed him. His voice stilled the raging winds and rain drenched lands dry and cracked in drought. His face was of perfect proportion. His body was tall and statuesque. No flaw marred his skin except three small birthmarks behind his right ear. They looked like three circles with hooked tops.

Mr. Covington's eyes popped open. The strange vision sent a burning sensation through his chest. Something about the familiar features of the man's face bothered him. The man looked like a younger version of him. The markings on the strange man unnerved him even more. He tried to shake off the eerie aura that enveloped him.

Mr. Covington turned his focus to his computer and searched the data base for name meanings. When the appropriate page appeared, he plugged in Khalid and hit search. The rotating hourglass on his computer irked him tremendously.

"Why is this taking so long?" he mumbled to himself.

Mr. Covington opened two new tabs on the screen and typed Erebus in one and Tucker in the other. The hourglasses began their dance as he clicked the mouse on the first browser. He took a long swallow from his bottled water and bit into an apple as he waited.

Within moments, the search revealed that Khalid was Arabic in origin. It derived from khalada which meant to last forever. Khalid meant eternal.

"That's interesting," Mr. Covington uttered. He took a bite into his apple then hit the next tab. To his displeasure, he read that Erebus was Greek for Erebos which meant nether darkness. It was the personification of primordial darkness.

"That is most bothersome," he whispered. "Darkness from under the earth? Darkness from before time? Sounds hellish to me."

Mr. Covington clicked on the last tab. Tucker was an English name that derived from Fuller which was a derivative of the Middle English name Tuck(en) which means full cloth.

"What does this mean?" he mumbled as we moved the cursor down the page. His eyes stretched wide as the he read that the Old English form of Tucker was Tucian which meant to torment. Mr. Covington picked up a pen and scribbled the name meanings on the paper. He wrote: *Khalid Erebus Tucker...Eternal Darkness To Torment.*

He shook his head slowly and dropped the pen onto his desk.

"God, damn that beast!" he wailed as he let tears fall like rain upon the damning words written on the paper, turning them into pitch black puddles. Now there was no doubt in his mind that the baby was a bringer of doom. The angel had impregnated his only child with something vile and horrible.

Mr. Covington pulled open his desk drawer and pulled out a small packet a doctor friend had delivered to him a week ago. Sadness filled him as he flipped it around in his fingers. He had to do what he had to do.

"This will make things right," he said as he looked at the prescription drug within his hand. "Lord forgive me," he whispered as he placed it upon his desk.

He picked up his pen and began to write a letter. He finished it and placed it inside a white envelope. In bold letters across the front of the envelope, he neatly wrote a name.

"Sky, I'm counting on you. I'm counting on you to bring this nightmare to an end," his voice trembled as he dropped hot wax onto the back of the envelope then pressed his seal into the wax.

41

"I've been having these dreams lately," James said as he sipped on a hot cup of coffee. He bowed his head and rubbed the back of his neck with his hands. "I just can't shake them. Night after night I resent going to sleep because I know they are going to come. That's why I drink so much coffee. I be so tired. I toss and turn all night long."

"What kinda dreams?" Luis asked. He sat across the table from James and looked at his watch. "If these chicks don't hurry up, we out." Luis looked around the restaurant for a sign of the young ladies he and James were supposed to meet for dinner. "Aminah would be late for her own funeral. She gets on my nerves with that. If she didn't know how to do the things she do, I would've cut her off a long time ago. And I'm sure that her friend is a super freak too." Luis lifted and dropped his eyebrows twice.

"I don't think I'm ready to date," James said, looking up from his coffee into Luis' impatient eyes. "I got too much going on. My head is all messed up. I'm so stressed out I probably couldn't even hold a decent conversation."

"Who said anything about dating? Hit it and quit it. You need somethin' to get your mind off Sadie and the best way to get over someone is wit' someone else. These chicks don't wanna talk. They wanna pair of shoes and some good lovin'."

"I guess," James sighed. "But they're barking up the wrong tree. I don't pay for dates or purchase sex. I don't buy strangers gifts 'cause they cute either. Shoot I'm cute and ain't no chick offering to buy me nothing." James laughed.

"Me either, but it's too late for them when they find that out." Luis laughed. "They can't resist me. They give up the goodies too quick and I ain't gotta buy sh...."

"You are so stupid," James laughed.

"I be strokin' so good they start to pay me!" Luis laughed as he did a little sex dance in his chair.

James shook his head.

"Don't embarrass me in here," James said as he looked around the room to make sure no one noticed Luis doing his sex dance. "Somebody might think we gay with you doing all that."

"I'm too fly to be gay," Luis said. "So what you been dreamin' 'bout?"

"It's hard to explain." James put his cup down and let his hands drop to the table. He leaned forward and said, "This voice is telling me that I should be with Sadie and we are going to rule the world. It says that the kid is mine, but I know it ain't mine 'cause I didn't sleep with Sadie, but the voice says that the kid is a Tucker and if I deny the child my name I will be throwing the world into chaos or something."

"It sounds like Sadie has been sneakin' in your room and whisperin' in yo ear telling you to be her baby's daddy." Luis laughed hysterically.

"It's not funny," James said. "I'm serious."

Luis stopped laughing.

"When I wake up, that same smell that Sadie has, be all over my room. Sometimes I can feel something in there with me," explained James. "Sometimes when I'm resting in bed, I can feel the weight shift on my bed as if something sat down or stood up. I look up and nothing is there. Other times I wake up because I sense that someone has turned on the light in my room. The light is so bright that it hurts through my eyelids, but when I force my eyes open my room is dark."

"That's wild dude," said Luis.

"I know. The crazy thing is that the dream has been reoccurring every night for weeks and that smell is always there when I wake up." James shook his head. "What if that thing is after me?"

"All I know is that it better stay in yo room," Luis snapped.

"Whatever." James cut his eyes. "You think I need to call Sadie?"

"No."

"What if she needs me?" James asked.

"She won't need you tonight," Luis replied. "Anyway, we have to talk about that later. Right now it's time to entertain the ladies."

Luis smiled and raised his hand for the ladies to see him across the room. The two women walked over. Hips wagging like a dog's tail. A short fair skinned woman who looked to be of Asian and eastern European descent with abnormally long yellow hair, surgically enhanced lips, and two balloons for breasts greeted Luis with a deep inappropriate kiss.

"James," Luis said. "This is my lady friend Aminah."

"Nice to meet you," James said as he extended his hand. She shook it.

"This is my friend Tori," Aminah said as she placed her hand on Tori's shoulder.

James smiled at the tall skinny golden haired woman. Her skin was as dark as his with glittery makeup caked all over it. Gray contacts hid the natural color of her eyes and she shared the same barely covered balloon breast condition as her friend. James extended his hand. When Tori's talon tipped hand accepted, he kissed it and offered her a seat. James looked at Luis with disdain because Luis knew darn well that James would not be attracted to a plastic woman. He barely liked women who wore too much makeup and Tori was fake and caked. He was into natural beauty. The sad thing was that both ladies probably looked incredible without all the fake hair, makeup, and boobs.

"Nice to meet you Tori," James said as politely as he could.

The ladies sat down.

"Have you been waiting long?" Aminah asked, popping gum as she spoke.

"Too long," Luis snapped. "What was the hold up?"

"I had to pick up Tori. She lives all the way in East Point. I had to drive all the way from Buckhead," Aminah whined. "You know how I hate to drive the big Benz."

"You act like that's real far?" Luis snapped again. "I told you about havin' me waitin'. Next time you'll be eating by yourself."

"Sorry, baby," Aminah rolled her eyes.

James shook his head and took another sip of coffee.

"Whatcho name is again shawdy?" Tori asked.

James eyes got big. He looked at Luis and Luis laughed aloud.

"James," he answered. If he wasn't a gentleman he would walk out of the door immediately, but he didn't want to be rude. He mentally started doing a countdown in his mind. He would stay no more than ten minutes. The gentleman in him had a short expiration date.

"You cute and I like your style. You look like a brotha who got a lil somethin'. Where you work at?" Tori cooed.

"I own my own car detailing business," James responded in the most monotone voice he could muster. "What do you do?"

"We dance." Tori pointed at herself then to Aminah.

"What kind of dance?" James asked facetiously. He knew full well that she meant that she was a stripper. "Ballet? Modern? Tap? African?"

"Imma exotic dancer," Tori said as she made a popping sound with her mouth. She did that after every sentence. "I work at the most popular club in the ATL. *POP* You should come and see me sometime. *POP* Me and Aminah is featured at my club. *POP* The top money makers. *POP* I would love to have a baller like you on my side. *POP*," Tori invited, flashing a smile revealing a diamond encrusted tooth.

"Maybe I will," James lied.

He hated strip clubs. He never understood why men paid to see something they could see for free. He looked at his watch then to the tattoo of two cherries with a tongue in between on Tori's neck. She had a matching tattoo on her left breast.

"Luis," James called. "I have to get up early for work in the morning. I'm gonna have to cut this night short. It was a pleasure to meet you Tori. I wish I could have spent more time with you. You seem like an interesting person to know."

Tori looked at her girlfriend in utter shock. Her face revealed a deep displeasure.

"I know he ain't walking out on a dime like me!" she screeched.

Aminah hunched her shoulders in confusion.

Luis tried hard to keep a smile from taking over his face.

James got up and dropped a generous amount of money on the table.

"Enjoy your meal," he said. He turned and walked out of the restaurant.

42

Sadie awoke with a huge smile on her face. She stretched and jump out of the bed. The radio played lightly as she danced her way into the bathroom to shower. She felt good. It had been a long time since she felt good. For the first time since the angel began visiting her she felt like something good was intended for her. The future seemed a bit promising. Sadie smiled as she turned on the shower and undressed. She wiped the gathering steam from the mirror and stared at her silver haired reflection. A small pudgy belly began to form. Sadie cupped her tummy and turned to the side. She stood staring into the fog until her image vanished. She looked down at her belly.

"Kido, I know everything will be all right. I can't wait to meet you Khalid. I can't wait to hold you."

Sadie climbed into the shower and let the water rinse over her. After about twenty minutes, she emerged from the steamy bathroom wrapped in a fluffy robe. She made her way down the hall to Sky's room. Sadie knocked three times. Sky opened the door.

"Yeah," Sky said, leaning against the door post. "Whatcha need?"

Sadie looked strange. A weird grin was plastered across her face and her eyes looked as bright as an innocent's, like one of those Precious Moments children.

"I feel like shopping today. You wanna go?" Sadie asked.

Sky answered, "Sounds good. Give me a few minutes to get dressed. I already showered. All I gotta do is pull my hair into a ponytail and throw on a sundress."

"Okay, I'll meet you at the front door in half an hour," Sadie said as she turned and headed back towards her room. "Today will be a great day," Sadie sang as she entered her room and dressed herself quickly.

Half an hour later, Sadie stood at the front door dressed in a rainbow colored halter dress with matching heels, jewelry, and headband. Within seconds, Sky was beside her wearing a similar styled sundress, but in a vivid purple.

"Are you ready to roll?" Sadie asked with a broad silly smile.

"Yeah," Sky responded as she looked at her friend with suspicious eyes. "You are acting way too happy. You creepin' me out!"

"I'm fine Sky. Be happy that I'm happy."

"If you say so," Sky mumbled.

The two ladies locked the door and made their way to the car.

The weather was beautiful. It was hot, but not too humid. Sadie let down the convertible top and they zoomed down the crowded street. Within minutes they pulled up to Lenox Square Mall. Sadie parked near the entrance and skipped into the mall.

"Do you want to shop for shoes first or jewelry?" Sadie asked.

Sky answered, "Jewelry! You know how I love to sparkle." Her cell phone rang. She pulled it from her purse and answered, "Hello."

"Sky?"

"This is she."

"This is Mr. Covington."

"Da..." Sky began, but was cut short.

"Shhhh. Don't say my name. I don't want Sadie to know that I'm speaking to you," Mr. Covington requested.

"Okay," Sky said as she flashed an awkward smile at Sadie.

"Who's that?" Sadie asked.

"This dude from New York," lied Sky. "Give me a sec. I'll catch up to you in a moment."

"Imma tell Forrest!" Sadie joked.

"Whatever! This ain't nothin'." Sky laughed.

"Umhum," Sadie hummed and walked into a nearby shoe store. She decided to wait for Sky to finish her phone call before they hunted for jewelry.

Sky sat down on a bench.

"What's going on Daddy C?" Sky asked.

"I need your help," he said. "Sadie can't have that baby. It would prove dangerous for her. Has she told you about the demon?"

"Yes," Sky responded. She kept looking over her shoulder for Sadie. An uneasy feeling fingered the bottom of her stomach.

"The baby belongs to it and Sadie must not give birth to that thing!"

"What am I supposed to do? She wants to keep it. I can't change her mind. It's her choice," questioned Sky.

Mr. Covington let out a loud sigh then continued, "If you love her you will help her. I sent a package to you. You should receive it very soon. I have enclosed instructions. Follow them. It's for the best."

"I just don't know Daddy C. It's according to what you're askin' me to do," Sky said reluctantly.

"I'm asking you to save your best friends life!" He snapped. "Sadie isn't pregnant by some unsavory man; she is pregnant by a thing!" He paused to calm himself. "I'm counting on you Sky. I don't know any other way to help her."

"I will try to help as much as I can, but you are making me nervous. Exactly what are you asking me to do?" Sky whispered into the phone, looking over her shoulder ensuring that Sadie was not nearby.

"I want you to do what needs to be done!" he shouted.

"But..." Sky started.

"I hope you see the light before it's too late. Take care of my baby," Mr. Covington whispered and hung up the phone.

Sky placed the phone back into her purse. Her heart drummed heavily against her garment. Exactly what was it that Mr. Covington wanted her to do? Sky had a feeling that it was something drastic and she was sure that she did not want to be a part of it.

43

It wasn't rare that James was alone. The house was quiet and empty often because of the men's busy schedules, but he felt more alone than normal. He was suddenly aware of his solo existence within the walls of his home as if he was alone in all of creation. He looked around the room and thought, *this is what Adam must have felt like when he opened his eyes to the world.* If James allowed his thought to be verbalized, he was sure that he would hear his voice echo against the walls. No televisions or radios were left on. No clothes tumbling in the dryer. No faucets dripping. No air blowing though the vents. No nothing. It was just quiet. Too quiet.

Forrest was at the hospital saving lives and Luis was out entertaining the most ghetto fabulous women James had ever seen. James shook his head and laughed under his breath. Only Luis could find women of that caliber. Maybe Luis arranged the date to make James laugh. If that was Luis' intention, he definitely succeeded. If a love connection was Luis' intention, he had totally missed the mark.

James walked into the kitchen and grabbed a bottle of water from the refrigerator. He sipped it slowly as he listened closely to the abnormal silence. The quietness of the house made him uncomfortable. So, he slowly walked through every room down stairs looking for something, nothing, just looking for the uneasiness to leave him. After finding nothing, but emptiness, he walked up the stairs. The silence became louder. Everything around him loomed as if every object pulsated with life. The pictures on the stairway wall seemed to be doorways to alternative worlds. The bedroom doors appeared to inhale and exhale. The plants in the hall looked to be a brighter green than usual.

James rushed into his room and hit the power button on his stereo. He needed noise. Only noise would banish the eerie feeling that was beginning to permeate his chest. He sat upon the bed and removed his shirt. James felt hot despite the cooling fan above his head. He fell back on his pillow and closed his eyes. He thought of Sadie and remembered how it felt to touch her. It seemed like eons since the last time they were intimate. His body ached for the moist warmth of hers. James adjusted himself and whispered Sadie's name into the silence.

A blast of thick odor rushed through his nostrils. He began to cough hysterically. James sprang up and tried to catch his breath, but the myrrh smell held his lungs with locked fists.

An invisible hand grabbed James' shoulders and he was pulled against a body tingling with inhuman power. James felt his heart halt. A voice whispered into his ear. His vision blurred. The presence was gone and James was left discombobulated on the side of the bed. He pulled his feet up on the bed and placed his head between his knees. Strange thoughts swam through his head. Visions of him heading a prominent family and of worldly power pulsating from his fingertips, of agonizing love and beautiful hatred, of blood raining from bodies impaled upon street signs, and of a time of total world peace. The visions dominated his thoughts in brilliant color, in flashes of real life images being acted out within his brain. The visions flashed faster and faster and then black, nothing, the silence returned.

He knew what he must do now. James took several deep breaths and picked up his cell phone.

"Hello," Sadie answered.

"Sadie, I love you."

"I love you too James."

"Forgive me," James begged. "I can't be without you. I have been a fool and I'm sorry for not supporting you when you needed me the most."

"You were forgiven long ago," Sadie whimpered. "It's not your fault. You did what anyone in your position would have done."

"I'm here now sweetheart. I can't lose you again Sadie. Marry me!"

"What about the baby?" Sadie asked as tears swam through her words.

"The baby is ours to raise. It is a part of you and I love every part of you," he confessed. "Will you be my wife?"

"Yes!" she cried.

"Then marry me quickly," James demanded. "We'll do it this weekend. We have wasted too much time already."

"Okay," Sadie wailed.

James disconnected the call and let the phone hit the floor. The heavy smell flooded James' nostrils again, this time drawing tears from his eyes.

"I have done what you have asked," James yelled. "Now leave me be and never come here again."

"As you wish," a voice echoed. "Never break our agreement and I will never come near you again "

"And Sadie? Will you leave her alone too?" James questioned. Anger dripped from every word.

The voice was gone.

"Do you hear me?" James yelled.

The odor faded as if it had never been.

"Will you leave Sadie alone too?"

James sat in the cool of his room, eyes glassy and fists as tight as nuts on bolts, listening for an answer that would never come.

44

It was two weeks before his trial was scheduled to begin and Oliver sat upon his bunk reading a large black book in hopes of distracting his thoughts. His parents came by often to see him and his friends showered him with letters and phone calls. But he was downcast. It bothered him that his verbose lawyer seemed to be at loss for words when Oliver questioned him. There were so many fears swimming around in Oliver's head, but for the moment the big black book would replace Oliver's fears with an adventurous tale that would conclude with a happy ending.

The fiend eyeballed Oliver angrily from across the cell. His eyes burned into Oliver's face like a sunbeam shooting through glass.

Oliver felt the heat of hatred and looked up from his book. He asked in a passionless tone, "Do you have a problem dude?"

The fiend nodded his head. His dangerous eyes locked with Oliver's as the fiend's left hand fiddled with something shiny tucked under his pillow.

"So, what do you want to do about it?" Oliver asked. He thought he caught a glimpse of a blade of some sorts.

The fiend stood up and punched his hand repeatedly. Something small was hidden inside the assaulting fist. It glinted between the cracks of his closed fingers.

"You haven't learned?" Oliver asked as he put down his book and stood up.

Oliver had absolutely no fear of the fiend. Oliver did not fear anything anymore. Not even the prospect of death. Maybe his life would end today and he would not have to worry about the outcome of a trial. After all, he would rather die than spend his life in prison for a crime he did not commit. He welcomed the fiend to battle. Maybe

Oliver would wash his hands in the fiend's blood and seal his fate within the dungeon he dwelled in. At least then his imprisonment would be just.

The cell door swung open and Kashard walked in.

"Chill out ladies," he commanded. He stared the fiend down with complete hatred in his eyes and then looked respectfully at Oliver.

Oliver and the fiend decided to war another day. They reluctantly sat back down on their bunks.

"How did the meeting with your lawyer go?" Oliver asked as he leaned back on his bed and picked up his book. He looked past Kashard and saw the fiend put the small blade under his pillow.

Kashard followed Oliver's eyes and walked over to the fiend's bed.

"What you got there?" Kashard asked. He pointed to the fiend's pillow.

"Nothing! It's a pillow. Never seen one?" the fiend growled. "Go head on!"

"Give it to me," Kashard threatened.

"You want it?" the fiend smiled big. "I would love to give it to you."

The fiend pulled the blade from under his pillow and tried to shove it into Kashard's belly. Kashard slapped the blade from the fiend's hand. The fiend dove towards the blade, but Kashard stepped in front of him and picked it up from the floor. Kashard backhand slapped the fiend across the face, knocking him backwards. The fiend stood up, breath heaving and eyes glaring wildly.

"Next time I won't be so nice," Kashard roared as he bumped chests with the fiend.

The fiend sat down on his bunk, but never let his eyes leave Kashard's. Unadulterated hate flowed through the fiend's body. Despite his anger he grinned. Vengeance would be his. All he had to do was wait.

Kashard walked to the bars and yelled for the guard. The guard came to the cell door.

"Here," Kashard said. "This piece of metal fell off the side of the bed. I think you should take it. It looks dangerous."

The guard looked down at the sharpened metal and shook his head. It was obvious someone tried to make a knife. He took the blade and walked away. Today he decided not to give the cellmates trouble. He was almost at the end of his shift. All he wanted to do was to go home and paperwork would add more time to his already dragging day.

Kashard sneered at the fiend, who was thankful that Kashard did not snitch, but was angry that Kashard tried to intimidate him.

"Next time I won't be so nice," Kashard repeated.

The fiend gave Kashard the middle finger and sat back on his bunk. He nodded his head up and down as he grinned and mumbled under his breath. He found comfort in the doom he was plotting.

Oliver ignored the fiend and flipped another page of his book then asked Kashard again about his meeting with his lawyer.

"It was good," Kashard replied. "That dude you got me is the man. He know what he doin'. I really think I might beat this thing."

"That's great Kashard. I hope justice is served," Oliver said.

"If justice was served, both you pigs would be dead by now!" the fiend interjected.

He was fully ignored by both men.

"I don't know how to thank you for getting that lawyer for me. You really saved my life and you will always be my homie for that," said Kashard.

"No problem," Oliver whispered. He was happy that Kashard was making progress with his case, but Oliver's life was still hanging in limbo. Mr. Money was doing all he could, but Oliver had the sneaking suspicion that things were not as good as Mr. Money claimed.

"How's your case going?" Kashard asked.

"I'm not sure," Oliver responded honestly. "My…" Oliver was cut off by a correctional officer.

"Oliver Snickermier, you have a visitor," the guard said.

"Who?" Oliver asked.

"A nice old lady," the guard answered and escorted him out of the cell.

Oliver and the guard arrived at the visiting room. Sitting at a table across the room was the older woman that Oliver remembered being at Dr. Putina's office. He rushed over to the table and sat down.

The woman looked Oliver in the eyes and then looked away. She was dressed in a tailored gray suit with matching shoes and fancy silver jewelry. He liked the silver. It reminded him of his own. She sat quietly as if she was contemplating the right words.

"Who are you?" Oliver asked as he sat down. "I remember you. You were in Dr. Putina's office after I left."

"My name is not important," she answered. "But what is important is that I know that you didn't kill Dr. Putina."

"Well, why won't you tell someone?" Oliver yelled. "If you can prove my innocence, why won't you help me?"

"Keep your voice down young man." She looked around the room. "I can't tell anyone. I wish I could, but I can't."

"Why not?" Oliver asked on the edge of hysteria.

"Because no one will believe me," she answered, avoiding his eyes.

"Well, why are you here?" he asked. He wanted to jump across the table and shake the woman until she spilled everything she knew or died of brain damage. At this point, it didn't matter which came first.

"Because I know you are innocent and I want to help you," she said. "I just don't know how.

"You can start by telling the truth lady!" Oliver shouted. Anger bubbled from his belly. Finally he had someone who could get him off the hook, but she didn't want to tell what happened.

"I shouldn't have come here," she said as she stood up to leave.

"If you don't sit down, I will tell everyone that you were at the scene of the crime and you are trying to frame me for a murder that you set up!" Oliver threatened.

She sat down.

"Who are you lady and what did you see?" Oliver asked through his teeth.

"My name is Ebbie Covington and I saw the professor get murdered by an angel."

Oliver's jaw dropped in disbelief. His only hope sat before his eyes with a claim no one in their right mind would believe.

"I am finished..." Oliver whispered under his breath. "Mrs. Covington, I don't quite understand you," Oliver stated. "What are you talking about?"

Mrs. Covington leaned closer to Oliver and whispered, "Dr. Putina was killed by an angel. She summoned him with an incantation. It came and killed her. I saw it with my own eyes. I know it sounds insane and I wouldn't believe me either, but I know what I saw."

Oliver's body stiffened. The thought of his freedom being flushed down the toilet made his body begin rigor mortis. There was no way she could help free him with her cockamamie story. But she was the only person that he knew was in the room after him and before the professor died. He closed his eyes and took a deep breath. Oliver leaned closer to Mrs. Covington and said, "Start from the beginning. Tell me what you saw."

Mrs. Covington told him about Sadie, the summoning of the angel, the death of the professor, and her escape from the campus. Oliver sat before her with breath abated, lingering on every word. Strangely, he believed her.

But how does this help him? The police would never believe her.

"I'm so sorry that you are suffering like this. This is all my fault. If I would have never contacted the professor, she would still be alive and you wouldn't be here," Mrs. Covington whined.

Oliver looked into her eyes. Anger filled his.

"You are right!" he spat. "This is your fault. You killed the professor and you pinned it on me!"

"No!" Mrs. Covington cried. "I didn't touch the professor. I'm not physically capable of hurting her like that!"

"But I'm not going to rot in jail for your crime. I'm calling my lawyer and I suggest you contact yours!" Oliver growled as he jumped up and the correctional officer escorted him from the room.

45

Sadie plopped down on a mall bench. Shoppers buzzed by her unaware of her baffled disposition. Tears rolled down her cheeks. Joyful sighs rumbled through her chest. Her heart leaped. She wanted to stand up and scream, scream with blissful exaltation. James loved her still and wanted to marry her. Turiel was right. James was hers again.

Sky rushed over to the bench where Sadie sat weeping. The talk with Mr. Covington already made Sky uncomfortable and now Sadie was sobbing in the middle of the mall. All the emotional pressure surrounding Sky made her want to just jump on a flight back to New York. She left New York in hopes of getting away from all the madness yet she found herself enveloped in chaos unimaginable.

"What's wrong? What happened?" Sky grabbed Sadie's shoulders gently. Sky's eyes revealed her worry as she tried to camouflage the fear in her voice. "Are you okay?" Sky secretly prayed that there had not been another angel visit.

Sadie looked into her friend's eyes and smiled. "I'm more than okay," she said. "I'm happier than I've been in a very long time." Sadie wiped the tears away, laughing in sighs of joy.

"Oh," Sky responded, confused by the entire situation. She leaned back on the bench in relief. She didn't know what to expect. Everything concerning Sadie was beyond the expectable. She put her arm around Sadie and asked, "So tell me the good news."

"James just called," Sadie grinned from ear to ear.

"And…" Sky urged.

"He asked me to marry him!" Sadie squealed. "He called out of the blue and asked me to marry him!"

"That's wonderful Sadie." Sky hugged her friend. "I'm glad y'all decided to work things out." Sky looked even more confused. Last she heard from Forrest was that James had no interest in getting back with Sadie. Sky forced a smile.

Sadie's countenance changed. Sky's lack of enthusiasm caused Sadie great displeasure. A threatening darkness grew within Sadie's eyes and a sinister smirk disfigured her face.

Sky pulled her arm away and stood up. Chills covered her body. For a moment she could not recognize Sadie's face for it had changed into something twisted and malefic. Sky took three steps backwards.

"I told you James would be my husband, but you didn't believe me," Sadie growled. "You told me that he was gone forever and no child could keep a man." Sadie's voice morphed into a hiss. "Well, he wants me and the baby!"

"Sadie calm down," Sky pleaded as she backed away some more. "I think you're over reacting. You lookin' and behavin' like a crazy woman!"

Sadie stood up. Her eyes grew more dangerous than ever. She stepped towards Sky with fists balled tight.

Sky's hand flew up and pushed against Sadie's chest. Sky's boney fingertips dug into Sadie's flesh hiding beneath the top of her rainbow sundress. Sky balled her free fist.

A small crowd gathered around the women hoping to see a physical altercation. Remarks flew through the air encouraging a hit to be thrown. Further down the walkway, a security guard walked quickly towards the commotion Sadie and Sky were causing.

"I don't know what's gotten into you, but whateva it is, you better back the hell up!" Sky yelled. Her face flushed as red as her hair. Her eyes became wild with anger and fear. "Sadie, I love you and I'm very happy for you and James, but if you don't back down, you and I are gonna be brawlin' in this mall! I don't wanna fight you, but I will defend myself."

The breathless security guard stepped between the ladies.

"Is there a problem here?" he asked with one hand on his flashlight as if it was a gun.

Sadie took a step backwards. The freakish darkness still dominated her eyes.

"No sir," Sadie answered. "My friend and I were just talking."

Sky's eyes locked with Sadie's.

"Are you okay, ma'am?" The guard asked Sky.

"I'm just fine," Sky answered not removing her eyes from Sadie. "Everything is okay."

"All right ladies. Don't make me have to come over here again. Next time I'll have to ask you to leave," the guard scolded them.

"No need," Sadie said to the guard. She smiled smugly and said, "I'm sorry. I don't know what got into me." Sadie sat back down on the bench. Sky reluctantly sat down beside her.

The guard went on his way and so did the onlookers in expressed disappointment.

"I'm sorry Sky," Sadie apologized. "I don't know why I behaved that way. I guess my hormones are going berserk. This baby has me acting a bit crazy."

Sky crossed her arms and nodded her head in disbelief of Sadie's words. She was sure that something more than hormones was causing Sadie to behave in such a way. There was never a time in their friendship when Sky felt closer to coming to physical blows. A matter of fact, she never remembered them ever arguing.

"Please forgive me," Sadie asked, this time the shadows seemed to have lifted from her face.

"I forgive you girl. Me and you ain't never got no problem," Sky lied. She was so angry that she felt hot heart beats in her head. "But I'm not in the mood to shop anymore. Let's go home."

"Okay," Sadie agreed. She stood up from the bench and followed Sky to the car.

The ride home was a quiet one. The music of the radio hung between the silence of the two friends. Sadie drove as Sky looked out of her window. Neither of them knew what to say. Sky pulled into the driveway. There was a small package sitting in front of the door.

"I wonder what that is," Sadie said as she hopped out of the car.

Sky knew it was the package from Mr. Covington. He said it would be coming soon. Sky wondered what kind of mischief making she was getting herself into. She hopped out of the car quickly and zoomed past Sadie to pick up the package.

Sadie looked at Sky curiously. *Why the big hurry?* She thought, but didn't say anything. Things were already strange between her and Sky so Sadie thought it best not to ask any questions.

46

Sky walked into her room and tossed the package onto the bed. She could only imagine what Mr. Covington had hidden inside that small cardboard box. If it had eyes, she was sure that it was watching her. Sky glanced at it occasionally as she undressed and changed into a tank top and yoga pants. She sat upon the bed and slowly opened the package and poured its contents upon the bed. There lay a white envelope with Sky's name written on it with a calligraphy pen. She forced a smile. She always loved the fancy way Mr. Covington wrote things. Everything about him was meticulous and classy. The ink was a rich dark purple and the back of the envelope was sealed by wax with *Covington* stamped into it.

Next to the envelope was a tiny mahogany box. Sky opened the box and found four small pills in its velvet center. Her eyebrows rose. Something about the pills made her uneasy. She closed the box and opened the letter. It read:

Sky,

I know what I am about to ask you will be difficult for you to understand, but it is very important that you carry out my plan. It will benefit us all in the future although it will cause much heartache now.

Within the box you will find mifepristone and misoprostol. They are abortion pills. Grind them up and put them into Sadie's food or drink. I know that this is a lot to ask, but the life of that child can mean the death of us all. I researched the names the angel told Sadie to name the child and it stands for all that is terrific and unholy. Do this thing and tell no one! Do it soon and call to keep me posted. Know that I ask you to perform such a foul deed out of sincere love for my daughter. After reading this letter, please destroy it.

> *Respectfully yours,*
> *Carlos Covington*

Tears ran down Sky's face as she silently wept. The thought of killing Sadie's child made her feel insane, but she knew what Mr. Covington spoke was the truth. She could see that the child had changed Sadie. Sadie now possessed a hard and biting edge to her personality that she never had before. Behind her eyes lurked something truly frightening bordering on dangerous.

Sky ripped the letter into tiny pieces then flushed it down the toilet. She picked up the small mahogany box from the bed and withdrew the pills, tucking them safely within the palm of her hand. She prayed that her nervousness would not cause her palms to moisten the pills.

Sky walked into the kitchen and pulled a grinding stone and bowl from the cabinet. Never did she think she would be grinding deadly dust in the same bowl where she had turned fragrant spices into tasty powders. Sky dropped the pills into the bowl and put the stone to work. In seconds the pills transformed into fine powder. The white dust looked as harmless as baby powder. Sky looked at the bowl and her heart felt so heavy within her chest that her ribs threatened to collapse under the weight. She swallowed hard and put a pot of hot water on the stove.

"Sadie," Sky called. Her voice trembled. She cleared her throat and called again. "Sadie!"

"Yes," Sadie answered from the other side of the apartment.

"Would you like some tea?"

"It's too hot for tea," Sadie answered.

"I can make yours ice tea."

"Okay fine," Sadie agreed. She really didn't like to drink without eating, but she assumed that Sky was making a peace offering so it would be rude not to accept. "I'll be in the living room. Would you like to watch a movie?"

"Sure," Sky answered as she mixed the powder with sugar, a large amount of sugar. She could not risk Sadie discovering the secret ingredient. After the tea pot whistled, she poured the hot water into the grinding bowl ensuring that the deadly sugar mixture would fully dissolve. She dropped in two peach tea bags and waited until the liquid was nice, brown, and cool before she poured it all over a tall glass of ice. A small prayer fluttered from her lips pleading to God that the only damage that would be done would be to the baby. Sky placed a tea bag in a large mug and poured herself a steaming cup. She placed both beverages on a serving tray. Something was missing. Sky stopped for a moment. Sadie needed to drink all of the tea. Sky could not risk for Sadie to take a sip like she usually did, leaving the rest to be discarded. Sky searched the room and her eyes rested upon the cookie jar. She opened it up and pulled out four iced oatmeal cookies. Sadie loved cookies and the ice tea would be the perfect pallet washer. Sky placed them on the tray and headed for the living room.

"What did you pick out?" Sky asked as she placed the tray upon the coffee table and sat on the couch next to Sadie.

"*Beaches*," Sadie answered.

Sky swallowed hard. Of all the movies in the world, why would Sadie pick out one about a best friend dying?

Sadie picked up the glass of ice tea and swirled it around letting the ice clink against the glass, cooling the liquid within. When she figured it was cold enough, she drank two deep gulps of the fatal brew.

Sky looked on. Her eyes searched for an immediate reaction. There was none. She exhaled nervously and watched as Sadie reached for the tray.

Sadie picked up a cookie and bit down. She followed with three more thirsty swallows. She took another bite of the cookie then finished the tea.

"That was good," she complimented. "What kind of tea was that? It was really sweet like I like it, but it had a bitter aftertaste."

Sky lifted her trembling cheeks into a smile as her heart prayed earnestly for her best friend's safety and replied, "Peach. I may have used too many tea bags."

47

"What's wrong with you?" Forrest asked as he walked past James' door. Forrest saw him balled up on the floor staring at the wall. His face was blank and his breathing was shallow.

James looked up in embarrassment. He didn't want to share his experience with Forrest. James knew that he would not understand. James pulled himself from the floor and sat on the edge of the bed.

"I'm cool," James mumbled.

"You don't look cool. You look like you have seen a ghost," Forrest said as he invited himself into the room and sat on the bed next to James. "What's going on man?"

Forrest walked close to James and attempted to put his hand on James' forehead to check his temperature, but James backed away, avoiding Forrest's hand.

"I'm okay," James said.

Forrest backed away. James' demeanor was disturbing, but Forrest knew he could not force James to talk so he decided to change the subject. Forrest lifted his nose in the air. The faint smell of myrrh filled his nostrils.

"Why is that smell here?" he asked.

"I don't know," James lied. "It was here when I came home."

Uneasiness filled Forrest. The thought of something supernatural being in their home made him want to move out.

"What's going on?" he repeated.

" It's Sadie," James started. "I..."

Forrest placed his hand on James' shoulder and said, "I know it's hard, but you have to get over her. It's not your fault and you should not feel guilty. Y'all had to part under the circumstances. She understands." He gripped James shoulder and turned James to face him. "You gotta stop beating yourself up. It's all for the best."

"I asked her to marry me," James whispered.

Forrest's face turned fire engine red. "When did this happen?" he asked.

"Before you came home. I called her and asked her to marry me. Everything became so clear," he whispered. "There's no reason for us to be apart. I love her and I don't want to be without her."

"Are you sure about this?" Forrest inquired. He did not understand how this could have happened. James was so against continuing his relationship with Sadie and now they were engaged again? Just the other day James spoke to him and Luis about how he was finally getting used to the idea of moving on. This didn't make sense. James was beyond freaked out about Sadie's baby and that spirit that haunted her. Now he wanted to marry into the Addams Family?

"I'm sure. I love her," James whispered as he looked away from Forrest. James wished he could tell Forrest about the revelation he received, but Forrest would say that James was being pressured by something unnatural to marry Sadie and that his heart wasn't sincerely in it. Forrest would try to talk him out of it. He would warn James about the danger involved. He would tell James that he was being too emotional and not thinking. Forrest would tell him to run for the hills because the angel was now after him. James did not want to hear any of it. He knew what he had to do.

"But you were so sure that you wanted to walk away. What changed your mind?" Forrest stood up and began to pace. "And what about the baby?"

"I realized how much I really loved her and needed her," James looked into Forrest's eyes.

Icy chills rolled down Forrest's arms as he saw the cold hardness within James' gaze.

"I love her so I have to love her child. The baby is ours and I'll be a father," James stated louder and clearer than anything he had said thus far. "She will be my wife.

We'll have a family. That's the way it will be." James stood up and stepped into Forrest's personal space.

Forrest backed out of the door and stepped into the hallway.

"If that is what you want brother, I will support you one hundred percent," Forrest said. "But..."

"But nothing," James snapped. "My mind is made up." He closed the door in Forrest's baffled face.

48

"AHHHHH," Sadie screamed. Her eyes popped open. Darkness filled the room. "AHHHHH!" She shrieked. Her teary eyes rested upon the bright digital clock which read 2:48 a.m. The pain shook her awake in the middle of the night. She held her belly and pulled in her legs. Her stomach cramped so badly that it felt as if hooks were inside her lower abdomen ripping her apart. The pain intensified every second.

"AHHHHHHH" she wailed. She rolled onto her other side. As her legs shifted, warm liquid covered her thighs. She reached down and let the wetness cover her fingers. Sadie looked at her scarlet fingertips and screamed again. "AHHHHHH!"

Blood drenched her night gown, her sheets, and her thighs. Sadie rolled onto the floor and crawled to the bathroom leaving a ruby trail behind her. She reached the toilet and pulled herself upon it. Large chunks of blood fell from her womb as she sat with her legs trembling and her free hand holding the edge of the sink.

Moments later Sky stood in front of Sadie's bedroom. She rested her hand upon the knob as she tried to steady her heartbeat. Guilt pressed upon her shoulders. Her eyes filled with moisture. Sky opened the door and walked into Sadie's bedroom. She had heard her friend's wailing from across the apartment. Sky slowly placed one foot in front of the other as she approached Sadie's bathroom door. Fear seized Sky's heart. She was afraid of what she might see and even more afraid of what she had caused. Sky hugged herself desperately as her eyes beheld the blood that covered Sadie's carpet in thin lines leading to the bathroom. Blood smeared beneath Sky's toes as her foot landed on the cold tile.

"Sadie," Sky called. She reached out and placed her hand upon Sadie's shoulder. Sadie looked up in complete and utter agony as she leaned forward on the toilet trying to keep her body balanced.

"My baby," Sadie cried. Tears and mucus covered Sadie's face. She looked in Sky's eyes pleading for deliverance. "Call 911."

Sky could not move. She wanted to call for help, but she also wanted to ensure that the baby would not be saved. She stood frozen, staring at her friend in blank horror.

"Sky!" Sadie screamed. She grabbed hold of Sky's tank top and pulled her down before her. Sky's knees splashed into a blood puddle. Her hand fell into another.

Sky looked at the blood on her hands and began to weep. *Murder!* She thought to herself. Her hands were dripping in the blood of her best friend. She looked into Sadie's fading eyes and pulled away from her.

"Help me!" Sadie groaned.

Sky ran to the phone and dialed 911. Bloody fingerprints dotted the phone's keypad. Blood covered Sky's hands and forearms like satin gloves. The crimson liquid seemed to draw Sky into a trance, but her stupor was broken by the voice of the 911 operator speaking in her ear. Sky told the operator everything she could then hung up and rushed over to Sadie. She refused to stay on the line because of the fear of incriminating herself.

"I'm so sorry," Sky cried. "Please be okay. Please, please be okay!"

Sadie looked up at Sky. Cramps and contractions alternated within her uterus. Sadie rocked back in forth while the warm liquid leaked from her body.

"My baby," she whispered. "I can't lose my baby." Sadie balled up as a fresh new wave of pain rocketed through her. "It hurts so bad!" she cried.

"I never meant to hurt you!" Sky blubbered. "Please be all right. Please Sadie. I didn't mean for this to happen."

Sadie looked up with confusion in her eyes. She was not sure if she heard correctly. The pain had her hearing things. Sky could not possibly be the cause of this.

"Please don't die," Sky wailed. "Please be okay."

More pain filled Sadie. It snatched the sound from her throat. She mouthed, "What are you talking about?"

Sky wrapped her arms around Sadie and pulled her from the toilet. Sky held her tight, rocking back and forth, both of them splattered in red.

"Help will be here soon. Just hold on," Sky pleaded. "Everything will be just fine."

Sadie's eyes became heavier and heavier. Her head rested upon the neck of her friend as she tried to fight the looming darkness of unconsciousness.

"Stay wit' me," Sky wailed. "I'm so sorry. I never meant to hurt you. Only the b..." Sky stopped mid-sentence. She held Sadie closer. "Please be okay."

Sadie's body stiffened at what she thought she heard. Her mouth opened to question, but her eyes closed and her consciousness was no more.

Sky buckled under Sadie's weight and slid upon the bathroom floor. Moments later the loud knocking of the door forced her to roll Sadie to the side and let the paramedics inside.

Sky stepped back and watched as they laid her best friend on a stretcher and took her from the apartment. Tears streamed from Sky's face, washing small streaks of blood from her flesh. Sky grabbed a robe and her cell phone and followed behind them and soon climbed into the cab of ambulance.

"What did we do Pappa C?" she cried under her breath. "What did we do?"

49

"What's going on?" James questioned as he stood in the hallway of the hospital.

Sky called Forrest and told him that Sadie was in the hospital and Forrest told James. James was livid with Sky for not telling him directly. He was so angry that he could barely look at her face.

"What's going on?" he asked again, this time with even more rage in his voice. Beads of sweat formed on his bald head as he breathed too close to Sky's face.

"You need to back up man," Forrest said as he lightly pushed James out of Sky's personal space. "She's just as concerned as you are."

"I didn't mean no disrespect," James lied. He did not know why he felt so angry with Sky. He knew that Sadie's condition was not Sky's fault, but for some reason he felt so much deep rooted wrath towards her. "I just want to know what happened to Sadie."

"I told you already," Sky said as she avoided James' eyes. "I heard her screaming in the middle of the night. When I got to her room, she was in the bathroom bleeding. I called 911 and they brought her here."

"Why didn't you call me? I'm her fiancé! You didn't think I should know?" James yelled.

"I wasn't thinking," Sky whispered.

"Calm down James. This is no one's fault. Sadie will be okay," Forrest said as he put his arm around Sky and issued James a warning with his eyes. "There is no need to make matters worse."

James looked away and began to pace the hallway.

"I'm going to go talk to the doctor to see what's going on. They know me here so maybe I can get more information," Forrest reassured them both. "Be nice you two," he scolded and made his way to the nurses' station.

"I'm sorry I didn't call you James. I wasn't thinking," Sky apologized. She spoke slowly and avoided his eyes in fear of him looking into them and seeing her involvement in Sadie's condition. "Everything happened so fast. After we arrived at the hospital, I was borderline hysterical and the only person I could think of calling was Forrest," she lied.

Forrest was not the only person she called. He was not even the first person she called. Sky called Mr. Covington and told him that Sadie was in the hospital. She was hysterically screaming her head off about how she thought she had murdered her friend and her baby. Mr. Covington was the one who calmed her down and told her that Sadie would be just fine and that getting rid of the baby was the best thing for everyone. Sky was not sure if she agreed with that or not, but it was much too late to rethink things. He finally convinced her to remain calm and to not allow guilt to cause her to confess to anything. After hanging up with him and crying like a baby in the emergency room bathroom, she then called Forrest.

"I'm sorry too," James lied. "I know it's not your fault. No one can control these things. I'm just worried."

James still could not shake the loathsome feeling that he felt for Sky at the moment. He had a dream the night before of Sky poisoning Sadie and trying to kill their baby. He woke up in a cold sweat and to the thick suffocating smell of myrrh. James was never a superstitious man nor did he believe in the power of dreams so he tried his best to dismiss it and watch TV until he fell asleep again. Now he wondered if the dream held any truth. He looked over at Sky and noticed that she was awfully nervous and avoided everyone's eyes. That was the total antithesis of her. Sky was always an in-your-face kind of person and she was always confident, overconfident even. From the first time he met her and from everything Sadie had told him about her, Sky did not seem to be capable of nervousness. Now she sat balled up with a frightened look in her eyes and she had been bouncing her knee non-stop since he arrived. James had a feeling that Sky knew more about Sadie's condition than she claimed.

"No worries," Sky replied as she looked down the hallway to avoid James' face.

A few minutes later, Forrest came back down the hall. James and Sky turned towards him with questioning eyes.

"I have great news." Forrest smiled.

Sky stood up and James walked over to Forrest.

"Sadie lost a lot of blood, but she and the baby will be just fine. It was a miracle!" he exclaimed. "With that amount of blood lost, the baby should have perished, but it clung on. Sadie is asleep, but she will recover fine," Forrest countenance fell. "But something strange was found in her system."

Sky sat back down and looked away. Her leg began to bounce faster than ever. James took a mental note of it, but did not allow his eyes to leave Forrest's face.

"What?" James asked.

"Abortion pills were found in her system. Double the normal dose of abortion pills," Forrest said, a frown bent his face. He turned to Sky. "I thought she was adamant about keeping her baby?"

"She was," James said between his teeth. His heart began to beat triple time.

Sky looked down and tears formed in her eyes. She said nothing.

"Do you know anything about this?" Forrest asked her as James' eyes burned a hole in her face.

"No," Sky lied.

"Are you sure?" James asked in a tone that would send chills down the devil's back.

"I'm sure," Sky mumbled as she swallowed a mouthful of tears.

"Something just doesn't add up," Forrest said.

"It sure as hell doesn't," James replied as his eyes zoned in on the side of Sky's face.

Forrest looked from James to Sky then back at James.

"Let's not jump to conclusions," Forrest said.

James had told him about the dream. The way James was looking at Sky made Forrest nervous and the coincidence was making him even more nervous. He had never seen Sky so humbled and afraid.

"The truth will come out soon enough. Until then," Forrest suggested. "Let's be thankful that Sadie and the baby are safe and sound."

50

Oliver's eyes popped open. He tried to sit up, but he could not move. His body was completely paralyzed and fear began to fill Oliver's heart. The sour smell of the fiend infiltrated his nostrils. Darkness suddenly covered Oliver's eyes. He could feel cushiony fabric on his face. Oliver tried to struggle, but nothing happened. It was too late. A sharp object pierced the side of his throat. Oliver could not force a sound to materialize. Warm blood leaked from his neck onto his bed.

"I don't hear yo slick talk now boy," the fiend whispered softly in Oliver's ear. "Yo little savior is sound asleep after the mickie I slipped him at dinner. I just finished doing to him what I'm going to do with you," he laughed. "You can't move too much yoself huh?" the fiend laughed again as he leaned in closer to Oliver's ear. "I have a little something for you too. You see, I have friends also and my friends work in the infirmary."

Oliver tried to lift himself, but he could not. He could move nothing, but could feel everything. The pressure of the fiend's knee on his chest made him think that his lungs would collapse under the weight. The smell of the fiend's breath made his stomach ache. The pillow fell from Oliver's face. He looked up into the eyes of his assailant.

The fiend smiled as he pushed the small ice pick he held into Oliver's chest. Oliver watched in horror as the metal point came toward him time and time again. He watched until the fiend and the blade blurred then faded to black.

Oliver Snickermier was no more.

51

Mrs. Covington lay in her bed, eyes swollen from perpetual weeping. It had been a week since she had seen Oliver Snickermier and at any minute she expected the police to kick her door in and haul her off to prison. She was sure that he was telling the police that she was Dr. Putina's murderer and that he was packing up his belongings so she could move into his cell. Mrs. Covington thought about visiting him again to beg for mercy, but that would be moot. Why would he exchange his freedom for hers?

The bedroom door opened. Mr. Covington peeped his head inside the door. Sadness filled his eyes as he looked upon his wife. He had never seen her so distraught. She had been crying for a week and she would not tell him what was wrong. Mr. Covington walked into the room and sat on the edge of her side of the bed. He leaned over and kissed her on the cheek.

"How are you feeling, baby?" he asked.

"I haven't been feeling very well," she whined. "So much has been going on in our family and the weight of it all is crushing me."

"I know, baby. I constantly worry about Sadie too," Mr. Covington replied. "We have to have faith that things will work out just fine. I've been praying a lot lately. Only God can help us through this time."

"God?" Mrs. Covington scoffed. "Why would God allow all of this stuff to happen in the first place? Sadie is a good person. Why her?"

"Baby I don't know. I just think that only God knows how to deliver us from these tribulations," Mr. Covington whispered as he stroked his wife's forehead.

Mrs. Covington frowned in disagreement. Anger was the only emotion she had towards God. She no longer doubted that God was real. She now just doubted that he was good, well-meaning or kind. God was responsible for all the evil that befell her family. They did not deserve this. Why should she want to put trust in such a vain and wrathful being? Mrs. Covington felt that God was only punishing her and her daughter because they refused to worship and stroke His ego. She felt that only a spitefully insecure creature would seek revenge for something so petty. Mrs. Covington's heart of flesh became a heart of stone.

Mr. Covington sensed his wife's agitation, but continued, "Maybe if we humbled ourselves in prayer, God will change things."

"I'll pray over my dead body," she snipped.

He decided to change the subject because he knew his wife would not change her mind. Mr. Covington mentally prayed for mercy and said, "Sky called while you were sleeping. Sadie is out of the hospital."

"Wonderful." Mrs. Covington smiled. "I'm so glad to hear that."

Mr. Covington looked away from his wife.

"I'm glad to hear that Sadie is doing fine, but I'm disappointed that the baby survived," he admitted.

"How can you say that about our grandchild?"

"Easily when I know that the baby will bring nothing, but more hurt and chaos into our family," Mr. Covington responded.

Mrs. Covington touched his leg and rubbed gently trying to calm his anger. She kissed his shoulder and said, "At least Sadie doesn't have to raise the child alone. James will be with her."

Mr. Covington said nothing.

The phone rang. Mr. Covington picked up the receiver and said hello. After about five minutes he hung up the phone and looked at his wife with a hint of sadness in his eyes.

"Who was that?" Mrs. Covington asked.

"Percy Flippin," Mr. Covington responded. "Do you remember that kid Oliver that's in jail for Olga Putina's murder?"

"I do," Mrs. Covington's voice trembled. She leaned back on her pillow and looked up at the ceiling. Her heart thumped chaotically. She wondered who Oliver told.

"He's dead," Mr. Covington said.

"What?" she bolted into a sitting position and looked her husband dead in the eye.

"He was killed in his prison cell days ago. He was stabbed to death by his cellmate," Mr. Covington answered.

Joy and relief filled Mrs. Covington's body. She felt guilty about her inner rejoicing, but she could not help it. The boy could not reveal her secret and the police would never suspect her. This was fortuitous! *Maybe God was merciful.* She thought then dismissed it quickly. All she wanted to do was to dry her eyes and jump out of the bed and dance, but dancing would be inappropriate when hearing of someone's death so she smiled into the pillow instead.

"I'm sorry to hear that," she mumbled as she tried to hide the relief in her voice. Deep down she felt sad for Oliver, but it was difficult to mourn for a death that saved her life. "We should send his family flowers for the funeral."

"We will do that," Mr. Covington said. "That's the least we can do," he said as he looked at his wife with suspicion in his eyes. The muffled excitement in her voice unnerved him to no end.

52

Two weeks had passed since Sadie was released from the hospital. Each time Sky looked upon Sadie's face, a sense of dread and guilt filled Sky. She found it harder and harder to even be in the same room with Sadie. Sky felt that she had betrayed Sadie in the worst possible way and felt mentally sick for giving Sadie those abortion pills. Sky could feel Sadie's suspicion of her. The way she looked at Sky made her skin crawl. Sadie fixed her own food and refused to even take a drink of water from Sky. The awful part of it all was that Sadie never accused Sky of anything. Sadie just watched Sky with piercing eyes and kept her distance.

Sky sat upon her bed with her hands folded on her lap. Forrest sat across from her on the vanity chair. She leaned forward and grabbed one of his hands. She kissed his fingers gently and pressed his palm upon her heart.

"I love you," she whispered.

"I love you too Sky," Forrest replied. A look of alarm flashed across his face. He hoped that she wasn't breaking up with him. The look in her eye looked like goodbye.

"It's time for me to leave here. I miss New York and I don't think Sadie and James want me around much longer," said Sky.

"Why would you say that? Sadie loves you," Forrest asked.

"And I love her too, but so much has changed between us. Nothing has been said, but I can feel the shift. I know when I have worn out my welcome," Sky answered. "Plus they will be a family soon and families need their private space."

Forrest grabbed both of her hands and pulled her close to him. He kissed her lips softly and pulled away.

"What about us?" he asked. "I don't want to see you leave."

"Forrest, you knew that I was just visitin'. My home is in New York. My life is in New York."

"I know that, but you and I have something real here. I don't want to let you go," Forrest said.

Sky leaned her forehead against his chest and whispered, "You are the love of my life. I don't want to let you go either. But..."

"But nothing. If you won't be with me in Atlanta, I'll be with you in New York!" Forrest exclaimed.

"I can't ask you to leave your job and your friends," Sky cried. "You love your life here."

"I love you more. Do you want us to be together?" Forrest asked.

Sky nodded her head.

"Well let's be together. When you leave, I will follow you there in a couple of weeks. All I have to do is arrange a job up there. It should take no time. My father is a doctor at New York University Hospital and he is well known in medical circles throughout the city," Forrest said. "If you will have me, I will be there. New York is home for me. I was raised in the heart of Manhattan."

"I would love for you to come, but I don't believe in shackin' up. I would never feel comfortable livin' with a man that I'm not married to."

"Sky," Forrest called.

"Yes," Sky answered.

"Will you be my wife?" he asked.

She nodded her head with tears in her eyes.

Forrest reached into his pocket and pulled out a beautiful black diamond ring.

"I've had this ring in my pocket for two weeks now. Thank you for allowing me to pull it out." He smiled and placed the ring upon her thin finger. "Fits just right."

Sky hugged him and kissed him deeply.

"When are you going home?" Forrest asked.

"I'll be leavin' in a week. I want to be here for Sadie and James' weddin'. It will be on Saturday and I have just a few days to get everything together. Of course it will be tiny, but it will still be fabulous. After the wedding I will leave Atlanta."

"Does Sadie know you're leaving?"

"No. I plan on tellin' her right before I leave for the airport. That way, James will be there to comfort her and they can come back here to an empty house. They can start their new life together."

Sadie stood listening from the hallway. Her eyes narrowed into sorrowful slants as she watched her best friend with her new fiancé. She overheard the entire conversation and sadness filled her heart. Deep down Sadie knew that Sky was right. It was time for her to go. Sadie loved her dearly, but she knew that Sky was responsible for the attempted miscarriage. Love and loathing competed within Sadie's heart every time Sky was in her presence. The only way Sadie felt that she could ever learn to forgive Sky is with Sky out of her home and out of her life for at least a little while. Plus, Sadie feared the angel. If it knew that Sky tried to destroy the child, it might destroy her.

"Goodbye," Sadie cried under her breath. She rubbed her belly and back peddled down the hallway. "I will miss you."

53

Sadie danced around her room as she prepared for her wedding on tomorrow. She neatly packed her wedding accessories in a small bag along with her make-up kit, toiletries, and hair products. Excitement filled her. She could not believe that her wedding day was so close. She looked over at her wedding dress which was hanging on the door and a big smile curled her face. Sadie turned her radio up higher as she twirled around and around. Joy, unspeakable joy is all she felt. Things were looking up. She was going to marry the man of her dreams. James accepted the baby as his own. Sky was getting married and going back to New York. Her father stopped pressuring her about getting rid of the baby and the angel was gone. Sadie felt like she was getting her old life back.

"Feel the rain on your skin. No one else can feel it for you..." she sang along with Natasha Bedingfield when the lyrics were suddenly ripped from her throat. Something was behind her. She could feel the warmth of a living thing and she could smell the undeniable scent of myrrh. Arms wrapped around her. She struggled against it, but was rendered helpless. Burning kisses singed the back of her neck and shoulders. Sadie whimpered after each peck. Angelic hands rested upon her stomach and thigh. Tears formed in her eyes as she felt her gown incinerate and fall from her skin in ashes.

"Noooo," she wailed as her nude body was carried into the air.

"This is our last night together..." Turiel uttered. "...before you give yourself to another. When I return to you, you will be spoiled and I will be forbidden to touch you; yet, I will love you still."

"Please don't," Sadie begged. It felt like thousands of hands fondled her all at once. She writhed around in sensory overload. Involuntary moans of pleasure mingled with moans of protest.

Turiel grabbed her hair and bit down gently on her bottom lip. Sadie pulled away, but was locked within his arms. She pounded his chest with balled fists, but each hit only fueled his passion for her. Soon she fell limp, exhausted from struggling.

Turiel's body melted into Sadie's forming a multi-limbed creature tumbling above the floor. Legs and arms intertwined. Lips burned with fiery kisses. Eyes rolled back and tongues licked. They swirled in a glowing ball of passion as Sadie groaned in soul numbing pleasure. Tears rained from her eyes as her body slowly floated unto the soft comforter of her bed. Turiel levitated above her, shining as bright as the sun. Sadie shielded her eyes as he transformed into a ball of hot light.

"I will always love you!" his voice echoed. The room dimmed and he was gone.

Sadie, a bruised and smoldering creature, curled herself in a ball and wept herself to sleep. Not even the torturing of Turiel would steal her rest from her. Sadie was determined to let nothing stop her from marrying the man she loved. Not even being raped by an angel on the night before her wedding.

54

Luis walked into the house carrying three tuxedos in his hands. "Yo!" he yelled into the empty living room. "Yo! Where everybody at?" Luis draped the suits across the back of the sofa and walked into the kitchen.

James and Forrest sat at the small kitchen table nibbling on potato chips and drinking bottles of water. They looked up at Luis and pointed to an empty seat.

"Y'all didn't hear me come in?" Luis asked as he pulled out a chair from the table and sat down.

"Naw man," James answered.

Forrest shook his head from side to side.

"I got the tuxes. They're so hot! When that suit hits my body, the sprinklers are gonna go off in the hotel," Luis bragged.

"Whateva," James laughed. The smile left his face and he looked over at his friends. "I'm gonna miss y'all."

"Me too," Forrest replied. "I can't believe I'm going back to New York. I thought I left that cold weather forever."

"It's gonna be real quiet without y'all. I guess I better have my harem move in to keep me company," Luis joked.

"I'm sure," James laughed. "It's an end of an era." He shook his head from side to side.

"I know we're all movin' on..." Luis mumbled. "...but make sure we stay boys forever."

"Without a doubt," James responded.

"You didn't have to say that," Forrest said as he rested his hand on Luis' shoulder. "We are forever." Forrest smile. "I like it when you get all sensitive," he said in a feminine voice.

James laughed so hard he almost choked.

Luis knocked Forrest's hand away. He shook his head and laughed.

"We gotta hurry up and get dressed. We gotta be at the hotel in less than two hours for the wedding," Luis said, changing the subject. He hated goodbyes.

"I know," James mumbled as he crunched on a potato chip.

"You ready?" Luis asked. "You sure you wanna marry that broad after all the crazy stuff she been through?"

"Yeah man. I love her," James responded as he stood up and walked out of the kitchen into the living room.

Luis followed close behind. Forrest tailed him. The men picked up their suits and draped them over their arms. James opened the front door and exited the house. Soon all three men piled into Luis' Mercedes station wagon, Forrest volunteered to drive, and pulled out of the driveway.

Luis leaned his head between the two front seats and said, "Jay, you sure you doin' the right thing. Marriage means forever. You sure you wanna be tied to that girl, that baby, and possibly that thing that keeps on bothering her?"

"He said yes," Forrest intervened. "Today is his wedding day. I'm sure he's under enough pressure already. So don't start in with all the questions. The time for questioning has passed."

"I'm not trying to stress you Jay. I just don't understand how you changed yo mind so quick," said Luis.

"It's not for you to understand," Forrest answered as James sat in the passenger seat staring quietly out of the window. The hotel that housed his wedding was only six blocks away.

"I ain't talkin' to you Forrest. Are you James' PR man now?" Luis snapped. "Jay, are you sure man? If you love her, I like her. I just want to make sure that you are okay. Feel me?"

"I feel you Lu," James answered. "I'm sure. I appreciate your concern, but everything is okay. I know what I'm getting myself into. I rather live with her than without her. Everything else don't matter." James pointed his finger. "Park over there," he said. "I want to be close to the door."

"Here we go fellas," Luis sang. "This is the last few hours of James' bachelorhood." Luis leaned closer to James. "You should have banged that fat booty stripper that you kept tipping last night."

James laughed, shaking his head from side to side.

"She was too much for me bro. A girl like that would mess a man up for life," James quipped. "You know she was bad if she got my dough. Strip clubs ain't my thang, but that chick was a sin to look at. I tell you, if I didn't love Sadie I would be in her bed right now knocking her back out!"

"Her butt looked like two basketballs!" Forrest laughed. "And her hips were huge! I can't believe that tiny waist of hers could hold up all that lower body. She has to have lower back problems. I should have given her my card in case she needs medical advice."

"You know you loved every bit of it," James joked. "Your eyes were about to pop out of your head."

"Hell yeah!" Luis yelled. "Sky ain't got none of that."

James laughed hysterically.

"Sky got what I need," Forrest replied with a big smirk on his face. "I admit that stripper was hot! Just watching her walk gave me heart palpitations."

The men laughed as Forrest parked the car. They exited the car and entered the hotel.

"Congratulations man," Luis uttered. "I really wish you happiness."

"Thanks," James replied as they quickly found their dressing rooms and began to prepare for the service.

55

Vivid purple flowers decorated golden cloth covered chairs sitting in five columns and five rows on each side of a purple satin isle. Statues of arrow pointing cherubs hung from the four corners of the room. Golden drapes dressed the tall windows that drenched the room in sunshine.

James, Luis, and Forrest stood in the front of the room dressed eloquently in black tuxedos. Mrs. Covington sat in the front row wearing a beautiful violet dress with matching hat and shoes. Amethyst jewelry sparkled from her ears, wrists, and neck as her hands rested upon her lap. James' parents sat on the row directly across from her. His mother wore a violet and white dress and a gardenia in her hair. James' father sat beside her in a simple tuxedo. Both looked at their son with adoring eyes.

About forty-five people made up the audience, almost an equal amount showing support for the bride and groom. The audience was beautifully dressed and of great variety. Nuns, strippers (Luis' friends), business executives, laymen, and artists came to celebrate with James and Sadie. They sat waiting with great joy and anticipation.

An older woman sat in the far corner with her fingers gently tickling the strings of a harp, filling the room with soft music. The harp player changed her song to something much louder and more dramatic. The audience stood on their feet. A pretty woman with long honey blond hair and bright blue eyes wearing a purple ruffled, t-strap, knee length dress pranced down the aisle carrying a bouquet of lilies. Sky followed next with her fiery red hair twisted up in a bun with soft curls gracing her neck. She wore a similar dress to the first woman's, but Sky's dress was mid-calf and strapless. Once the two women took their places across from Luis and Forrest, the harp player began to play the wedding march.

Sadie Covington stepped down the aisle to the rhythm of the wedding march. She wore a fitted white dress with a bright purple sash around her waist. A rhinestone and amethyst tiara sat upon her silver curls and amethyst jewelry sparkled from her ears and neck. In her hand she held lilies dyed violet. He father, dressed impeccably in a black tuxedo, was on her arm as they made their way to James who was smiling wider than anyone could deem possible.

Sadie's father presented her to James and the minister began the ceremony. The couple waxed poetic with hand written vows, exchanged beautiful rings, and kissed with unspeakable passion. Soon they were pronounced man and wife before their small applauding audience. As the couple turned to make their exit from the hotel as husband and wife, a shadow passed over the crowd in a flash. Everyone looked upward, but saw nothing. The smell of myrrh filled the room and the crowd applauded once again. They assumed the couple released the smell of incense as a part of the ceremony; little did they know, a demon passed above them with envy in his eyes.

56

"You look absolutely stunning," Sky complimented with tears in her eyes. "I'm so glad that things worked out for you and James. You two are beautiful together." Sky smiled as she pulled one of Sadie's soft curls.

"Thank you for being here," Sadie said. It was difficult to look into Sky's eyes. Every time she did, her heart flooded with hurt and the thought of losing her baby made her livid. "I thought this day would never come."

"But it did and you have the love of your life," said Sky as she walked Sadie to the limousine that waited outside of the hotel to take her and James to the airport for a quick honeymoon.

"Yes it did." Sadie was careful to avoid eye contact at all costs. She loved her best friend so much, but the disappointment in her made her chest ache. This was Sadie's day and the last thing she wanted was painful thoughts to dominate her mind.

Sadie and Sky stood outside the car. James was already inside laughing and talking to his friends as his head hung out of the window.

"You two have fun," Sky said. "I'll be gone when you get back. Newlyweds need their privacy and I've been in Atlanta long enough. New York is callin' my name."

Sadie turned to face her friend. For the first time that day she looked Sky in the eye. Sky looked so beautiful. Sadie smiled.

"I will miss you," Sadie said as she grabbed Sky and held her close. "I love you and I want you to know that I forgive you."

Sky's body stiffened. Tears poured down her face. She didn't know what to say. Sadie knew that Sky was guilty of trying to terminate her pregnancy yet she loved her still.

"I love you too," Sky wept. "I'm so sorry. I never meant to hurt you. I thought I was doin' the right thing. Pappa C..."

Sadie pulled away and searched Sky's eyes. Sadie had no idea that her father was behind Sky's actions. Now things made more sense. Sky was only doing what Mr. Covington asked her to do. Sadie pulled Sky close once again and whispered, "It's okay. I understand everything. Go home. Be happy. Marry Forrest. Everything will be okay."

"Thank you," Sky wept. "I'll miss you more than you know."

The two women embraced once again before Sadie entered the limousine and headed to the airport. Sky climbed into a rental car which already held all of her belongings, and headed to the airport also. In two hours she would be back in the city that never sleeps.

57

"That was such a beautiful ceremony," Mrs. Covington said as she and Mr. Covington settled into their seats on the plane. "I'm so happy that they finally tied the knot. Sadie has been through so much. She deserves to be happy. Sadie looked stunning."

"Yes she did," answered Mr. Covington. "She looked more beautiful than ever before."

"I hate that our trip was so short. I didn't even get a chance to talk to Sadie and James before they left. Everyone ran out of the wedding like the hotel was on fire," Mrs. Covington complained. "And they jumped into their car so quickly. They didn't even thank the guests. Young people these days are way too inconsiderate."

"Well, we all have lots to do and the wedding was very last minute. I'm sure Sadie and James were happy that people showed up and I'm sure Sadie will send everyone a thank you card for coming and for gifts," Mr. Covington mumbled as he closed his eyes hinting that he wanted to take a nap.

"You've been so quiet lately," said Mrs. Covington. "What's going on with you? You can't even carry on a conversation over three minutes anymore. Most of the time I feel like I'm talking to myself."

Mr. Covington opened one eye and said, "I tell you what, tell me what's going on with you and I'll tell you what's going on with me." Annoyance was in his voice. He was tired. He needed sleep, even if it was only for an hour.

"What do you mean?" she asked.

"I mean that you were in a deep depression, but as soon as you found out that Oliver kid died you were resurrected from the dead. Not to mention, you never explained to me why you were on campus the day Dr. Putina died." He sat up and leaned closer to her face. "So Ebbie, you tell me. What's going on with you?"

Mrs. Covington looked out of the airplane window. She knew this day would come. She contemplated whether she should lie or tell the truth or maybe she could just sit and say nothing. Usually if she ignored her husband long enough he would just change the subject or go on about his business.

"Come on, Ebbie. You know, all I wanted to do was nap and you wanted to talk. Now that I'm talking you have nothing to say," Mr. Covington chided. "Answer me woman!"

"Lower your voice, Carlos," Mrs. Covington whispered. "You're in a bad mood. I don't want to talk anymore."

"Too bad. You started it. Now finish it," he snapped.

Mrs. Covington knew that this time he would not let her pass. She had to start talking and soon. Usually Mr. Covington was a laid back person, but when he was in one of his moods he could become loud and obnoxious and people being around would not stop him from acting out.

"Oliver's death didn't make me happy. I dare you assume that," Mrs. Covington snapped. "And, I was on campus for a meeting with Dr. Putina."

"You want me to get upset don't you?" he asked with much irritation in his tone. "I'm asking you to be frank with me and you are not cooperating," his voice was elevating. Other passengers began to stare at them.

"Okay!" Mrs. Covington hissed through her teeth. "What do you want to know?"

"I want to know everything."

Mrs. Covington took a deep breath and began, "I was worried about Sadie. I called the professor and asked her if she knew anything about driving away spirits. I offered her five thousand dollars to summon the angel and drive him away from Sadie." Tears formed in Mrs. Covington's eyes. She continued, "I went to her office. Oliver was there, but he was leaving as I was coming in. He

was as high as a kite. Anyway, Dr. Putina summoned the angel and he came. He killed her. He disappeared. I picked up the professor's planner and ran. I felt guilty and visited Oliver a couple of weeks ago. I wanted to tell him that I knew he was innocent. I told him an angel killed the professor. Of course he didn't believe me. He threatened to turn me into the police, but was killed before he could say a word."

Mr. Covington sat with his mouth open. He was in complete shock. He knew that his wife was involved somehow, but he never suspected this. Sympathy filled his heart. He wanted to cry for her. He knew that she had to swallow so much pride to even talk to Dr. Putina and to know that Mrs. Covington's entire belief system had been shattered by actually seeing the angel had to be devastating on top of witnessing a murder. All this time he resented her because he thought she still did not believe.

Mr. Covington grabbed his wife and wrapped her within his arms. She wept heavily. He kissed the top of her head and promised not to let go until she asked him to.

"It's okay, baby," he whispered. "It's okay."

58

Purple and pink colored the sky as the bright orange sun dipped beyond the horizon. The beach was sprinkled with waving palms and couples snuggling under the romantic heavens. The warm Mexican weather felt wonderful to James as he stood on the balcony of an eloquent hotel. It was more beautiful in person than it was in the pamphlet. He turned and leaned on the balcony and let his eyes rest upon his wife inside the room. *My wife.* He thought. Sadie was finally his wife and he felt good despite all the odds. He loved her. He lusted for her. And now he had to have her.

Burnt orange and turquoise walls with tropical paintings surrounded Sadie as she lay sprawled across the large round bed covered with rose pedals. Yellow sheer curtains surrounded the bed. Sadie's head rested within a nest of plush red pillows. She wore nothing, but a big smile.

"Everything is so beautiful here," Sadie said as she hummed along with Prince singing *When 2 R N Love.*

"Yes it is," James agreed as a naughty smile curled his lips. He let his eyes wash across Sadie's nude form. Her skin was smooth and flawlessly brown. Toned muscles covered her entire body. His eyes rested upon her full breasts and dark nipples. They looked inviting and ready to be caressed. James licked his lips and let his eyes fall upon her rounded belly and the silver triangle beneath it.

Sadie blushed heavily. She loved when James devoured her with his eyes. He made her feel like a school girl.

James slowly made his way to her. He slowly undressed and tossed his clothes in various directions then lowered himself upon the bed.

"I have missed you so much," he whispered into Sadie's ear and began to nibble her lobes lightly. Firm kisses where showered upon her neck and chest. Slower more sensuous kisses began as his lips reached her breast. He kissed them both softly, nibbled a bit then trailed down her stomach and disappeared into the lush silver below.

Sadie's body twisted in pleasure as James kissed her forbidden fruit. The warmth of his mouth and the strength of his hands trapped her within the walls of ecstasy. Her hands gripped his head with every wave of orgasm After climax, Sadie pulled his face to hers and greedily drank from his mouth, ravished his neck, suckled his chest, and French kissed her king's scepter. James entered her and she wrapped her legs around him. They were one. At last, they were finally one.

59

"How was your trip?" Mrs. Covington's voice echoed through the phone. She sat at her kitchen table folding napkins.

"It was wonderful mom," Sadie answered. Her and James had been back from their honeymoon for over a week and they were just getting into their new routine as husband and wife. "Mexico was so beautiful and James and I really needed the vacation. You have no idea how good it felt to get away from it all."

"I'm glad to hear that all went well. After all you've been through, you both deserve to be happy," Mrs. Covington said.

"You believe me Momma?" Sadie asked with surprise in her voice. She assumed that her mother would never believe the preternatural story about the baby. Sadie wondered what made her change her mind, if she changed her mind.

"Yes, I believe you," Mrs. Covington reluctantly answered. The conversation made her uneasy. She was afraid that she would have to admit that she saw the angel with her own eyes and she was not comfortable reliving Dr. Putina's murder.

"But why?" Sadie asked, puzzled by her mother's sudden change of heart. "What made you believe me?"

Mrs. Covington cleared her throat and said, "Because you are my daughter and I love you. If you say something bad happened to you, I know you are not a liar; therefore, I have to trust your word. All the details, I'm not comfortable with, but I am comfortable with the fact that you speak the truth."

"Oh Momma," Sadie cried. "You have no idea how much that means to me. I thought that you were the only one who didn't believe me."

"Don't cry, baby," Mrs. Covington instructed as she looked up and saw Mr. Covington standing in the kitchen entrance.

"Is that Sadie?" Mr. Covington asked.

"Yes," Mrs. Covington answered.

"How long have they been back?" he asked.

"For about a week," Mrs. Covington answered as she laid the phone on her shoulder after telling Sadie to hold on a moment.

"I've left Sadie at least five messages. Ask her why she hasn't returned my calls," Mr. Covington requested.

"Why don't you ask her yourself," Mrs. Covington said as she passed the phone to her husband.

Mr. Covington grabbed the phone and asked, "Sadie, why haven't I heard from you."

Sadie was quiet for a moment. She wasn't sure how to respond. Anger filled her when she thought of her father instructing Sky to kill the baby. But the anger was wavering because she knew her father did what he did out of love. But does love excuse attempted murder?

He did not like the sound of silence.

"Put mom back on the phone," Sadie hissed.

"No. Answer my question," he demanded.

"I didn't return your calls because I didn't want to talk to you," she snapped.

Mr. Covington was wounded by her answer.

"Why, baby?" he asked.

"You tried to kill my baby!" she yelled into the phone. "You told my best friend to poison me so that I would miscarry!"

Mr. Covington's facial expression hardened. With a voice void of compassion he stated, "It was for your own good. You carry a beast within your belly and you don't have sense enough to get rid of it so I tried to do it for you. My only regret is getting Sky involved."

"Carlos you didn't!" Mrs. Covington yelled from behind him. "I can't believe you would put Sadie in such danger. Have you lost your mind?"

Mr. Covington ignored his wife and spoke into the phone, "I love you and I wanted to protect you. I failed. Now it's up to you to correct things."

"Daddy, I'm having this baby. If you want to be in my life, you have to accept that fact. Do I make myself clear?" Sadie belted through the phone.

"Crystal clear," he mumbled. Mr. Covington knew he would never get through to her, but he did not want her to banish him from her life. He needed to remain close to her in order to protect her even if it meant being the grandfather of a nephilim.

"Are you sure you understand?" Sadie asked. "There cannot be any more attempts on my child's life. I will forgive you this once because you are my father, but only this once. Next time you will make yourself my enemy."

Never had Mr. Covington heard such venom in Sadie's voice. It was like he was on the phone with a perfect stranger. Each time he spoke to her she seemed more and more hard and cold. He wondered if it was the baby that was affecting her personality.

"Answer me!" she yelled.

"I understand," he replied and handed the phone over to Mrs. Covington before he exited the kitchen with a long and worried face.

"I'm sorry, baby. I didn't know," Mrs. Covington apologized for her husband. "I can't believe Carlos would go that far. And Sky..." Mrs. Covington paused. "What he did was inexcusable; but, Sadie you have to know that he did it because he thought he was saving you."

"It's okay, Momma. He did what he felt was right. If he does it again I will be forced to do what I think is right," Sadie snapped and hung up the phone.

Mrs. Covington sat holding the phone with her mouth open and heart reeling.

60

Months had passed since Sky and Forrest left Atlanta for New York. They married shortly after they settled in. Things seemed to be going well and their new life in the big city was a wonderful one. Sky called Sadie every so often to check on her. Forrest did the same for James and Luis.

Luis was all alone in the big house. At first he felt lonely, but he soon found two new roommates, Aminah and Tori. Needless to say, he was having the time of his life.

James and Sadie was now a comfortable married couple with happiness surrounding them constantly. Turiel had not reared his ugly head since the night before their wedding. It seemed as if the Tuckers were now at peace.

The Covingtons were doing quite well despite their worries in Florida. Mr. Covington immersed himself in his work and Mrs. Covington resumed giving piano lessons. When they had free time, they busied themselves with plays, museums, and concerts. Anything to keep their minds off Sadie and the baby.

Everything seemed to have settled down. The chaos was slowly melting into normal life once again as the world kept on spinning. The seasons had changed so quickly. Now the hot Georgia sun had turned into cold clear sunshine. The cycle of life was well into motion.

Sadie walked around the shopping mall like a penguin with swollen feet. She wobbled with every step as she popped grapes into her mouth every few seconds. Bags hung over her forearm as she searched through her large purse for her car keys. It was time to go home. Her feet were tired. She had bought the perfect outfit for her and the baby to wear home from the hospital. She purchased black and red Ralph Lauren sweaters and Levi jeans for her and the baby. They would be warm and stylish when they left the hospital.

Sadie plopped down in a chair in the middle of the food court and continued searching her purse for her car keys. She could not seem to find them anywhere.

"Where are my keys?" she whined out loud. Sadie felt so exhausted at the moment. All she wanted to do was to get into her bed. She felt so heavy, like a lumbering beast. The baby seemed to weigh a ton. Constant heartburn plagued her. Her mom kept telling her that it meant that the baby had a head full of hair. Sadie wished it was bald.

Finally Sadie found her keys and pulled them from the bag.

"Thank God," she sighed. At the mention of God, the baby kicked Sadie so hard that she winced in pain.

Sadie pushed herself up and started wobbling towards the exit. Within five minutes she found her car and began to toss her bags into the back seat. A sharp pain ripped through the bottom of her stomach. It felt like a menstrual cramp times fifty.

"Ahhhhh," she cried as she opened the door and fell into the driver's seat. She waited until the pain subsided then pulled her legs inside and started up the car. She put the car in reverse and pulled out of the parking lot. The pain frightened Sadie, but it had left as quickly as it had come. After driving for about fifteen minutes the pain came again, but this time it was much more grueling. She was thankful that she was sitting at a red light.

"Ahhhhh," Sadie wailed as she tried to keep her eyes open and on the road. She fumbled around in her purse for her cell phone. The pain gradually subsided. Sadie drove on. Home was now only five minutes away.

Sadie's car pulled into her parking deck and she hopped out as fast as she could. She entered the building and rushed through her front door.

"James," she called through the apartment. "James!"

"Yes, baby," James rushed into the living room wearing a bath towel, his skin carrying drops of water. "What's going on?"

"I think I may be in labor," Sadie cried as she held her swollen belly and plopped down on the couch.

"About how many minutes apart are the contractions?" James asked with an ounce of panic on his face. He sat next to her, water dripping on the sofa.

"Fifteen minutes apart.....ahhhhhhh!" Sadie cried. Another contraction shook her core. Her back fell against the sofa pillows as she squealed in pain. "I think they're coming faster."

"About how much faster?" James inquired as he grabbed her hand.

"Ten minutes," she whined as the pain weakened. "Do you think we should call the doctor?"

James jumped up and grabbed the cordless phone. He pulled the doctor's number off of the refrigerator and dialed it quickly. The doctor instructed them to make their way to the hospital when the contractions became five minutes apart. James hung up the phone and relayed the information to Sadie. He then ran into the room and dressed himself quickly. He brought Sadie's suitcase into the living room and sat it by the door.

"How are you feeling, baby?" he asked. James was breathing just as hard as she was.

Sadie looked at the face of her cell phone to check the time. She placed it back in her coat pocket as a new pain developed.

"Ahhhhhhhh," she cried again. "The contractions are now about seven minutes apart."

"I'm going to pack up the car. I'll be back up to get you in a few minutes," James said as he grabbed Sadie's suitcase and exited the apartment.

Sadie closed her eyes as the pain washed over her. Never in her life had she felt such agony. She grabbed her stomach and allowed the tears to come. She took a deep breath. The air within the room shifted. For a moment her pain subsided. Myrrh filled her nostrils. A bright light filled the room. James entered the apartment and the light was gone. James rushed to her side coughing hard from the odor.

"Are you okay?" James asked as he pulled Sadie to her feet. "Did that thing come back here?" he asked in supreme anger.

"I don't know," she said. "I think you frightened him away."

"That demon better keep away!" James threatened as he and Sadie exited the apartment. Behind them the sound of wings fluttered.

61

The delivery room was a pleasant temperature. Floral wallpaper decorated the walls and a comfortable bench with plenty of cushion sat against the wall next to the hospital bed. Sadie paced the floor trying to help the baby drop and to cause further dilation.

The pain came in waves, but Sadie was too prideful to ask for medication. She walked across the room grimacing with every step. James sat on the bench watching her impatiently. It seemed as if the baby was taking his sweet time.

SPLASH! Sadie's water broke leaving a giant puddle on the floor. James paged the nurse and they were in the room within seconds. After Sadie climbed into bed, they checked her and discovered that she was fully dilated. The nurse paged the doctor and they began to prepare Sadie for labor.

"It's time!" James said to himself. He could barely contain his excitement. He took his place beside his wife and waited patiently for the doctor to come.

"Ahhhhh!" Sadie wailed.

"Don't push!" the nurse instructed as the surgical tech prepped Sadie. "Hold on."

"Ahhhhh...." Sadie cried. "I can't!"

The nurse looked under the sheet and saw that the baby's head was crowning. The child was coming and there was nothing anyone could do to stop it. Before the doctor could get into the room, the child's entire head was protruding from Sadie's womb.

"Ahhhh...." Sadie cried. The sound of the baby's voice quickly blended with hers.

The sight of the child bursting from Sadie's womb almost made James hit the floor cold. He took a deep breath and painted a smile on. His head felt dizzy as the doctor presented the slimy baby to James to cut the cord. He did it with trembling hands praying that he wouldn't maim the child.

"It's a healthy boy!" the doctor shouted as she handed the blood smeared child to Sadie.

Sadie opened her arms to welcome her son. Chestnut skin, a head full of curly hair, full lips, he was beautiful. A tired, but loving smile covered Sadie's face. She whispered to the baby, "Welcome to the world Khalid. Mommy and daddy were waiting for you."

62

The clock on the wall read 3:00 a.m. Sadie, James, and Khalid all lay at rest. Sadie lay nestled under the white sheets of the hospital bed as James lay on the bench. Little Khalid lay in his clear baby bed sleeping soundly.

Darkness filled the room save for a small dull light above Sadie's bed. Silence and calm surrounded the family as they slept. Faint snores drifted through the air. Occasional smiles indicated sweet dreams.

Turiel stepped out of nothingness and hovered over the sleeping child. He bent over the bed, his wings folded behind him. For a moment he stared at the child. The boy was strong and beautiful, all ten pounds of him. His long body filled the bed completely. A look of fascination and glee filled the unholy intruder.

Khalid's eyes fluttered as his tiny lips moved in a suckling motion.

Turiel lifted the child from his bed. He kissed the boy three times behind his right ear. Instantly, three looped marks appeared on the baby's skin. They were tiny, but very distinct markings. The baby did not stir. It seemed to find solace in the arms of the angel.

"It is done." Turiel whispered as he placed the child back into his bed. The angel moved away from the slumbering child. "Goodbye my son." Turiel whispered and was gone.

63

"Mr. Covington," James said as he gave Mr. Covington a big hug. "You are a proud grandfather! How does it feel?"

"Wonderful," Mr. Covington lied. Every inch of his skin felt like cockroaches were crisscrossing over it. The demon had come to fruition. Mr. Covington felt helpless in the scheme of things. There was nothing he could do, but let fate take the reins. What was to be was to be. *God have mercy.* Mr. Covington was thankful for the couch underneath him because if he were standing his body would quickly meet the floor.

"I can't believe I'm a dad!" James grinned. "And look how big he is already. That boy is gonna be a giant!" James laughed.

Again Mr. Covington found no humor in the truth. He forced a smile to his face, but he was pretty sure that his facial expression displayed pain more than happiness. He looked over to his wife who was Eskimo kissing the baby nose to nose. Mr. Covington leaned his head against the pillows and closed his eyes to whisper a silent prayer. He was tired. More tired than he had ever been in his life. All of a sudden he felt old. He wanted to sleep for a millennium. Maybe when he awoke, he would realize that this all was just a horrible nightmare.

Mr. and Mrs. Covington flew to Atlanta to see their one month old grandson and Mrs. Covington hasn't stop gushing over and kissing on Sadie and the baby since they landed.

"I'm sleepy guys. Do you mind if I go to the guest room and take a nap?" Mr. Covington asked.

"Daddy you haven't held Khalid yet," Sadie whined.

A look of irritation crossed James face.

"Mrs. Covington, I'm so glad you're here. Now the baby will see more faces than Sadie's. She seems just fine with Khalid in your arms. Your daughter is so protective over Khalid that even I barely get to touch him," James laughed dryly. It was true. Sadie guarded the baby with her life. It was rare that Khalid was not in close proximity to her. She claimed the reason she wanted no one around was because the baby was too young and she didn't want people to breathe on him and possibly make him sick. James understood that, but he was Khalid's father. Sadie watched James like a hawk when he held the baby. She hovered over him constantly and seemed very paranoid every time he touched the child. It also irritated him that she constantly referred to the child as her baby.

Mrs. Covington looked up and smiled. She kissed the baby on the cheek and turned to her husband and asked, "Carlos, are you ready to hold your grandson?" Before waiting for an answer, Mrs. Covington shoved Khalid into his grandfather's arms.

Mr. Covington wanted nothing to do with the child, but if he openly expressed his feelings his entire family would be crushed by his coldness. He held the child in his arms. The warmth of the baby softened his heart. Mr. Covington unknowingly smiled. Maybe evil could not dwell in something so small. Maybe Khalid would simply be a hero and not something sinister. After all, the Bible said that the nephilim were heroes of old. Maybe Khalid would be a savior instead of a satan.

"See there Carlos, he is as sweet as pie," Mrs. Covington smiled as she got up from the sofa to grab her purse.

Mr. Covington tickled the baby's chin with his pointer finger. Khalid grabbed onto his grandfather's finger firmly. Mr. Covington felt the abnormal strength in the tiny little hand.

"I knew you would love him instantly Daddy. How could you not?" Sadie asked with a smile on her face. She rested her head on her father's shoulder and felt at ease. All of the loves of her life surrounded her. This was the closest she knew she would ever get to heaven.

Mr. Covington let his nose rest in the silkiness of the baby's hair. He forgot how sweet babies smelled. Mr. Covington kissed the boy gently behind his ear. His lips fell upon raised skin.

"Sadie," Mrs. Covington called. "I'm trying to have a silver rattle engraved. I need you to spell the baby's name so I will know how many letters to pay for."

"K-h-a-l-i-d E-r-e-b-u-s Tucker," Sadie answered.

"That's six letters for Khalid. Six letters for Erebus and six letters for Tucker," Mrs. Covington said aloud as she multiplied the cost of engraving.

Mr. Covington pulled his face away from the baby's and folded the child's ear downward. The markings were clear. Mr. Covington's heart dropped. All color left his skin. Mr. Covington frantically pulled his finger from the baby's fist. It seemed as if the child would not let go. Mr. Covington jerked away wildly and tossed the child into Sadie's lap.

The baby screamed and began to cry.

"Daddy what's wrong with you!" Sadie huffed.

"Can't you people see what's going on?" Mr. Covington yelled.

"What on earth are you talking about?" Mrs. Covington screamed. "And why did you toss the baby like a rag doll. You could've hurt him!"

"Are you people blind?" Mr. Covington howled. He jumped up from the couch and ran into the back room. He returned with a Bible in his hand.

"Daddy what are you doing?" Sadie asked as she held Khalid pressed to her bosom. James put his arm around his wife to calm her.

Mrs. Covington stood dumbfounded.

Mr. Covington began to flip the pages so hard that many ripped from the seams and fell to the floor. The book trembled within his hands. Mr. Covington looked like a crazed maniac as he searched the scriptures,

"Are y'all blind?" Mr. Covington screamed, slobber flying from his lips. He finally came to the scripture he was searching for.

"Calm down Carlos," Mrs. Covington said as she rushed towards him. "Whatever it is that's bothering you, I'm sure we can fix it. Don't you think you're overreacting a bit?"

He shot a glance so cold that he stopped her in her tracks. She backed up and huddled with Sadie and James.

Mr. Covington began to read:

"And I saw another beast coming up out of the earth...And it does great wonders...And it causes all, both small and great, rich and poor, free and bond, to receive a mark on their right hand, or in their foreheads, even that not any might buy or sell except those having the mark, or the name of the beast, or the number of its name. Here is the wisdom. Let him having reason count the number of the beast, for it is the number of a man. And its number is six hundred and sixty-six." Revelations 11:13-18

Mr. Covington slammed the book shut and fell to his knees. Tears streamed down his face. The old man's body trembled like he was having a seizure. He screamed, "God have mercy!" At that moment the baby opened his eyes and looked directly at his grandfather instantly silencing him. The whites of Khalid's eyes turned black and a stretched out inhuman sneer bent his mouth. The baby placed his pointed finger over his mouth as if he was saying *shhh*.

Mr. Covington's heart stopped within his chest. A failed attempt to inhale sent his balance rocking. His eyes rolled back in his head.

"Carlos!" Mrs. Covington ran to him.

He fell straight on his face and was gone. God was merciful, at least to Mr. Covington.

END NOTES

[i] translation by: R.H. Charles Oxford: The Clarendon Press

[ii] Translated from the Slavonic by W. R. Morfill, M.A

[iii] translation by: R.H. Charles Oxford: The Clarendon Press

[iv] http://www.deliriumsrealm.com

Violette L. Meier, a happily married mother, writer, painter, poet, and native of Atlanta, Georgia earned her BA in English at Clark Atlanta University and her MDiv at the Interdenominational Theological Center. Writing since her preteen years, she has written over 1,200 poems (a few have been published on numerous poetry sites and in poetry anthologies), and 25 short stories (1 has been made into a movie). She is the author of *The First Chronicle of Zayashariya: Out of Night, Violette Ardor: A Volume of Poetry, Angel Crush, and This Sickness We Call Love.* Her website is www.violettemeier.com.

24094738R00157

Made in the USA
San Bernardino, CA
02 February 2019